GUILTY

UNTIL PROVEN INNOCENT

CONRAD JONES

Copyright © 2018 Conrad Jones

The right of Conrad Jones to be identified as the Author of the Work has been asserted by him in accordance Copyright, Designs and Patents Act 1988.

First published in 2018 by Bloodhound Books

Apart from any use permitted under UK copyright law, this publication may only be reproduced, stored, or transmitted, in any form, or by any means, with prior permission in writing of the publisher or, in the case of reprographic production, in accordance with the terms of licences issued by the Copyright Licensing Agency.

All characters in this publication are fictitious and any resemblance to real persons, living or dead, is purely coincidental.

www.bloodhoundbooks.com

Print ISBN 978-1-912604-79-1

Also By Conrad Jones

DI Braddick Series

Brick (Book 1)
Shadows (Book 2)

Standalone

The Journey

PROLOGUE

He turned down the radio so he could hear the muffled cries for help coming from the boot. The victim's voice had been strong at first, full of anger. The energy and venom were waning. He was incoherent now, sounding almost demented. A thin smile touched his lips as he listened to the anguish. He would drive around for a while, taking an hour or so to reach his lair; it would feel like an age for his victim. There was fear in his voice and he savoured his fear. Listening to him plead for help excited him. He had no sympathy for him, only hatred and anger. It was his own fault that he was where he was; he had asked for everything that was about to happen to him. Retribution. That's what it was. He would make him understand what he had done when he was broken, when he was helpless. It wouldn't take long to break this one. He could tell. Some were stronger than others. At the end, they were always the same: sorry and apologetic, but their apologies were too late. They would beg for mercy at the end but there was none to be had. Where was the mercy when he had needed it? Nowhere, that's where.

He had realised a long time ago that the world was short on mercy. Mercy and giving the benefit of the doubt were gifts that humans talked about, but rarely delivered. People are fickle. One minute you're loved and respected, the next you're a pariah. Given the right circumstances, lifelong friends could become enemies in the blink of an eye. Innocent until proven guilty – that was how it was supposed to be. It was bullshit. Mercy and forgiveness were rare. They were commodities that not many could afford.

He could hear him sobbing again. The anger had dissipated and burnt out – it always did. They always started out angry, shouting abuse and screaming threats. That was when they realised they were in the grip of evil. There was no going back. This was where they would meet their end, screaming, begging for mercy. Yet still they threatened him. He had heard it all. It didn't matter. Nothing would stop him. That was the point: to show them how it felt to be helpless. They had to feel the total desolation of being helpless and alone, teetering on a knife edge between life and death, the pain so intense that death was the desirable option. Being helpless was all part of the horror they had to suffer so they could understand what they had done. Fear blurred the reality in their minds. When they realised that they couldn't break the wire that was bound around their wrists and ankles, they would change; they couldn't stop him hurting them, and they couldn't talk their way out. Once that was accepted, the threats would subside. They would realise that he wasn't about to release them, not now, not soon, not ever. Once it had sunk in that this wasn't a situation with a happy ending, their spirit would weaken, and eventually break. The adrenalin waned from their bloodstream and they would resort to seeking mercy. But there was no mercy.

They had nothing but pain and suffering to look forward to. Pain and suffering and fear. The fear in their eyes was what drove him. It fuelled him. It was the price they paid for what they had done. They would never be found. Their loved ones would never know why they didn't come home. They would suffer too. They would always wonder where they were and what had happened to them. They would always miss them, always grieve for them. That made him happy. He had suffered and now it was their turn. Every action had a reaction: yin and yang, karma, an eye for an eye, whichever universal power people believed in. This was revenge, and it worked for him. It would be a long night for his victim, a very long night indeed. He lit a cigarette while he listened to the dulcet tones of suffering coming from the boot.

CHAPTER 1

Richard Vigne looked across the living room at his twins. They were good-looking kids, even if he said so himself. His son, Jake, was engrossed in an online game on his iPad, playing against his best friend who lived across town. His daughter, Jaki, was on her phone, texting at a million miles an hour. They hadn't spoken for at least an hour. Interaction with his teenage offspring was often limited to grunts and groans, every question an intrusion into their virtual worlds. Sometimes, he wondered if they could answer a question with a complete sentence without rolling their eyes towards the ceiling, but generally they were nice kids. Their grandparents said they were ruined, and he blamed his wife for being soft when they were toddlers; she, in turn, blamed him for being soft when they became teenagers. The older they got, the harder it was to impose and police any boundaries, no matter how well intentioned. Richard had given up trying to discipline them. He preferred being the approachable parent, the one who would slip them a tenner when mum had already said no. There were no issues at their school, which was where he worked. They didn't take drugs, drink or smoke. Academically, they were above average, they were polite and well-mannered. They seemed to be popular, well-balanced individuals, liked by the pupils and staff. Most importantly, they were healthy. As far as Richard was concerned, that was all that mattered. If they remained healthy, they would find their way in life, eventually.

Richard smiled at them, checked his watch, and turned the channel to BBC, set for *Match of the Day*.

'What are you doing, Dad?' Jaki asked, annoyed, hardly looking up from her phone.

'What does it look like I'm doing? I'm putting the football on,' Richard replied, calmly. He scratched the dark stubble on his chin and rubbed his shaven head with his palm. It was an anxiety thing – if he sensed an argument brewing, he rubbed his head – and he knew he did it.

'It's Saturday night. Saturday night is football time.' Jaki pulled a pained expression. 'Don't look so surprised. It's a tradition. Downtrodden fathers across the country seek the sanctuary of *Match of the Day*. It's a tiny piece of sanity in a mad world,' he said. 'Saturday has been football time for many years, way before you were born.'

'In the old days before the wheel,' Jake muttered.

'I heard that, cheeky bugger,' Richard warned.

'Oh, Dad. That's so unfair. I was watching that programme!' Jaki moaned, the pain on her face deepening. Her long blonde hair framed her pretty face.

'You weren't,' he said, glancing at her.

Richard had a suspicion that Jaki's lips had recently changed shape, along with half of the girls in her year group. Some of them looked fish-like. He had broached the subject with Celia but she'd fobbed him off, saying he was a dinosaur. He wasn't sure he agreed with that analogy. Not being consulted about his daughter having injections in her face had irritated him, but he could live with it. It wasn't the end of the world. He would have said yes, eventually. One angry female in the house was difficult enough to deal with, two were impossible. She was glaring at him, sulkily. The pout emphasised her lip fillers.

'I was watching it!'

'No, Jak, you weren't watching it. You were texting.'

'I can do both.'

'What was it about?' Richard asked.

'What was what about?'

'What was the programme, that you were watching, about?'

'That one that you just turned over?'

'What was it?'

'It was about the girls and the guys competing against each other,' she mumbled. She hadn't been paying attention, but it wasn't football and that was the point. 'I can't remember the name of it, to be honest.'

'Oh, come on, Jak. If it was so engrossing, what was it called?'

'I can't remember.'

'That's because you were texting and not watching it.'

'I was doing both.'

'I bought the television and I pay the licence fee.'

'Mum pays it, actually,' Jaki said, correcting him.

'Same thing,' Richard replied. He gave her a look. It was a 'don't push it' look. 'I'm not arguing with you. We're watching the football.'

'That's so unfair!'

'Stop moaning, Jak,' Jake said, nudging her. The family always shortened her name. 'We're watching the football and that's that.' Jake grinned sarcastically. His blond hair was cropped at the sides and spiked on top.

'But I was watching that programme,' she protested.

'You don't even know what it was called,' Jake teased.

'I do.'

'You don't.'

'I'll miss the end!'

'No one cares.'

'I care.'

'We don't.'

'Shut up, stupid.'

'I'm sick of watching your reality-crap programmes anyway.' Jake looked at his dad. 'Aren't we, Dad?'

'What?' Richard asked, half listening.

'I said, we're sick of watching reality programmes, aren't we?'

'Sick of the sight of them,' Richard said, winking. 'Six-packs and orange people everywhere.'

'That's why she watches them,' Jake chuckled. 'She's orange too.'

The twins smiled and nudged each other. They looked like bookends, sitting on the settee in their Adidas tracksuits.

'But you already know the results of the games,' Jaki argued. She sat forward, and pouted to emphasise her point. Richard looked at her side-on. She had definitely had her lips done. 'What is the point in watching it when you know what happens?'

'Because we want to watch the games, retard,' Jake muttered.

'Jake!' Richard said, sternly. 'I don't want to hear you using that word about your sister again.'

'Tell her to stop being one then,' Jake protested. He caught her profile too. 'Have you had your lips done?' he asked.

'Shut your face!' She blushed and covered her mouth, hiding her lips from her dad. 'You're such a knob sometimes!' It was obvious from the side that she had, and all the girls in school were having fillers. Jake realised that his dad hadn't been consulted; from the expression on his face it was obvious. He decided to shut up, not wanting to get his twin into hot water.

'Retard,' Jake replied.

'I am not the retard. Watching football when you already know the scores is retarded.' Jaki stood up and walked towards the door, her nose in the air, offended. 'I do not see the point.'

'I don't see the point in a lot of things that you do,' Jake called after her.

'Like what, stupid?' she answered from the doorway.

'What is the point in putting that cream on your skin and turning yourself orange like all your Oompa Loompa friends?' Jake replied as she left the room. 'And as for those eyelashes, you look like a couple of spiders have died on your face.'

'You're such a knobhead,' Jaki countered from the hallway. She fluttered her spider-like lashes self-consciously and glanced in the mirror, pouting. Were her lips that obvious? They would settle down in a few days. Maybe she had overdone it with the fake tan. She got a drink from the kitchen and walked back into the room, plonking herself next to her twin. He looked at her and stuck out his tongue, making his lips look bigger. 'You're so immature,' she said, shaking her head in disgust. 'No wonder April Morris won't go out with you.'

'I don't even like April Morris,' Jake said, embarrassed. He had a massive crush on her if the truth be known, but she had a boyfriend who was seventeen and had his own car. A black BMW. The only way a seventeen-year-old could buy a car like that was by having rich parents or selling coke. Jake couldn't compete with either.

'Oh, really?' Jaki teased. 'I'll tell her you're not interested any more. She'll be heartbroken, not.'

'Tell her what you want. I'm not bothered.'

'I've seen the text messages you sent to her,' Jaki said, shaking her head. It was Jake's turn to blush. 'They come over a bit desperate, if you ask me.'

'Maybe I am desperate, but I'm not orange,' Jake said, grinning. Her words stung a bit, but he knew April Morris was way out of his league. He went back to his game, keeping one eye on the television. Jaki finished her drink and stood up. 'If you're going to get another drink,' he said, 'I'll have a Tango, unless you've used it all in your bath.'

'Knobhead.'

'Oompa Loompa.'

'Will you two pack it in?' Richard snapped. 'I'm trying to watch this.'

Jaki handed her brother a glass of orange. Despite their bickering, they worshipped each other. She sat down and pretended to be bored by the football. The sport didn't interest her but some of those thighs made her blush. Richard frowned when a phone pinged. He looked at the twins, annoyed by the intrusion.

'Don't look at us like that. It was your phone, Dad,' Jaki said, chuckling.

'Was it?' Richard was shocked.

'Yes!'

'It's never made that noise before,' he said, frowning.

'Sounded like an alert from Messenger,' Jake said. Richard looked at him blankly. 'It's Facebook, Dad.'

Richard pulled a face. Facebook wasn't really his thing. He had a profile page on the school site but he never looked at it – teachers avoided it, for obvious reasons. He picked up his phone and looked at the message:

Richard Vigne, we know what you did with Nikki Haley and we're going to tell everyone. We know where you live, paedo. We're onto you. The information will be sent to your employers, the press and the police.

Richard inhaled sharply and sat upright. He nearly choked. The kids glanced at him, concerned expressions on their faces.

'What's up, Dad?' Jake asked, distracted from his game. He eyed his dad briefly. His face was pale, almost grey. It wasn't like his dad to be shocked by something; he looked baffled but didn't reply. He was staring at the screen. 'Something wrong, Dad?'

'No, no. Nothing is wrong,' Richard said, shaking his head. He sat back and reread the message, trying to keep calm. He looked at the sender's name. It had come from a Facebook group called Predator Hunters Northwest. His hands were shaking as he looked at their page. It appeared to be a vigilante group that focused on trapping paedophiles online. There were dozens of pictures of men getting arrested when they turned up to meet someone they had thought was a child, and finding out that the person they had been grooming was, in fact, a group of vigilantes who were setting a trap. He scrolled through the discussions with trembling fingers. His mouth dropped open when he saw a grainy picture of a man talking to a young girl. He didn't recognise the place, and he didn't recognise the girl. The man in the picture didn't look like him, but it wasn't clear. Beneath the picture was his name:

This scumbag is Richard Vigne. He's a teacher and a paedophile. Address to follow. Please like, share, and tweet as many times as you can. We need to stop this monster being anywhere near children.

Richard was winded as if he had been punched in the stomach. Fear gripped his guts with icy fingers and twisted his intestines. He wanted to scream at the screen. *It isn't me! It isn't me!* Who were these idiots and why were they sending him such vile messages? His head was spinning. His heart was pounding so fast in his chest he thought it was going to explode. He could barely draw breath. His teeth were grinding painfully against each other. Someone had made a mistake. A huge mistake. A massive mistake. As far as mistakes go, this one was fucking monumental. He clicked back to the message on his phone and replied:

The picture on your Facebook page is not me. You have got the wrong man. Take my name off it!

'Are you sure you're okay, Dad?' Jaki asked, concerned. 'You look like you've seen a ghost.'

Richard looked at her. His mouth opened, as if he was going to speak, but no words came out. He heard Celia's voice shouting for him from the kitchen, but he could barely understand her words. His body was numb; fear and shock coursed through his veins. They were going to tell his employers and the police what, exactly? He couldn't think straight. Panic set in.

'Richard,' Celia called again, 'can you come in here, please?' He looked at his screen and swallowed hard. 'Richard,' she shouted. The volume of her voice had increased and there was an edge to it. She was mad about something. His breath stuck in his chest, he couldn't move. 'Richard! Can you hear me?'

'Mum is shouting you,' Jaki said, sitting down again. 'Pass me the remote on your way out, please.' She grinned sarcastically.

'I'm watching this,' Jake snapped. Jaki huffed and stormed out, slamming the door behind her.

The door opened again and Celia walked in. Her long blonde hair was tied up into a ponytail. The twins had inherited their good looks from her. She was lean and fit for thirty-six, and turned heads wherever she went. Her blue eyes were piercing and there was anger in them.

'Didn't you hear me?' she asked, holding her iPad in one hand and a large glass of white wine in the other. Richard looked at her blankly. He thought about answering but couldn't find the words. She had her really-pissed-off look on her face.

His mind was frozen with fear. 'I'm talking to you, Richard. Did you hear me?'

'Sorry,' he mumbled, pushing his phone between his leg and the armchair, wanting to push it right down into the material where it could never be recovered. His face flushed red, embarrassed and confused. 'I didn't hear you. I was watching the football.'

'You can hear me now?'

'Of course.'

'Pause it. I need to speak to you,' she said, gesturing with her head. 'Come into the kitchen, please.'

Her eyes were wide and accusing, he could see the tension on her face. She was pissed off about something. He could hardly move; his limbs were lead. What was wrong with her? What could he say anyway? *Now isn't a good time, Celia. I've just been called a paedophile online.* He hadn't done anything, but the accusation was enough to stun him. It was impossible to respond normally.

'Richard,' she snapped, trying to keep the anger from her voice. 'I need to speak to you in the kitchen, right now.'

'Okay, okay.' Richard pushed himself out of the chair and walked unsteadily towards the door. Jake watched him, concerned. Something was going on. Adult stuff probably. There was tension in the air. It was worse at the weekends when Mum didn't have to get up early. She would drink until her words were slurred, and berate Dad about underachieving because he wouldn't apply for the deputy head position. The next morning, she would make a cooked breakfast for the family and be completely oblivious to what a bitch she had been. Jake wasn't going to get married and put up with that shit, that was for sure. Any girlfriend who gave him a hard time would be down the road straight away. Then he thought about April Morris's breasts. If he was honest, she could say whatever she wanted to him.

Celia led the way and walked into the kitchen; her pink tracksuit clung to her hips, flattering her shape. She glided across dark slate tiles to the island, which acted as a breakfast bar. When they'd first met, Richard was smitten – he still was. She was the prettiest woman on the planet as far as he was concerned.

'Close the door, Richard.'

His throat was dry and he felt parched as he closed the kitchen door. The light reflected from white high-gloss units, almost dazzling him. He looked at her and waited.

'I don't want you to panic,' she whispered. She gestured for him to move closer.

'Panic about what?'

'I've had a message,' she said. 'Not a very nice message.'

'Let me see,' Richard said, feeling his stomach clench.

'What the fuck is this all about?' she whispered, pointing to her iPad. Richard stepped closer to look at the screen. There was an email open. The sender was Predator Hunter Northwest, at an AOL address. He tried to swallow but couldn't. Celia stared at him while he read the content:

Dear Mrs Vigne,
    This may come as a shock to you, but we feel we should let you know that your husband, Richard, had a relationship with a minor. Her name was Nikki Haley. Nikki tried to commit suicide a month ago as a direct result of the affair. Your husband is a paedophile and should not be allowed anywhere near children. It has come to our attention that he is employed as a teacher, which is like letting a fox into a henhouse. The information has been sent to the police and the press and his employers. We intend to make this public and feel it is only fair to warn you, as you have children of your own.

Regards

The words sank in and struck home. Every letter was a dagger in his guts. He was going to vomit. He read and reread the message. Celia watched him intently, analysing his every move. He could feel her eyes boring into him, searching for the truth. His legs were shaking, threatening to collapse beneath him. His mind was in turmoil, nothing was working properly. He felt guilty.

'Richard?'

'What?' he stuttered.

'Why can't I hear you denying this?' Celia said, her voice strained. She looked into his eyes. Her bottom lip began to quiver. 'Please tell me this is a hoax, or someone's idea of a sick joke?' Richard looked at her then back at the screen. He shook his head. 'Richard, tell me this isn't true. Who are these people?'

'I don't know.'

'Do you know a girl called Nikki Haley?' Tears filled Celia's eyes. She waited, but he didn't deny knowing her. She shook her head in disbelief. 'You need to tell me that this is a lie, Richard.'

The kitchen door opened and Jake stepped in. His eyes were almost bulging out of his head. He was holding his iPad.

'Dad,' he said, panicking. 'Someone has posted some shit about you on Facebook.'

'What do you mean?' Richard stammered. 'What does it say?'

'It says you're a paedo, Dad.'

Richard couldn't believe what was happening. Why had they done this to him?

'Delete it immediately,' Celia said, angrily.

'I can't delete it,' Jake said, shaking his head.

'Of course you can. Get it off your page now, and block the sender.'

'Mum,' Jake tried to explain. 'You don't understand.'

'Don't argue with me, Jake,' Celia snapped. She took a large glug of wine and stared at Richard. Richard stared back, his mouth open, shocked and stunned into silence. 'Just do it.'

'I can't, Mum,' Jake insisted. 'It's not on my timeline, it's been posted on the school page.'

'The school page?' Celia repeated, eyes widening. 'Let me see.' She read the posts. 'I don't believe this is happening.'

Richard and Celia exchanged glances. There were no words. They stared at Jake as if he were a talking bear. It couldn't be real. The school page was active and well used.

'Has anyone read it yet?' Celia asked, her voice cracked, panic setting in. The ramifications were echoing around her mind.

'There are over a hundred comments on it already,' Jake added, quietly.

'Richard?' Celia pleaded, her voice soft. She took a deep breath and shook her head sympathetically. 'Can you please explain what the fuck is going on?'

'No.' It was all he could manage. 'I can't explain it.'

'Who are these people?'

'I don't know,' he said, quietly. 'I wish I did.'

'Why would someone say that, Dad?' Jake asked, astounded. His phone beeped three times in quick succession. He looked at the screen and then at his father. 'My friends are texting me, asking me what it's all about.' Richard wanted to curl up and die. It was bad enough without his kids being sucked into the situation. He knew only too well how cruel kids could be to each other. 'What do I tell them, Dad?'

'Don't tell them anything,' Richard said. He couldn't think of anything to tell them. *Hey, Jake, is it true your dad's a paedo? How do you answer that?*

'Richard,' Celia said. She grabbed his arms and shook him gently. 'Will you answer me and tell me what is going on, please?' Richard shook his head and looked away. He couldn't find the words to answer. Whatever he said would be wrong.

'I honestly don't have a clue.'

'Richard, do you know this girl?'

'What was the name?' Richard asked, frowning.

'Nikki Haley.'

'The name doesn't ring a bell.'

'It doesn't ring a bell?' Celia repeated, shaking her head. 'You're making it sound like you might know her, but conveniently can't remember.'

'I'm racking my brains here to make sense of this, Celia. Do you know how many teenage girls I've taught over the years?'

'Who said she was a pupil?' Celia asked.

'I'm assuming.'

'Why would you assume that?' she asked, confused. 'Have you taught a girl called Nikki Haley?'

'Not that I can remember,' Richard mumbled. He tried to get a grip. 'Anyway, it doesn't matter if I have.' Celia stared at him open-mouthed. She was shocked and confused. 'I haven't so much as touched any of my students, never mind had a relationship with them, so her name is irrelevant.'

The kitchen door opened again and Jaki appeared, a look of horror on her face. 'OMG,' she gasped, 'have you seen this shit on Facebook?' She looked from her dad to her mum and then at her brother. It was obvious they had. 'Dad? What is going on?'

'Will you say something, please?' Celia pleaded.

'What would you like me to say?' Richard sighed, his anger rising. He could feel the blood pumping through his veins. Three pairs of eyes stared at him, questioning, confused, accusing, but most of all disappointed. A random Facebook group had accused him of being a paedophile, and the three people he loved unconditionally were looking at him with uncertainty in their eyes. It was breaking his heart. 'What can I say to make this better?'

'You could deny knowing this Nikki Haley girl for a start.' Celia said, angrily.

'Okay. I don't know anyone called Nikki Haley,' he said, shrugging. 'Does that help?'

'Not really,' Celia replied, quietly.

'There isn't much I can say really, is there?' Richard said, shrugging. He was at a loss to explain it.

'Dad!' Jaki hissed. She was horrified. 'Do you have any idea how embarrassing this is?' she said, throwing her arms in the air. 'OMG, I will never be able to show my face in school again. This is an absolute nightmare. We'll have to move to another area.'

Richard looked at her in disbelief. He hadn't noticed how selfish she had become. 'My Snapchat is going ballistic. None of my friends will ever talk to me again.'

'Thanks for your concern, Jak,' Richard said. 'Obviously this is all about you, and what your friends will think. Don't worry about what it could do to my career.'

'Sorry, Dad,' Jaki mumbled. She walked over to him and hugged him, placing her head on his chest. He held her tightly and breathed in the scent of her hair. His eyes caught Celia's and she looked away. The show of affection made him feel stronger. 'Why would anyone do such a shitty thing to you?' she said, hugging her dad. 'Who would say such a thing about you, Dad?'

'I don't know,' Richard said, ruffling her hair. 'Someone has got their wires crossed. It's just a mistake.'

'We need to call the police, Richard,' Celia said, pulling herself together. 'Call them now before too much damage is done.'

'Here, Dad,' Jake said, holding out his phone. 'Mum is right. Call the police.' Richard stared at the phone. 'Call them, Dad, before people start to believe it.'

Jake's words seemed to reach into the dark place Richard was hiding. Celia watched his expression change: his eyes focused, the muscles in his jaw tightened. He looked at the phone and shook his head. She was nauseous. He still hadn't denied it. Not properly. Not convincingly.

'Will you get my phone from the other room, son?' Richard asked. 'It's on the armchair.' Jake nodded and ran through into the living room. Jaki stared at her dad in disbelief. He could feel their uncertainty in the way they were looking at him. He needed to get a grip of the situation.

'This is all complete bullshit,' he said, finally. Their expressions changed immediately. Celia looked relieved. 'I have no idea where this group has got this information, but they have got the wrong man. It is total bullshit.' Jake came back into the kitchen in a hurry. He handed the mobile to his dad. 'Thanks, son.' He scrolled through his contacts until he found the number he wanted.

It rang a few times before being answered. 'Helen, it's Richard,' he said. He listened for a moment. 'Yes, we've seen it, that's why I'm ringing. You're the page admin, so you can remove it. I need that post taken down and the group blocked from the school page, and I need it done now.' He listened again and nodded. 'That's great, Helen. I can't thank you enough.' There was another silence as he let her speak. 'I will be calling them next, see you tomorrow.' He ended the call and looked at his family, one by one. 'Right, listen to me. Helen Wright is the school page admin. She will remove the post immediately. We do not panic, understand?' Celia and the twins nodded but didn't look convinced. 'Go on your Facebook profiles and check your security settings are locked so no one can contact you, or see your list of friends. I don't want these idiots contacting anyone else we know. Then, go on the group page and block them.' They looked at him in silence. 'What are you waiting for? Do it right now, please!' he said, clapping his hands to get them going, even Celia moved quickly. 'I'm going to speak to the police, although I'm not sure that a crime has been committed.'

He was wrestling back some control; the accusations had been a terrible shock. A person's reputation could be destroyed in minutes on social media. He had seen teachers' careers ruined by false accusations before. If you throw enough shit at a wall, some of it sticks. Tarnished reputations were rarely rebuilt. The perception is always 'no smoke without fire' – especially for a teacher. He would have to manage the situation – take control and stay in control – or risk losing everything he had worked for. He dialled the police non-emergency number and smiled at Celia, hoping to reassure her. She tried to return it but failed miserably. He could see uncertainty in her eyes, mistrust on her face. He couldn't blame her for that. At the beginning of their relationship she was convinced she had caught him out. She thought he was still sleeping with his ex-girlfriend. He wasn't. They had remained friends but he had never cheated on Celia with her. Celia had suffered severe bouts of bulimia, anorexia, and depression throughout their marriage. There were underlying mental health issues that she had refused to recognise existed, and that he just accepted as the norm. There had been unfounded accusations of infidelity all through the marriage. She couldn't help herself. He said she was insecure and she said he was a cheating bastard. Even when things were good, there was always suspicion in their relationship. It was in her eyes, her voice and her actions; she was forever checking his pockets and looking at his social media accounts. He knew she checked his phone regularly so he removed the password and left it lying around so she could check it, at will, to alleviate her jealousy. Many men wouldn't have put up with the constant accusations, but he wasn't one of them. She was Celia, beautiful but flawed. He loved her, always had and always would.

She watched him as he made the phone call. He looked away from her and said hello, giving his name and address and some details. Celia watched him intensely and googled the name Nikki Haley: nothing came up locally. The profile of an American ambassador to the United Nations was top of the search, and she didn't look like a minor. She deleted the search from her history.

Richard dialled the speaking clock and cut off the call immediately. He paced up and down the kitchen, talking loudly and clearly, as he explained what had happened to nobody.

CHAPTER 2

He watched them talking for over half an hour; some were angry, some were emotional, some were animated, pointing fingers and apportioning blame. They were a ragtag bunch of misfits. There were passive members of the gathering and aggressive members – some bullied others. They were angry that their latest sting had failed. He was their target and he had turned the tables on them. They had arrived, hidden, and waited patiently, and then realised he was not coming. They had pretended to be a twelve-year-old boy, that he had been grooming online, and he was supposed to be a fifty-year-old paedophile called Paul. He had strung them along for months – chatting, building a friendship, flirting – until they were convinced they had caught a predator. They had thought they were more intelligent than him, and that was a mistake. Most of the group were below average intelligence, that was obvious. The men wearing camouflage gear, or black combat trousers and boots, were the real idiots. They believed they were a militia: soldiers of justice. If guns were legal, they would be the ones who owned machine guns to go hunting rabbits. They genuinely believed they were tracking predators, hunting paedophiles, but the hunters were actually the hunted. Not that they knew it until it was too late.

They were disappointed and deflated. A lot of time and effort had been invested in setting up the sting, but their victim hadn't turned up. When one of their missions failed, everyone blamed everybody else for tipping off the paedo by bragging online. The group was a mishmash of ages, social standing and levels of intelligence – some of them weren't too bright, sharing everything on their Facebook page, leaving discretion to chance. On the other hand, some thought they were Jason Bourne, communicating online in code with the other deluded idiots. The rest of the bunch would be somewhere in the middle. As a group they appeared to be unlikely friends, having little in common. One thing they did have in common today, though, was disappointment. The anticlimax was palpable. Some talked more than others and some didn't talk at all. He watched and waited, calm yet excited. His pulse was beating steadily. The urge to walk amongst them, and tell them how stupid they were, was overwhelming. He had to sit tight. Patience would pay dividends tonight. He wiped his sweaty palms against his pants.

Eventually they separated, and went in different directions, like a herd of bison stampeding away from hunting hyenas. They were powerful and dangerous as a pack, but once they'd dispersed, their leaders gone, they were weak individuals and easy prey. He waited for them to scatter. He was tense and ready to begin the chase. Excitement coursed through his veins. Another one of them would die tonight. Not that anyone would notice. Most of them were pathetic losers looking for something to belong to, something to give purpose to their sad lives. They were loners, social misfits trying to fit in somewhere. He knew some of them were victims of abuse themselves. They bleated all over the Internet, to anyone that would listen, about what a tough time they'd had growing up. One of them claimed to be a victim of Jimmy Savile. Fucking liar. He wasn't old enough by at least ten years. Some of them wore their troubled upbringing like a badge of honour. Shut up, grow up, and get on with your life, that was his view. Stop whinging about what happened twenty years ago; it isn't the reason you're divorced, living in a bedsit and claiming benefits. It's because you spent your life looking backwards, feeling sorry for yourself, that you didn't see what was in front of you until it was too late. Joining the predator hunting group was their way of hitting back. Well, two can play that game and there is only one winner. Hunting them was simple enough, and if he picked his targets carefully, suspicion would never be raised. He could go on killing them forever and a day. No one would miss them, or notice they were gone, for months. As the group separated, he identified his target and followed him at a safe distance.

His target looked both ways and crossed the road, heading for the train station at the edge of a sprawling housing estate. He knew he would take that route as it was the same one he had used the last three times the group had been on a hunt. The road leading to Hough Green Station was badly lit, narrow and lined with trees. A small car park was lit by a single streetlight. Its dull yellow glow cast shadows all around. The wind was blowing and a fine rain began to pour, soaking him as he followed the man, closing the distance between them. His footsteps echoed between the dark walls. At one point the target turned around, glancing over his shoulder. They locked eyes for a second but his prey didn't sense the danger that was approaching. Idiot. He seemed nervous, walking alone in the dark in such an isolated spot, but his camouflage outfit and army boots made him look tough. He wanted to be a soldier, hunting the enemy. His eyes told a different story. Underneath the uniform was a terrified boy, alone and vulnerable. The rest of the pack had gone. He saw the flash of fear in the target's eyes, but he didn't run. Some people were stupid. The target walked quicker, widening the gap between them. He slowed, not wanting to spook him. Not yet.

The unmanned station was deserted as he reached the sandstone steps that descended onto the platform. Litter and leaves hurtled past his feet while he looked over the gantry at the westbound platform. There he was, hood up, leaning against the wall. He was sheltering from the elements. A brave crusader returning home alone. He didn't look like a predator hunter. Sausage roll hunter, maybe. He was a spineless coward hiding behind a group, pretending to be of some benefit to society. It gave him a feeling of worth. He had no idea how much damage the group caused to innocent people when their amateur searches went wrong. They ruined lives. They were keyboard warriors, untrained and unintelligent with no concept of the carnage they left behind when they outed innocent men. Families were torn apart and lives were ruined. Children were parted from their parents and careers ended, all because they got it wrong.

In his case, they had got it right, but that wasn't the point. He had lost everything because of them. The jail time was hell for him. Four years of his life, mostly spent in solitary because other criminals viewed him as vermin. He had been beaten badly, scalded with tea that had been mixed with so much sugar that the liquid clung to the skin, prison napalm, and slashed with a carpet blade attached to a toothbrush. All of that paled into insignificance in comparison to the months before the trial. His life had disintegrated in front of his eyes. Friends, family and workmates abandoned him. He lost his girlfriend and three stepchildren, his job, his friends, and his house in the space of three months. He'd rebuilt his life and they had demolished it again. That was nearly as bad as suffocating in a dingy cell. He couldn't blame them for his crimes, but he could blame them for being sent to prison. They had tricked him and set a trap. There was no one else to blame. It was completely their fault. They were bullies and they ganged up on people. They interfered in people's lives. They were vigilantes who thought there would be no repercussions for them. Well, they were wrong. Very wrong. The ramifications of their interference would echo through their shallow lives and beyond. He would make sure of that.

He watched his target from the footbridge; he glanced up but didn't register the danger. He walked down the steps and along the platform, stopping beneath an overhanging roof to escape the rain. He waited until he could see the lights of the Liverpool train appearing around a long bend in the distance. It wouldn't be long now. The target lit a cigarette and sucked deeply on it, releasing the smoke through his nostrils. He was watching the approaching train without a care in the world. It was too good an opportunity to miss; he was going to tail him home, but this was too easy. The platform was deserted. Smoking was the perfect cover to approach him without raising the alarm.

'Have you got a light, please?' he asked. The target nodded, and reached into his pocket for a lighter. He lit his cigarette and blew out the smoke. 'Thanks.'

'No problem.'

'Shit weather, isn't it?'

'Really shit.'

'Do I know you?'

'I don't think so.' His target looked concerned. There was a twinkle of fear in his eyes. Suspicion made his eyes narrow slightly. Not much, but enough to display that he was spooked. Good.

'Yes, I do recognise you.' He smiled and pointed a finger. 'You're Dave, aren't you?' he asked. 'Dave Rutland. I recognise your face.'

'Yes, that's right,' the target answered, uncertainty in his voice. He looked frightened. Predator hunter? The closest he had been to a predator was Chester Zoo. 'How do you know my name?'

'Facebook,' he answered. 'You're friends with some of the same people I am.'

'Small world, eh?' Dave Rutland said, relaxing.

'It's a small world. Thanks for the light.' He turned, as if to walk away, and flicked open a telescopic baton. 'Are you still in the predator group on Facebook?'

'Yes,' Dave said, smiling. He looked excited. 'That's where I've been tonight.'

'Really,' he said, smiling coldly.

'Yes. I'm on my way home from there.'

'Catch anyone?'

'No, not tonight,' Dave said, shaking his head. 'The dirty paedo didn't show up. We'll get him next time.'

'Unless he gets you first.' There was a glimmer of confusion in Dave's eyes. He swung around quickly, striking him across the side of his head with the truncheon. Dave collapsed on the spot. His knees buckled and he crumpled into a rainwater puddle. A second blow sent him further into the darkness. 'How does that feel?' He could hear his attackers voice and he knew he was being dragged across the platform. He also knew his jaw was broken. 'Like a rat in a trap, eh, Dave?' Rainwater soaked Dave's clothes but he couldn't resist. 'Not nice feeling helpless, is it, Dave?' One of his boots caught on the concrete. His attacker pulled him clear. 'You thought you were a tough guy, didn't you, Dave?' Dave mumbled but couldn't speak. Blood dribbled from his mouth. 'Not so tough now, are you, Dave?' The platform became darker as he was dragged along. 'I was going to follow you home and kill you there, but this is too good an opportunity to miss.' There was pain as his head jerked around. 'Have you ever wondered what it would be like to see your life coming to an end before your eyes, and not be able to lift a finger, Dave?'

It was pitch black where the platform turned into a ramp that led onto the tracks. He felt someone lifting him, and then the sensation of falling, floating through the night. It wasn't a pleasant sensation. Hitting the rails wasn't pleasant either. His head cracked against one, fracturing his skull; his knees hit the other, twisting them painfully. He heard himself moaning in agony yet felt detached from it. A bright light pierced his mind and a roaring sound filled his thoughts as the train thundered towards him. His eyes flickered open, sensing danger. He saw the oncoming juggernaut and opened his mouth to scream. The sound of the brakes squealing was painful; there was a catastrophic impact and a second of excruciating pain, and then nothing.

He watched the train trundle over David Rutland. It dragged his body beneath its wheels, dismembering it over two hundred yards, before screeching to a halt further down the platform. He stayed in the shadows and moved towards the steps. He hid in a dark recess to watch the aftermath. Time seemed to stand still. He could see a light in the driver's cab. The driver was female and she was animated on the emergency phone, no doubt reporting a jumper. She didn't leave the train and she didn't open the doors for the passengers to leave. He heard a muffled announcement over the train's loud speakers but he couldn't decipher her words. It was twenty minutes before the first ambulance arrived. A second one pulled up fifteen minutes after that. A single fire engine arrived and the firemen searched for body parts. A police car arrived to secure the scene and to guide passengers from the station to where they would have to wait for a replacement bus service. He left his hiding place and mingled with them as they climbed the sandstone steps to the access road and the car park. Some of them were sympathetic to the plight of those who suffered mental illness, while others were not so accommodating. Getting home was far more important than a stranger's need to end their life beneath a train.

'Poor soul must have been in a very dark place,' one voice said.

'Selfish twat,' another replied. 'That driver will never be the same again.'

'Fuck him. It's going to cost me a fortune in a cab.'

'I've got work in the morning.'

He listened to the heated debate as they walked through the rain. When they reached the car park, he pulled up his hood and walked towards the main road. Ten minutes later, he was in a black cab on his way home. Job done for tonight.

CHAPTER 3

Richard took a deep breath when he had finished his conversation with the imaginary police officer. He went to the fridge and took out a can of sugar-free cola, placing the ice-cold tin against his forehead. It soothed the growing headache for a few seconds. He closed his eyes and wished that he could wake up in bed to find this was all a bad dream. He would swap places in the most frightening nightmare ever if he could; this was worse than any nightmare he had ever experienced. He felt light-headed and anxious, angry and frightened. The sense of wrongdoing was overwhelming, despite being innocent. He felt guilty for being accused, which was madness, but he couldn't help it. Guilt was seeping through his bones where it had no business being.

'What did the police say?' Celia asked. She stared at her iPad, searching for any more posts about it. She had been inundated with messages from her friends. They had all said: private message me if you need to chat, which really meant: what the fuck is going on? Tell me everything. Did he do it?

Most of them were written with fake concern. Sympathetic on the face of it, but just plain nosey beneath the sentiment: I'm so sorry you have to go through this, you seem such a happy couple, which meant: is it true? Is Richard a paedophile? She batted away the enquiries politely, trying to sound positive, and grateful for their interference.

Richard shrugged and looked at her. 'They said the group hadn't committed a criminal offence and that it's a civil matter.' He opened the tin and drank greedily from it. 'They said they will look into it, but they didn't think there was much they could do.'

'That's crap,' Celia snapped.

'What is?'

'It's a criminal offence. I can think of at least three offences. Tomorrow, I'm going to take advice from some of my colleagues and I'm going after them. I'm going to crucify these bastards!' Celia emptied her wine and walked to the fridge. She opened the door and took out an empty bottle of white wine, tutting angrily. 'I'll sue them for defamation.'

'Who?' Richard asked.

'Who what?'

'Who will you sue?'

'Whoever is responsible for posting that filth, of course!'

'It's a Facebook group.' Richard shrugged. 'The best way to get rid of them is to report them to Facebook and say they have been threatening me.' Celia reached for her iPad to do it. 'I've already done it,' Richard said, 'but feel free to report them again. With a bit of luck, they'll shut down the page and that will be the end of it. They can't have any evidence to back up their claims because it never happened.'

'I hope that's true, because if you've cheated on me again…' Celia said, biting her lip. She shook her head and closed her eyes, already sorry for what she had said. He didn't deserve that.

'Cheated on you again?' Richard challenged her. He'd had enough accusations for one night. 'There's no *again*, Celia. You made an accusation a year before the twins were born. That was fifteen years ago, Celia, and what I really don't need right now is you turning a drama into a fucking crisis.' He glared at her. She was usually the dominant personality but Richard had his moments. There were times when it was better to back off than keep prodding him. The look in his eyes told her that this was one of them. 'I need you to believe me and I need your support right now.'

'I'm sorry.'

'So am I,' Richard said.

'I can't believe they think they can make accusations like that and get away with it,' Celia said, dropping the bottle noisily into the recycling. 'You're a teacher, for Christ's sake, and they have the gall to post that on the school page. I don't understand the mentality of someone doing that, unless they think they have evidence.' She realised it sounded negative, suspicious even. 'I cannot believe they used the school Facebook page. It's like trial by Internet.'

'Well, it isn't there now,' Richard said. 'Hopefully, it's a storm in a teacup. No one will believe them. No one we care about at least.'

'Let's hope so,' Celia said, opening another bottle. She saw Richard watching her, disapproval in his eyes. 'What?' she asked, flippantly, filling up her glass. The glass held half the bottle without looking full. 'Is there a problem?'

'No problem,' Richard answered, shrugging. It was his turn to feel disappointed.

'If ever I needed a glass of wine, it's right now.'

'I'm going to finish watching the football while you pickle yourself,' he joked, but Celia's face said she hadn't found it funny.

'You're accused of being a paedophile online and you're going to sit and watch the football?'

'What would you suggest I do, Celia?' he asked, shrugging. He felt sick with worry, but what could he do about it? Things would play out in the end. He couldn't predict what would happen next, no one could. All he could do was react to each situation as it arose; dwelling on what a group of strangers might do next was both pointless and depressing. 'The damage is done and we've done what we can. I can't change anything right now. We'll have to see what tomorrow brings.'

'I wish I had your ability to remain calm,' she said, half-smiling. She meant it too, it was one of his traits that she'd fallen in love with. Nothing rattled him. When her world was being shaken to the core, he was her rock. 'Tell me this will blow over, Richard.'

'This will blow over, Celia,' he said, nodding. 'There is no truth or substance behind the accusations. We have nothing to worry about.' He walked to her and took her hands in his. Their eyes locked, both searching for the truth.

Has he done anything wrong?
Does she think I have done anything wrong?

They kissed briefly and he held her. It was like hugging a distant relative, she was tense and uncomfortable. 'Someone has messed up. They have the wrong man.'

'I'm sorry,' she said, kissing his cheek. 'I overreacted. It was a shock.'

'That's an understatement,' he said, smiling.

'What, me overreacting or the shock?'

'Both.'

'Thank you.'

'My hands are still shaking,' Richard said.

'Mine too.' He squeezed her again. Her phone rang and she showed him the screen. It was Silvia Booth, member of the school board and self-appointed queen bee. 'I'll have to talk to her.'

Richard nodded and walked out of the kitchen into the living room, closing the door. She stared at the door and had a gulp of her wine before answering.

Jake was on his laptop in conversation with his friends, deflecting questions about the accusations. Rumours were spreading like wildfire. Not everyone had seen the posts before they were removed – most had heard them second- or third-hand. They had heard that Mr Vigne was having a relationship with a minor. The name of the alleged minor, Nikki Haley, had been omitted from communications, leaving an opening for speculation about who Richard Vigne had been having an affair with. Jake was frantically trying to firefight the chat. Some people were guessing who the girl was. April Morris had been mentioned a few times because she liked older boys. Older boys? Her boyfriend was seventeen, for fuck's sake. His dad wasn't just older, he was actually old. He looked at his dad and shook his head.

'This is going viral, Dad,' he said, frowning. 'Some people are making shit up. I'm trying to put them straight.'

'That's what people do when they don't know the truth,' Richard said, pressing play, 'they make shit up.'

'They shouldn't.'

'Why not?' Richard asked. Jake looked confused. 'Everybody else does. The newspapers do it every day. If they don't know what happened, they make shit up. If television reporters don't know the truth, they make shit up.' He shrugged. 'If politicians get asked a difficult question that they don't know the answer to, what do they do?'

'Make shit up,' Jake answered.

'Correct. It's human nature, son.' Richard watched the football but wasn't really seeing it. 'We have a burning desire to know the truth, to know what happened. Films, soap operas, books, are consumed by millions because we want to know what happens. And if people don't know, they make it up.'

'I can't keep up with all the questions, Dad,' Jake said, shaking his head.

'Don't try, son. The jungle drums will be beating tonight, let them,' Richard said, shrugging. 'They're going to speculate whether you tell them what happened or not. You're bound to say it's not true, aren't you?' Jake nodded. 'I'm your dad. Most people won't believe you anyway. They'll make their own minds up.' He turned down the television and stood up. 'I'm going to bed. I've had enough excitement for one night.' He ruffled Jake's hair and hugged him. It felt normal. That was reassuring. 'Night, Jake. Don't worry. This will all blow over.' Jake nodded and half-smiled.

'Night, son.'

'Night, Dad.'

Richard walked out of the living room into the hallway. The wooden floor felt cool and soothing beneath his feet. His stomach was in knots. He checked the lock on the front door and climbed the stairs. Jaki was lying on her bed, typing furiously on her laptop. She looked up at her dad and shook her head in disbelief.

'This is a nightmare, Dad,' she said. Her voice sounded strained. 'Why are people so shitty to each other?'

'Because it's human nature to be shitty to one another,' he said. 'It will pass, Jak,' he sighed.

'Melanie Brand's father has posted that he is going to make sure the school suspend you while they look into the allegations,' she said, turning her laptop around so he could read the screen. 'He's head of the parents' committee.'

'I know who Kevin Brand is, Jak,' Richard said, reading the post. It was on the school page. It disappeared when he was halfway through reading it. Jak gasped and looked at him.

'What happened, Dad?'

'That will be Helen deleting comments. She's a diamond.' The page froze for a second and vanished. Richard sighed with relief. 'She's taken the page down. That will stop all the speculation for tonight.'

'Not on Snapchat and Twitter it won't,' Jak said, shaking her head. 'Half the school are on there, gossiping.'

'Luckily, I have no concept of what that means, and hopefully, neither will most of the people that matter,' he said. He bent down and hugged her. She tensed briefly before relaxing. It was enough to make him feel sick inside. His own daughter had doubts. They may be tiny, insignificant, unfounded and natural, nevertheless, they were there and that cut him deeply. 'Night, Jak. I'm sorry that you've had to go through this. I know exactly what schoolkids are like. There's not a shred of truth to this. It will blow over, I promise.' She hugged him properly this time and it felt good. 'Night night,' he said, kissing her forehead.

'Night, Dad,' she replied.

'Shall I close this door?'

'Yes, please.'

He pulled the door closed and headed to bed. It seemed like an age before he could sleep, and when he did, his dreams were dark and twisted. His sheets were damp with sweat when he awoke. It was dark and the shadows seemed to crowd in on him. He switched on the bedside lamp and patted the empty spot next to him. Celia hadn't come to bed; she often slept on the couch after too much wine, but this time, the fact she had stayed downstairs seemed to have more significance.

CHAPTER 4

Detective Superintendent Marcus Braddick pulled up in his Evoque and parked next to three marked police cars and a CSI van. A couple of dog walkers had braved the wind but they didn't look like they were enjoying themselves. There was no sign of any law enforcement personnel. He assumed they would all be on the beach, on the other side of the dunes. He switched off the engine and reached for his mobile before opening the door. The wind whistled through the gap, chilling him to the core. He grabbed a parka from the back seat and wrestled into it. As he zipped it up, he climbed out of the vehicle and pulled the hood over his bald head. Sand stung his black skin and made him squint. He closed the door and walked towards the path. The wind was roaring in from Liverpool Bay, across the beach, over the dunes and on to the mainland. It carried fine grains of sand with it; each granule was a painful projectile. He lowered his head and followed the path around the boating lake towards the dunes. It was longer than it looked and he was walking against the wind. To his left were the docks at Bootle. Stacks of multicoloured containers towered above the ships that were moored there. Nearby, a wind turbine rotated rapidly, at odds with its surroundings. It made an eerie whistling sound as it turned. To his right, the dunes went on as far as the eye could see. Thick green grasses topped the higher peaks. Parallel to them, Victorian terraces hugged the coast for miles into the distance. The boating lake was empty, its waters dark and choppy.

Braddick tried to remember the last time he had been here. His ex, Louise, had been fascinated by the iron statues. Sir Antony Gormley's iron men had transformed the beach and made it a tourist attraction. He couldn't decide how many years ago it was. It was too many. Life had hurtled past him since then. He envisioned her pretty face in the sunshine and couldn't remember why they had split up; not that it mattered. His thoughts ran through his mind as he headed for the path to the beach. The path was a few hundred yards long and climbed between the dunes, twisting its way up a gentle slope to a wide concrete promenade. When he reached the top, he paused to take in the view. It was a view that stopped people in their tracks and took away their breath. The wide sands were dotted with the iron men, staring out to sea, each one waiting to be submersed by the oncoming sea. Beyond the beach, the sea shimmered in the sunshine, and dozens of white wind turbines appeared to hover above the waves on the horizon.

Braddick pushed his hands into his pockets and looked around. A few hundred yards to his right he spotted uniformed officers creating a cordon and the CSI unit at work. His DS, Sadie Myers, waved at him. She was leaning on one of the iron statues, watching the forensic officers at work. Her fur-lined hood was flapping in the wind and her long red hair was tied at the back of her head into a tight bun. Braddick had never seen hair so ginger. She was the archetypical redhead: pale skin and freckles. He waved back and trudged down the promenade, through deep drifts of sand, until he reached some stone steps that led down to the beach. The salty tang of sea air filled his senses. Wide banks of seaweed, driftwood and debris striped the beach, marking the limit of the last tide. Razor shells crunched beneath his feet; seemingly, tens of thousands of them had been washed up in the storms – along with a body. Bodies on the beach were nothing new, and rarely attracted the interest of Merseyside's major investigation team, but this one was special. Initial reports indicated it had been encased in wire mesh and weighted; the body had been dumped by someone who didn't want it to surface. It clearly wasn't suicide, and it wasn't accidental, which left murder as the cause, hence the call to MIT. As he approached, Sadie smiled, and gestured with her head.

'Nasty one, this,' she said. 'The victim was wearing a United shirt.' She turned and looked out to sea, her expression serious. 'We've removed it to save his family any embarrassment.' She grinned. Braddick shook his head. He tried very hard not to smile but couldn't help it. 'Got you,' she said, 'made you smile.'

'Very funny,' Braddick said, nodding. 'The old ones are the best, eh, sergeant?'

'Don't be like that,' Sadie said. 'I've been standing here for two hours, freezing my tits off. I had to amuse myself somehow.' She stamped her Ugg boots in the sand, shifting her weight from one leg to the other in a vain attempt to keep warm. Her jeans were faded and worn. 'I love this place in the summer, I come here with the dog a lot, but today, I'm not feeling it.'

'It's a bit fresh,' Braddick said, rubbing his hands together. 'Who is our victim?'

'Doctor Libby said he would give me his initial findings when he has finished, whatever "finished" means,' Sadie said, eyebrows raised. She frowned. 'That was an hour and fifty minutes ago. I'm sure he does it to wind me up. Now you've arrived, I bet he comes over in less than five minutes.' She lowered her voice. 'He's always brown-nosing you.'

'That's not an image I need in my head.'

'Fiver says he does.'

'Tenner,' Braddick said, sealing the bet with a handshake. As if he had heard them, Graham Libby took off his glasses and walked over to them. Braddick could feel Sadie smiling behind her hand. That would cost him a drink. He nodded hello as the doctor approached.

'Braddick,' he said, cleaning his glasses on his blue forensic suit. 'Sorry to keep you waiting, sergeant,' he added, turning to Sadie. 'I didn't want to move our friend here until I was sure which bits washed up with him, and which bits belong to him.' He put his glasses back on and gestured for them to follow him to the corpse. Braddick frowned when the smell of decay reached him. Sadie handed him a small jar of tiger balm and he dabbed a blob beneath his nostrils. It helped a little, but there was something about a body that had decomposed in the water. The stench was cloying, choking almost.

'You can see from the state of decomposition that he's been in the water a while.' The bloated flesh was swollen, and protruded between the mesh in places.

'Roughly how long?' Braddick asked.

'Considering how cold the water is, probably three weeks or so. I'll have a better idea once we're back in the lab.' He shifted his weight and knelt. 'You see this here,' he said, pointing to some strands of seaweed in the wire. Braddick nodded. 'This type of algae is found in freshwater.' He paused, and pointed further down the left leg. 'This is saltwater seaweed. He was put in the water up river and he's floated down here into the bay. The storms lifted him from the bottom and dumped him here.'

He looked up the river, his eyes drawn by a Mersey ferry that was approaching the Woodside terminal across the river on the Wirral. The grey waters crashed against the hull, turning white, before splashing back into the water.

'How far up river? That's the question,' Sadie said.

Braddick glanced at her, that *was* the key question. The doctor was clearly right – if the body had been in the sea for two weeks, it would have been far out in the bay by now. Too far out to be washed ashore.

'I read a study that suggested a body could travel as much as a mile a day in the river,' Sadie said.

'Which study?'

'The university published it.'

'I read some of it, but threw it in the bin when I realised they didn't use bodies to do the study,' Graham Libby said. 'They used weighted floats. It isn't worth the paper it's written on.' He dismissed it a little too vehemently. 'Unless human bodies are used, there are too many variables to make it accurate. Water temperature, the time between death and being put into the water, body fat percentage, depth and flow of the river, tidal flows, phase of the moon, the list goes on and on.' He shook his head. 'You might as well pick a number between one and ten and double it.'

'I did wonder how accurate it was when I read it,' Sadie said, nodding. 'I wasn't convinced.' She smiled, revealing straight white teeth. She was a naturally pretty woman. Her green eyes had a sparkle of mischief in them.

'You were right not to be convinced, sergeant.' The doctor rubbed his chin, deep in thought. 'Last month there was an article about a motorcyclist killed in a crash in California. He was thrown from his bike, over a bridge, and into a river. Three days later he was pulled from the water, 175 miles downriver.' He paused for effect.

'Nearly sixty miles a day?' Sadie asked.

'He was obese so he floated quickly, and the water was warm so he decomposed rapidly. When they found him, the local police guessed he had been in the water for a month, from the state of decomposition, but they found his ID and ran a search. Of course, they had the bike but no body. They knew when the crash had happened, and realised he had only been in the water three days.' He pointed at the body. 'That university study is piffle. Real bodies have to be used.'

'Fascinating,' Sadie said. It was interesting, but the doctor was prone to going off track. She looked at their victim to bring back his focus. 'I wonder where he was put in.'

'Unfortunately, I can't tell you that.'

'Okay, what do we know?' Braddick asked. He noticed Sadie was blushing; she blushed a lot. Her skin was so pale it was obvious when she was embarrassed. He winked at her. The doctor was prone to the odd rant too. He was an opinionated buffoon but very good at his job.

'We know that he's male, somewhere between twenty-five and forty. I'll give you a more accurate number later.' The doctor pointed to the right arm. 'Can you see the fine cuts here, and here?' he asked. Braddick moved closer. The flesh was swollen and rotten, but there were obvious wounds in the skin. They looked fine but deep. 'There are dozens of cuts like this all over the body. The cuts are so deep that the bones are scarred.' Braddick looked closer. Many of the bones were exposed and clearly visible. They looked unnaturally white against the sand and seaweed. 'These cuts were made slowly and the killer went as deep as possible – the bones stopped the blade going any deeper.' He pointed to the skull. 'His eyelids, nose and lips are missing. At first, I thought maybe the sea life had nibbled on him, but then I noticed some of the wounds are precise. The bottom-feeders have removed flesh to a degree, but there are dozens of surgical wounds too. Someone removed his genitals, fingers, toes, tongue, and most of his face. This man was encased in wire mesh, tortured to death, and dumped in the river.' He pointed to some crisscross patterns on the arms. 'These marks indicate that the killer wrapped him in mesh ante mortem. He must have struggled against the wire.'

'What a way to go,' Sadie said.

'Is there any good news?' Braddick asked.

'Yes,' the doctor replied, bluntly. Braddick waited for him to expand. The silence was annoying. 'His teeth are still intact. We should be able to identify him from his dental records.'

'As long as we find out who he is,' Braddick said.

'Good luck with that one,' the doctor retorted.

'The killer overlooked that,' Sadie said. 'Why go to all that trouble and leave the teeth? Was it a mistake?'

'I don't think so.' The doctor shook his head. He looked out at the wind farm in the distance. 'He went to a lot of trouble wrapping the body in mesh. Look at the way he's weaved the sections together with wire. It's very intricate.' The detectives exchanged glances. 'Every limb is encased and weighted, yet still exposed to the elements. The flesh would be eaten, and would rot away, but the skeleton would remain intact at the bottom of the sea. He didn't overlook the teeth, he overlooked the power of storm Dennis.' He gestured to the sea. 'It's a freak of nature that his body was brought up. Your killer didn't get sloppy, he didn't count on us ever finding him.'

'Let's get Google onto the missing persons lists. Tell him to start with addresses in the city, and work outwards.' Google was the nickname of a detective sergeant who had an uncanny knack of knowing things that most people didn't. 'If we can identify him, it will give us a starting point,' Braddick said, shivering against the wind. 'Thanks, Graham. Keep me up to date.' He nodded to the doctor. Dr Libby turned back to the body without a word. 'There's nothing more to do here. Leave the tidying up to uniform, Sadie,' Braddick said, turning away. 'Walk back to the car with me.'

'You don't have to say that twice,' Sadie said, jogging to catch up with him. 'I'm bloody freezing.'

'Me too. I need a large coffee.'

'Sounds good. Your turn to buy them.'

'It's always my turn.'

'What do you think?' Sadie asked.

'Early days yet,' he said. He lowered his head to protect his eyes from the shifting sand.

'You saw what I saw though, yes?'

'Yes.' Braddick nodded. There was something familiar about the way the body had been disposed of. 'There was something that tugged at the memory bank.'

'The wire mesh,' Sadie said, studying his face for a reaction. He looked at her and she knew she was right. 'I thought the same thing as soon as I saw it; the way it was fastened together?'

Braddick nodded. 'We've seen something very similar before.'

CHAPTER 5

Richard left the house before Celia and the twins were awake. It was still dark and the rain was pouring down. The traffic was light as he navigated the route to school. It was a journey that he had made Monday to Friday for eleven years. Today was different. Today, he was driving towards a firing squad. It was surreal. He was anxious and panicking about the reception he would get. His colleagues wouldn't believe the accusations, would they? Surely not. The pupils wouldn't; he was very popular with the kids he taught, and he had never so much as laid a finger on any of them. They would know it was all lies. It was the parents who concerned him. Some of them knew him, but most didn't. Not all the parents interacted with the school. A lot of them couldn't give a shit. There were parents who had never been to parents' evening, not caring how their children were performing or behaving. He was a stranger to them, a stranger they entrusted the safety of their children to. All he could do was have faith in the trust he had built up throughout his career. Today would be a test of faith.

He parked his car in the usual spot and grabbed his laptop case. The lights inside the school were already burning brightly. Some of the teachers liked to arrive early to set up lessons, or complete their marking in peace. He took a deep breath and climbed out of the car, into the rain. The indicator lights blinked as he locked it and ran towards the main entrance. He pushed open the doors with his shoulder and stepped inside. The caretaker's room was empty: door open, kettle on. The administration office was open, lights glowing. Mrs Kelly, the school secretary, was sat at her desk; her trademark packet of mint imperials to her right, a teacup and saucer to her left. She was the first person in the building each morning, and the last to leave each night, although, he wasn't sure what she did any more. Most of the school secretary's administration work had been digitalised. The headmaster couldn't bring himself to make her redundant. He couldn't recall her taking a sick day in all the years he had been there. She called all the teachers by their surnames. He had been Mr Vigne every school day for eleven years. 'Morning, Mr Vigne' on his way in, 'Goodnight, Mr Vigne' on his way home. She was like part of the furniture. Richard hoped that the school's loyalty to her, would be mirrored in his case.

The wind caught the door and it slammed closed behind him, making him jump. His nerves were on edge. Disturbed by the noise, Mrs Kelly looked up. She focused on his face, her expression frozen. He saw the look in her eyes: mistrust, uncertainty and disappointment. She looked flustered, as if she didn't know what to say. He smiled at her but she didn't return it. It was like being punched in the guts. Mrs Kelly wasn't sure if he could be a paedophile or not. His spirits sank a little. He raised a hand in greeting. She had to respond.

'Morning, Mr Vigne,' she mumbled, looking down at her desk too quickly.

'Morning, Mrs Kelly,' Richard replied, his voice upbeat. It wasn't the best start. His nerves were jangling and Mrs Kelly's reaction had done nothing to settle them. 'The weather is shocking this morning,' he added. He had to act naturally, as if the allegations were of no consequence to him. It was the only way to deal with the uncertainty that he would undoubtedly encounter. He had seen it in the eyes of his family, it was only natural; human nature made people suspicious. It was part of the survival instinct. He couldn't expect people to be normal. 'It was bad yesterday, but today is absolutely shocking. How was your journey in? Terrible, I bet.'

Mrs Kelly looked up and nodded her head.

'It was terrible, Mr Vigne,' she agreed. 'I was soaked by the time my bus arrived this morning.'

'Was it late again?' Richard asked, frowning. It was a stupid question. It was always late, but he wanted to get her talking.

'It's always late,' she said.

And when it does arrive, there's nowhere to sit. He had heard it more times than he could remember.

'And when it did arrive, there was nowhere to sit,' she complained.

'I hope someone gave up their seat for you.'

'Eventually. Manners and respect for your elders aren't what they used to be.'

'It's time you learned to drive,' he teased.

'Not at my age.' She waved her hand to dismiss his comment, just as she had done for years. 'It's too late for that now.'

'Nonsense,' Richard said, shaking his head, 'it's never too late. See you later.' He left the office and walked towards the staffroom. Apart from her initial reaction, she had been normal. It was to be expected, accusations like that made people very uncomfortable. If it was somebody else who had been accused, would he feel awkward himself? Of course he would.

He walked down the corridor and took a flight of stairs to the top floor. The caretaker was there, changing a bulb. He looked down from his ladder and saluted.

'Morning, Ted,' Richard said, returning the greeting.

'Morning, Mr Vigne. Shocking weather today.'

'Absolutely shocking.'

'I'll be putting the doormats down when I've done this,' Ted said. 'Otherwise the little darlings will be slipping all over the place, and we don't want any broken heads, do we?'

'Definitely not,' Richard replied over his shoulder. 'It's not the little darlings we have to worry about, it's their parents. Where there's blame, there's a claim.'

Ted laughed, and climbed down his ladder. There was no difference in his manner, although the chances of Ted being online were zero. He wouldn't be aware of any accusations yet. Richard paused outside the staffroom, his fingers on the door handle for a second. The sound of conversation drifted from inside. His nerves were on edge as he entered. Three of his colleagues were sitting drinking tea; two supply teachers, who he didn't know very well, were standing next to the coffee machine. Their conversation stopped as he stepped in and closed the door. 'Morning,' he said. He could feel their eyes on him, searching for any signs of guilt.

'Morning,' they replied in unison. The two female teachers exchanged glances. One of them raised an eyebrow, surprised to see him. The supply teachers walked towards the door and left without saying a word. He didn't know them anyway. Despite that, they had voted with their feet. He felt the pressure building. 'Shocking weather out there,' he said. Nobody commented. 'Yesterday was bad, but today is terrible.'

'How much sleep did you get?' Bill Edwards asked, cutting through the small talk. He was a history teacher, and had been at the school since it opened. He wore a three-piece suit and a dickie bow tie every day; his greying beard showed evidence of his breakfast. Porridge by the looks of it.

'Not much,' Richard sighed.

'I saw some of the activity on the school page before it was removed,' Bill said. 'Some people ought to be ashamed of themselves, crucifying a man before they know all the facts.'

'It's human nature, Bill.'

'Pardon my language,' Bill said, lowering his voice, 'but who the fuck are these people, making ridiculous accusations like that on a school page?'

'I honestly don't know,' Richard replied. He sat down and put his laptop on the seat next to him. Despite Bill's efforts, the atmosphere was tainted. 'They're an online vigilante group with the wrong information.'

'Wrong information?' Bill tutted. 'Well, you need to sue the arse off them.'

'That's Celia's job.'

'I hope you've reported them to the police,' Bill said, frowning.

'Yes.' Richard swallowed hard. Being normal was more difficult than he had thought. 'They're going to look into the group.'

'Look into them?' Bill said, shaking his head. 'They need locking up.'

'I'm sure it will all blow over, once people realise it's a mistake.'

'Do you want some tea, while you tell us all about it?' Bill asked.

'Yes please. Although there's not much to tell.'

'How's Celia?' a maths teacher called Susan asked. She had been at the school a few months at the most, and Richard didn't think they had exchanged more than a dozen words since she had arrived, yet, here she was, asking about his wife. Two-faced bitch. He wanted to tell her to mind her own business, but alienating people wasn't the best idea.

'She's fine, thank you for asking,' he replied. He half-smiled, but she didn't return it. She looked straight through him.

'It must have been a terrible shock for her,' she commented.

'It was a bit of a shock to me, to be honest,' Richard joked. Susan didn't laugh. Bill handed him a cup of tea. 'Thanks, Bill.'

'So, what happened?' Bill asked, sitting down heavily. He looked at Richard with sympathy; there was no suspicion there, unlike his female colleagues. They believed it was possible. He could tell by their expressions. Richard was gym fit, and popular with the pupils. The older girls flirted around him sometimes, and they didn't like that. *He's a man, and men think with their dicks* – it was written all over their faces. No smoke without fire. Richard sipped his tea while he thought about the answer. He was about to speak, when the staffroom door opened.

'Richard,' the headmaster said, popping his head around the door. His white eyebrows dominated his face. He seemed nervous, looking around the staffroom as if he might catch something nasty.

'Morning, Charles,' Richard said, greeting him with a smile. It wasn't returned. It was beginning to look like smiling was a waste of time. His father had told him that a smile would disarm all but the most difficult of people. It didn't seem to be working today.

'I was hoping to catch you early. I thought I'd seen your car outside.' Richard felt his stomach clench. Of course his car was outside. What did he mean, he *thought* he'd seen his car? He had either seen it, or he hadn't. There was trouble ahead. The headmaster never came into the staffroom. Not ever. 'Can I have a word with you, in my office, please?' He paused, and gestured to the cup. 'Bring your tea with you.'

Richard stood up and looked at Bill. Bill looked concerned. The females swapped glances again. *He's guilty. Mr Vigne has been screwing a pupil.* They didn't say a word, but that's what he heard in his mind. He put down his teacup and picked up his briefcase. No one said anything as he left the room. This wasn't going as well as he would have liked. The headmaster walked quickly towards his office, which was four doors away. Richard lagged a few steps behind. They didn't speak until they were inside and the door was closed. The atmosphere was tense.

'I'm assuming you saw the allegations posted on the Internet last night?' Richard said, taking the initiative.

'I didn't see them myself.' The head frowned and cleared his throat, uncomfortable with the situation. He had always avoided conflict. Some of the more aggressive teachers walked all over him. 'But I've been made aware of them, in no uncertain terms.' He coughed again. 'It's a terrible business.'

'You realise it's all nonsense?'

The headmaster didn't answer. He stood facing the window for a moment, watching the trees bending in the wind; their bare branches threatened to break. He gathered his thoughts before speaking. The silence was deafening.

'This is a terrible business, Richard,' he began. 'A terrible, terrible business.'

'Look, Charles,' Richard interrupted, 'this is all rubbish. A vigilante group has got the wrong information and targeted the wrong man. It's social media gone mad.'

'I'll say it is,' Charles agreed. 'Sit down, please.' Richard sat, and put his laptop on the floor near his feet. 'How are your family?'

'They're shattered by it, obviously.'

'Obviously.'

'It's probably the worst thing a man can be accused of, especially a teacher,' Richard said, sighing. 'The twins are mortally embarrassed and Celia looks like she wants to shoot me.' Richard shrugged. 'It's like she's blaming me for these idiots posting it in the first place.'

'That good, eh?'

'Worse, Charles.' Richard shook his head and squeezed his nose between his finger and thumb. The pressure was increasing. 'You have no idea what it's been like. They could have said anything but that.'

'It's an emotive subject, especially in our position.'

'I could hold up a bank and get caught red-handed and people wouldn't look at me like they are right now. I've only been here fifteen minutes and I feel like a pariah.'

'People are shocked, Richard,' Charles said.

'Not as shocked as I am.'

'You have an advantage over them.'

'What is that?' Richard asked, confused.

'You know whether the allegations are true or not.' Charles steepled his fingers and placed them under his chin. 'Our teachers and parents don't.'

'Oh, come on, Charles,' Richard snapped. 'Anyone could post anything about anyone on that page. It doesn't mean that it's true.'

'Nevertheless, when accusations are made, investigations must follow.'

'What are you saying?' Richard felt sick. He had a point: it wasn't for them to prove he was lying, it was for him to prove he was innocent. He was surrounded by kids every day, the slightest suspicion of wrongdoing had to be investigated.

'What I'm saying, is that I've been on the phone half the night and most of the morning,' Charles said. 'Teachers, parents, members of the school board, the governors, the police–'

'The police?' Richard interrupted him again. He felt his guts tighten.

'They have received the same information, Richard.' Charles looked concerned. 'They will be investigating the allegations.' There was a long silence. Richard felt frozen to his chair. 'You haven't spoken to them?' Richard shook his head. He couldn't find the words to form an answer. 'Do you know the girl that they're accusing you of having a relationship with?' Charles asked. Richard shook his head again. 'You're sure?'

'Yes, I'm fucking sure!' Richard snapped. How could this be happening? People were listening to a group of strangers, rather than a man they had known and trusted for years. He took a deep breath and put his head in his hands. 'I don't believe this is happening to me. How long have you known me, Charles?' Charles shifted uncomfortably in his chair. 'You know this is all lies, don't you?'

'I want to believe it's all lies, Richard, and if you say it is, then unless I'm persuaded otherwise, with evidence, I believe you.' Charles stood and walked to the window again. The ledge was cluttered with reference books and wilted pot plants. 'What I believe is of no consequence to the board or the governors, Richard.' He turned and looked at him, eye to eye. 'I have a responsibility to the parents and pupils of this school. You understand, don't you?' Richard sensed what was coming. 'Until this is all cleared up, I need you to take some leave.'

'Are you suspending me?'

'No. I'm offering you paid leave while these allegations are disproved.' Charles raised his hands and shrugged. 'We cannot take the risk until then. It's a perfectly reasonable request and, in hindsight, I'm sure you'll see why I have chosen this course of action. Go and see the police. Sort this out and clear your name, Richard.' Richard nodded. He could see the sense in it. Charles was backed into a corner, just as he had been. He was a teacher accused of having a relationship with a minor. There were no choices. He had to be removed from the school until proven innocent. 'If this is an unfounded, malicious attack on an innocent man, it shouldn't take you long to disprove it, should it?'

'Everyone will think I'm guilty,' Richard said.

'I don't think they will.'

'If you suspend me, I mean,' Richard explained. 'If you suspend me from my duties, people will think I'm guilty. My kids will be taunted and bullied.'

'You're on paid leave,' Charles said. His voice was calm and soothing. 'I will personally make sure the twins are not bullied.' Richard shook his head. 'I have no choice, Richard. Sorting this out shouldn't take more than a few days, surely? You have my word, the twins will not be mithered by anyone.'

'That's a promise you can't keep, Charles. The Internet is a jungle at the best of times.' He ran his hands over his scalp. 'Imagine what it will be like when word gets out that their dad has been suspended from school for being a paedo.' Richard shrugged and stood up. 'Can you protect them from that, Charles?' Charles looked at his hands. 'Can you, Charles?' He waited for an answer, but there wasn't one. 'No, I didn't think so.'

'Go to the police, Richard,' Charles urged. 'Do it before they come to you. Sort this thing out and we can put it behind us and forget it.'

'What world are you living in, Charles?'

'What do you mean?'

'Once I walk out of this building, on suspension, the label is fixed, and as far as the twins are concerned, they'll be burdened with it all their lives.' Richard paused. His eyes filled with tears; the frustration was crippling him. 'Jake and Jaki, the twins whose dad is a paedo, you know them?' he said. Charles squirmed. 'It doesn't matter how or when I prove my innocence, mud sticks – especially for teenagers. Come on, Charles, you know what will happen to them. Please don't suspend me.'

'It's a holiday.'

'Bullshit. And everyone will say it is bullshit. I'm being suspended.'

'I don't have any choice, Richard.'

'It's Wednesday today. Give me until the weekend to clear this up. If I haven't, then I'll take your offer of leave from Monday,' Richard said, leaning forward, his elbows on the desk. 'I'm begging you to give me the chance to sort this out without a suspension.'

'The governors won't wear it, Richard. I had to work hard to get them to agree to paid leave.' Charles stood up again. 'They wanted you suspended without pay.'

'Three days, Charles. That's all I'm asking for. This could ruin the twins' education. They don't need this so close to their final year.' Charles looked like he was thinking about it. Richard could see him considering his words. 'Come on. I've been here for eleven years. When has there been the slightest indication that a child was in danger?' Charles sighed and shook his head. 'Please, Charles, don't suspend me.' Charles pondered on his words. Richard could see a light at the end of the tunnel. 'Please. For the sake of my kids.'

'I suppose we could ride out the storm until the weekend,' Charles conceded. 'There will be eruptions from the governors.'

'I don't have anything on my record. They offered me the deputy head position two years ago, remind them of that,' Richard insisted. 'I'm not likely to start running around the school molesting people, for heaven's sake.'

A knock on the door interrupted their conversation. The headmaster straightened his tie and walked to the door. He opened it to see Mrs Kelly, standing in the corridor, flanked by two uniformed police officers.

'The police are here, headmaster,' Mrs Kelly said, shaking.

'I can see that, Mrs Kelly,' he said, nodding to the policemen. 'How can I help?'

'We're here to speak to Richard Vigne. Is he with you?'

'Yes. Come in, please.' He opened the door and ushered them in. Mrs Kelly looked stunned. 'Thank you, Mrs Kelly, go back to your office. I'll manage this,' he said, closing the door.

Richard saw the uniforms and almost had a heart attack. His breath came in short gasps. His nightmare had become ten times worse. The police had come into the school to talk to him. Uniformed officers were in the school. The twins would be taunted to distraction. Every man and his dog would know within the hour. How could they be so insensitive? Anger boiled in his belly. He was going to explode.

'Why have you come into school to talk to me?' Richard asked, trying to remain calm. 'This is outrageous.'

'We're not here to talk to you, Mr Vigne,' one of the officers said, 'we're here to arrest you.'

CHAPTER 6

Braddick stepped out of the lift into the open-plan office space that was home to the major investigation team. Through the windows to his right, a Mersey ferry was docking at the Pier Head; the waters looked green today. To his left, the giant Ferris wheel turned slowly at the Albert Docks. Its white girders seemed to glow against the background of dark rainclouds. Sadie was already there, which didn't surprise him. She drove her Golf like it was a racing car. If she could get away with putting the blue lights on the roof to go to Tesco, she would. There was a buzz spreading through the room, and the sound of excited chatter filled the air. The details of the body on the beach were being discussed. He breathed in the atmosphere and savoured it. This was what made him tick. The thrill of the chase was life itself to him. Real life had passed him by while he'd followed his career, and now it was too late; a mortgage, marriage, holidays abroad, kids, grandkids, a dog – they were never going to happen. There were successful officers who had all that, but something had to suffer: their family or their career. Something had to give somewhere. He admired those who got the balance almost right, but he didn't fit into that slot and he embraced the fact. Sadie waved a hand, summoning him to her desk.

Braddick walked over. On her screen she had images of three bodies that had been encased in wire mesh. Each limb was wrapped separately, the heads and necks covered in a single piece; a seam ran up the back of the head. The wirework along the seams was detailed. It looked like it had been stitched with silver.

'This is very similar to what we've seen today,' she said, pointing to the screen. She looked at Braddick for confirmation.

He nodded that he agreed, but there was uncertainty in his eyes. 'What are you thinking?'

'It's similar, but it's not identical,' he said. 'What we saw today was far more intricate.'

'He's moved on, developed?'

'Maybe. Assuming it's the same person.'

'When have we seen this before, or anything similar? Never,' she said, excited, answering her own question. 'It's the same person, but he's become more proficient, more skilled.'

'When was this?'

'Seven years ago. I've pulled the latest files,' she said, gesturing to the screen. 'The cold case unit picked it up in January last year and shelved it in September. They hit a brick wall, just like the first investigation did.' She paused. 'Eventually, they filed it as unsolved.'

'Interesting,' Braddick said, nodding. 'Who investigated the cold case?'

'A DI named Lewis,' Sadie read out. 'Do you know him?'

'I know of him. He's a good detective. Send the files to me and distribute it to the team, please,' Braddick said, looking around. 'Alec Ramsay worked the original case, didn't he?'

'Yes,' Sadie said. 'Miles and Brian were on the original case.'

'Miles, Brian,' Braddick called. He gestured for the two veteran detectives to join them. Their colleagues called them the Smiths, as they shared the surname. They walked to the desk and looked at the screen.

'That's a blast from the past,' Miles said. His silver hair was cut neatly to his head. 'It has to be … seven years ago?' he said, turning to Brian.

'Yes, at least.' Brian grimaced. He loosened his tie and stroked his moustache nervously. The images had disturbed his memories. 'I had some sleepless nights on that case, I can tell you. It was like banging our heads against a brick wall.'

'They tried to throw us off the scent at every turn.'

'I've never known intimidation like it – before or since.'

'That bad?' Braddick asked, shaking his head.

'I had dog shit put through my letterbox, and someone posted pictures of the missus, walking home from the gym, on the Internet. They said if I wasn't scared, she would be,' Miles recalled. 'He had his car torched the next night,' he continued, nodding towards Brian.

'Really?' Sadie said.

'They set fire to it on the drive,' Brian said. 'Nearly burnt the house down. The wife didn't sleep properly for over a year. She still has nightmares.'

'Who was putting the pressure on you?' Braddick asked, frowning. 'The Karpovs, the Farrells?'

'That's the problem,' Miles said. 'We didn't have a clue.'

'Run it by me again,' Braddick said. 'I saw the pictures when the cold case unit picked it up, but I only glanced over the files. It was the wirework that stood out to me.'

'It's unique alright,' Brian agreed. 'The first time we encountered it, the river police had seen a van approaching the water near Ellesmere Port at about midnight,' Brian began. 'They slowed their boat down and put their spotlight on it from the water and it must have spooked the driver. He panicked and tried to reverse away, but crashed into a wall and knocked himself out. The passenger escaped and ran away over the fields. When uniform arrived, they found the three bodies in the back of the van. It was obvious they were set to be dumped in the Mersey. They called MIT, and the governor put us on it.'

'We had the driver in the cells for forty-eight hours. Hugh Collins, his name was,' Miles said. 'He was a local scallywag, loosely connected to Eddie Farrell and the Karpovs.' A murmur ran through the room at the mention of the Russian mob. 'His story was that he had no idea what was in the back of the van, and he'd been hired, under duress, to drive it that night. He said the passenger was a bloke called Harvey something.'

'Harvey Fitch,' Brian said.

'That's right, Fitch,' Miles said nodding. 'Collins said Fitch had hired him because he'd lost his licence on a DD charge and had to make a delivery of bent gear for his boss. Collins reckoned he didn't have a clue there were dead bodies in the back, and blamed Fitch for everything.'

'We checked him out and he had lost his licence, like Collins said, but we never found him,' Brian said, shrugging. 'Fitch disappeared off the face of the earth. He never went home again. No bank activity, no phone calls, texts, Internet usage, nothing. He just vanished.'

'Did he have money?' Sadie asked.

'Nope. Not enough to disappear,' Miles said, shaking his head. 'He was well down the food chain.'

'Then what happened?'

'We had to release Collins, and he went down the same black hole as Fitch; he was never seen again. They both simply vanished,' Brian added.

'All our enquiries went nowhere,' said Miles.

'No one was saying anything about the victims in the van. They turned out to be Albanians, rivals of the Karpovs, but that was all we knew about them" Brian explained.

'We only had the first names for two of them. The third was identified by his cousin, but he was deported a week later. There was no record of them entering the country, no National Insurance numbers, no dental records, nothing.'

'We canvassed for months. Even our informers were mute. As soon as we mentioned the wire mesh to anyone, we hit zero. I've never seen anything like it – before or since. Whoever was responsible for this handiwork was protected, and no one would break the silence.'

'The Karpovs had a grip on the city back then though, right?' Braddick asked. 'They took people out of the game all the time.'

'Not like this, guv,' Miles said, shaking his head. 'This was different. Alec Ramsay was convinced it was pure fear; we thought it was the Karpovs protecting their cleaner, but Alec thought otherwise,' he recalled.

'Why?' Braddick asked.

'Call it a hunch, if you like,' Miles said, shrugging. 'He thought it was pure fear of the consequences of talking. Any other time, there were people queueing up to give us stuff on the Karpovs, but not this time.'

'It's true,' Brian agreed. 'There was always someone, somewhere, who would give us a name in confidence for the right price, but not for this guy. No one was talking, not even for money. Alec said only the fear of being found out could do that. They were scared that, if they spoke out, the cleaner would find out. It was a total blackout, and one other thing.'

'Which is?' Sadie asked.

'Alec reckoned they had a source on our side.'

'He said he had an idea who it was, but he never did tell,' Brian said. 'Took it with him when he retired. Nothing like that has happened since, until this body was washed up. We've all seen bodies wrapped and weighted down, but not like this. This guy makes an artwork of wrapping them.' Brian pointed to the seams. 'It's not just about making them sink, so they never come up, he enjoys this. Alec said he would be excited by it and that he'd be proud of his work.'

'I don't understand why Alec would keep his hunch to himself?' Sadie said. 'Why not ask you to look into it?'

'He said that if it ever became more than a suspicion, he would order an investigation, but, until then, he couldn't say more than that. He said there was a good chance his hunch was bollocks, and he couldn't give us a name as it could ruin them if he was wrong. It was never mentioned again so we assumed he had ruled it out.'

'Ruin them?' Braddick said, rubbing the stubble on his chin. 'If he was worried about someone's reputation, they might be in the job?'

'Maybe,' Miles said. 'We always thought the cleaner was connected to the force, or the medical profession, because of the surgical wounds to the victim.'

'Or in forensics,' Brian chipped in.

'That would tie in with why Alec wouldn't reveal his suspicion,' Braddick said. 'He may have been protecting a colleague in case he was wrong.'

'Maybe,' Miles agreed.

'Are you still in touch with him?' Braddick asked. Miles and Brian exchanged glances.

'With Alec?' Miles asked.

'Yes.'

'I send him a text every now and then,' Miles said.

'Is he back in this country?'

'Yes. He's been back over a year.'

'We need to go and have a chat with him,' Braddick said, turning to Sadie. 'It could be useful.'

'We could go, if you like?' Miles said. 'We worked with him for ten years.'

'No. I've got something in mind for you two.' Braddick shook his head and tapped the keyboard. The images of the Albanians, encapsulated in mesh, appeared on a bank of screens that were used for briefings. 'Listen up,' he said, walking towards the screens. 'Google?'

'Yes, guv?'

'You're on missing persons for our new victim.'

'I'm already on it.'

'I want your team out and about, talking to anyone potentially related to the victim.' Google nodded. 'Have you pulled the missing list for the city centre?'

'Yes. We're looking at eight hundred plus names.'

'That should keep you busy for a while. Miles, Brian, I want you two to revisit your initial investigation.' They looked devastated. 'It's been seven years, things have changed. The power shift is unrecognisable now. People may be more willing to talk about what happened back then. Take your teams and interview everyone who is still alive. Put some pressure on. Shake the trees as hard as you can and let's see what falls out.' He pointed to the screen. 'Someone knows who did this and I want them found.

I want a name. This guy thinks he's in the clear. He thinks we've given up looking for him.' The detectives nodded, determined expressions on their faces. 'We'll meet back here tonight, at seven o'clock.'

'Yes, guv.'

'Keep me in the loop if anything comes up.'

***

He watched the unconscious man twitching. The man's eyes flickered before they opened; he looked around, nervously, unaware of where he was. When he realised he was tied up, he began to struggle. This made him smile. It gave him a warm glow.

'Darren Parks,' he said. His voice echoed in the darkness. 'Stop struggling. You'll need your strength.'

'Who the fuck are you?' Parks asked, angrily. 'What is this place?' He shivered. The smell of the sea was choking. It was cold and wet and dark. The only light came from his captor's torch. 'Untie me!'

'Save your strength.'

'Who are you?' Parks shouted. 'Why am I here?'

'You may remember me,' he said. 'You and your idiot friends put me away for four years.' Parks looked confused. 'Your group took four years of my life.' 'What group?' Parks asked. He looked terrified as he struggled against his bonds. 'What the fuck are you talking about?'

'The predator hunters.'

'Are you fucking kidding me?' Parks asked, scowling. 'I haven't had anything to do with them for months. Untie me!'

'You were there when they trapped me. I remember your face. I never forget a face.' He smiled. 'You'll never forget mine.'

'Untie me, you fucking nonce!' Parks shouted. 'Help me.' His voice echoed from the walls, 'Help me!'

'Don't shout. No one can hear you, Darren.' The man shone his torch around the tunnel. 'Look around you.' Parks twisted his head as far around as he could. The dark brick tunnel was covered in seaweed and slime. Water dripping was the only sound he could hear. 'We're under the city, close to the river,' he said. 'The tide is out at the moment; it's due to turn soon. When it does, this place will flood. You might be able to float for a while, but not all night. Eventually the cold will sap your energy. You'll become exhausted and you'll give up and drown. Can you imagine how that moment will feel when you give up?'

'This is sick.' Parks became angry. 'Untie me, you pervert!'

'Nasty, nasty,' the man said, shaking his head. 'You'll have plenty of time to reflect on your attitude. It *will* change.'

'Fuck you,' Parks screamed. 'Help me!'

'No one is coming to help you,' the man said. 'This is where your journey ends.' Parks looked around frantically. 'There's no way out. Accept it.'

'Fuck you!'

'The anger will pass. It always does.'

'Why are you doing this to me?' Parks began crying. Frustration was driving him mad. 'Why the fucking hell are you doing this to me?'

'I told you,' the man said. 'You're a predator hunter. It's not so much fun when you're the prey, is it?'

'Look,' Parks said, trying to remain calm. 'I'm not even in the group any more. I left it months ago.'

'I know you did,' the man said. 'That put you at the top of the list.'

'What?'

'You left the group. Now there is no connection at all. There's nothing to connect you to the others.'

'What others?' Parks asked. 'What are you talking about?'

'You don't think you're the first, do you?'

'I don't know.'

'You're not the first. And you won't be the last.'

'Please let me go. I'm sorry for what happened to you.'

'Ah,' the man said, 'the apology phase.'

'I am sorry,' Parks said, nodding. His lips were quivering. 'I'm very sorry. Please, let me go.'

'No.'

'Please.'

'I asked you to let me go. But you said no,' the man said.

'What?'

'When you were waiting for the police to arrive,' the man said, 'you were holding my arm.' Recognition dawned, he could see it in his eyes. 'I asked you to let me go, but you said no.'

'Fucking hell,' Parks said beneath his breath, 'I remember you. I'm sorry.'

'Sorry that you had me locked up, or sorry I came back for you?'

'I'm sorry if you went to jail,' Parks said, panicking. 'I am truly sorry. Please, I couldn't be any sorrier. I didn't know what would happen to you. Please, let me go.'

'No.'

'I have a wife and children. Please…' Parks said, beginning to panic. 'Please, think about them?'

'But you don't see them, Darren.' The man shook his head and sighed. 'Your kids live with your wife's new boyfriend.'

'How do you know that?' Parks said, frowning.

'He has your kids' names tattooed on his leg. I personally think it was too soon, but who am I to judge them?'

'How do you know?'

'I hunted you,' the man said, smiling. 'I watched you and the people around you. I followed your wife's posts on Facebook. Some people bare their souls on there, don't you think? You haven't paid for your children for twelve months. You won't be missed.'

'Please,' Parks said, crying. 'Don't leave me here. I've got money. You can have it all. Just let me go.'

'You don't have any money.'

'I don't,' Parks jabbered, 'but I'll get some. I'll steal it. Just tell me how much you want.'

'Do you feel helpless?'

'What?'

'Do you feel helpless, Darren?'

'Yes,' Parks said, nodding. 'I do. I feel very helpless. I'm very sorry for what happened to you. Please, let me go.'

'Imagine how helpless you will feel when the water begins to rise.' The man smiled. 'You will be in total darkness, cold, hungry, thirsty, and it will be your decision when you give up struggling.'

'Don't do this,' Parks said. He was becoming hysterical. 'I'm begging you, please!'

'Goodbye, Darren Parks,' the man said, closing the manhole cover. Darren Parks began to scream. He stayed a while and listened, until the screams subsided and were replaced by incoherent sobbing. He said he was sorry a thousand times before he succumbed to the river. Saying sorry wasn't good enough. Not nearly good enough.

CHAPTER 7

Richard Vigne felt his world disintegrating around him as he was handcuffed and led away. It was so cruel. He had virtually convinced the headteacher not to suspend him; he knew he was about to agree to letting him stay in his post until the weekend. He had been so close, he knew it. Things would have been okay if the police hadn't turned up and cuffed him. They had snatched hope from him at the last minute. This would change everything. Being arrested at work was a game changer. There was no coming back. The headmaster had stared at him, accusingly, shaking his head. The police arriving had changed his opinion. He thought Richard had been lying to him, he could see it in his eyes. As the police led him away, the headmaster picked up the phone; he would be speaking to the school governors before Richard had even left the building. Bill and the other teachers were standing outside the staffroom, watching. They muttered to each other as he passed by, shaking their heads, looking at him with accusing eyes. In their opinion, he was already guilty. *The police don't arrest people for no reason.* It was obvious from their expressions; each suspicious glance was like a dagger through the heart. Ted, the caretaker, looked on from his ladders, bemused. He didn't have a clue what was going on. Mrs Kelly looked horrified as they passed by her office. She shuffled paper around her desk, pretending not to watch him being marched away. Richard couldn't look any of them in the eye. The embarrassment was too much. Defending himself at this point was useless – no one was listening. Onlookers would know the police don't arrest people without reasonable grounds; there was some evidence of wrongdoing somewhere, and that was all they needed to know. An unsubstantiated accusation online now looked to be substantiated. Before first break, the entire school would know that Mr Vigne had been cuffed and put in the back of a van for being a paedophile. He could feel hot, stinging tears forming. The thought of the twins being at school was crippling him. They would be under a barrage of abuse. Kids were cruel to each other at the best of times. It would be open season on the twins when word got around. They would be torn apart verbally. He couldn't bear the thought of them being bullied. This was so unfair and he was totally helpless, unable to stop it. The wheels of justice were in motion and he was being dragged along, like it or not. Guilty until proven innocent. There was nothing to do but hold on tight and hope the end of the nightmare was near. The truth would rise to the surface. It had to.

Richard heard the policeman read him his rights but he didn't reply. Saying nothing was better than saying something wrong. Nervous, frightened, confused and anxious was no state of mind to be in when answering questions. He didn't protest and he didn't struggle. The officers were unnecessarily rough when they put him in the van; their manner was abrupt and aggressive. He banged his head on the roof and couldn't help but think it wasn't an accident. Maybe they already thought he was a paedophile, before he was even questioned. The accusation was enough to colour people's perception of him as a human being. They sat him in a tiny cell, no bigger than the inside of a wardrobe, and cuffed him to a plastic shelf that acted as a stool. A Perspex screen was closed to confine him. It had holes in it so he could breath. He had seen something similar at the zoo when the twins were young. When they closed the van doors, and he was alone, in silence, the seriousness of his situation hit him hard. Tears ran freely. He had never felt so alone and helpless. What would Celia say about him being arrested at work? She was insecure at the best of times; this would pour fuel on the fire. His guts twisted and he felt physically sick. How would the twins find out, Facebook? Twitter? Or their friends, gossiping about their dad getting arrested for being a kiddie fiddler? He closed his eyes, banged his head on the wall, and choked back a cry of anguish. It turned into a wailing sound. He was hurting like he had never hurt before. No one was there to see him sobbing, so he didn't try to stop. He let it flow, and at one point he could hardly catch his breath. Snot ran from his nose and he couldn't wipe it off. What had he done to be treated like an animal? He was thirsty, he needed the toilet, and he had snot hanging from his nostrils. This wasn't right. He was a schoolteacher, with teenage children of his own. They couldn't treat him like this, he thought. Unless they have evidence of wrongdoing. What evidence could they possibly have? He had never crossed the line with a pupil and never would. What on earth could they think he had done? The thought rattled around his head. What was it? There must be something for them to be able to do this, but what? A million questions rattled around his head and the same answers came up every time: either they had the wrong man, or someone was lying.

He felt the vehicle stop and heard voices barking orders. The back doors opened and he was bundled into Huyton police station, where he was processed and searched. His belt and laces were removed and his belongings were sealed in a clear plastic bag. He was offered legal representation and he requested that they call Celia and ask her to arrange representation. The custody sergeant recognised the name of the practice where she worked. His face darkened. They specialised in defending scumbags, scumbags with money, and they were good at it. The best. Celia would get him a brief, a good one. Richard asked for a drink. They reluctantly agreed and he was pushed into a cell to wait. His eyes were sore from crying. The vinyl covered mattress was grubby and the stainless-steel toilet in the corner stank. Urine and vomit tainted the air, masked slightly by the smell of disinfectant. Another prisoner, further down the corridor, was kicking the cell door and shouting a tirade of abuse at anyone who could hear him. He wanted a cigarette and a cup of tea. Apparently, the custody sergeant liked it up the arse, and his mother sucked cocks on Lime Street Station. The prisoner was determined to let everyone know these facts. Richard didn't think he would be getting either tea or a cigarette any time soon.

Two hours ticked painfully by, the time dragging until he heard the door unlock. A uniformed officer opened the door and gestured for him to step out. He led him in silence to a row of small interview rooms. The officer stopped and opened a door, standing aside so Richard could enter. He was to sit next to his solicitor, who he hadn't met before. The man stood and shook his hand. Richard was relieved. He was half expecting Celia to be sitting there, scowling. He was conscious that his eyes were red and swollen; it was clear he had been affected emotionally.

'The detectives will be along shortly,' the officer grunted. He looked at Richard's eyes but didn't show any sympathy. Richard didn't want, or expect sympathy. Crying didn't make him look innocent – he realised guilty men cried. Not tears of remorse for their victims, but because they had been caught. They cried for themselves. No one would feel sorry for him until he could prove his innocence.

'Thank you, constable,' his brief replied politely. He turned to Richard and nodded. 'I'm Emmerson Graff.'

'I'm Richard. Nice to meet you. Celia has mentioned your name,' Richard said. 'Thank you for coming.'

'Celia asked me to represent you.' The grey-haired man was immaculately dressed in a navy-blue suit, his hair smoothed back. He had a calm manner about him. 'How are you coping?' he asked, noticing his client's distress. It was clear that Richard had been crying a lot.

'Coping?' Richard said, shaking his head. 'I'm not sure I'm coping with anything, to be honest. I haven't got a clue what I've been arrested for.' His voice cracked and he stopped to compose himself. 'My feet haven't touched the ground since last night. This entire thing is like a surreal nightmare. If it hadn't happened to me, I wouldn't believe it could happen to anyone.'

'The detention process is designed to rattle the suspect. To unsettle them, you understand. It is no disgrace to be upset.

It's completely normal.' His voice was gentle, well-spoken. 'You've never been arrested before?' Emmerson asked.

'Not so much as a parking ticket,' Richard said, frowning. 'I thought Celia would have told you I have never been in trouble?'

'Oh, she did,' Emmerson said, smiling. 'But in my experience, husbands and wives can be frugal with the truth. Just because she doesn't know, doesn't mean it didn't happen. I'm here to represent you at her request, but my working relationship with your wife is now irrelevant. What we say between us will remain between us, unless you decide to tell her otherwise.'

'I understand. Thank you.'

'Good,' Emmerson said, nodding. His face became stern. 'Now we have that straight, I have a question.'

'Okay.'

'Are you aware of any corroborating evidence the police may have at this point?'

'Corroborating what, exactly?'

'Any impropriety.'

'I haven't done anything, inappropriate or otherwise.'

'Good. In that case, we won't be here long.' Emmerson paused and lowered his tone. 'Let me explain how this works. I'm here to keep you at liberty if charged with anything, and, if possible, I want to make sure you're not charged with anything at all.' Richard nodded that he understood. Emmerson seemed sharp-witted, maybe a little aloof, but at least the man was straight. It made Richard relax a little. 'We'll be as cooperative as we can while they are asking questions. I want you to answer anything they ask at this point, however, if they produce any evidence we're not happy with, I may advise a different course of action.'

'Namely?'

'A "no comment" interview might be our game plan, but it is only a last resort. We'll see what they throw at us first.' Richard felt nervous. It was the not knowing that was the worst of it. He had a million questions for Emmerson, but his mind was blank. The door opened and two female detectives walked in. One of them was superior in rank to the other, it was obvious from the way she held herself. She was attractive, wearing a dark trouser suit, auburn hair to her shoulders. There was a hint of Calvin Klein perfume. Not much, just enough. Her eyes were bright blue, full of life and intelligence. Her colleague was frumpy and overweight. She looked at Richard like he was something she'd stepped in. Emmerson stood up and offered his hand.

'Detective Superintendent Joanne Jones,' he said, smiling. They shook hands. 'I heard you'd moved to the child protection unit. Congratulations on your promotion.' Emmerson turned to Richard. 'Superintendent Jones was previously a DCI with the drug squad. She's one of only five females in the Merseyside force to have made Superintendent. Quite an achievement.' Richard nodded, bemused. He didn't know if he was supposed to congratulate her, greet her or keep quiet. She eyed him, searching for chinks in his armour. He could feel her analysing him. She studied his face, her eyes looked in his, red and puffy. He felt embarrassed that he had been crying. Her eyes showed uncertainty. Emmerson sensed it too. 'This is my client, Richard Vigne. A man with no criminal record and a previously untarnished reputation.' He paused and leaned forward slightly. 'Clearly this experience has disturbed my client, and I'd like this interview conducted in a manner that will not cause any further upset.'

'I'm sorry but I don't have a selection of interview techniques, Mr Graff.' The superintendent said, smiling. There was no warmth in the smile. It was challenging Emmerson. 'I'll be asking your client some questions, he'll either answer them truthfully, or he won't. The choice is his.' She pointed to a camera, mounted in the corner above them. 'This interview is being recorded, Mr Vigne. I'm Detective Superintendent Jones, and this is Detective Sergeant Young,' Joanne Jones said, ignoring Emmerson's introduction. Emmerson was talented at smoothing interviews. He could be both charming and articulate, while dismantling the evidence against his client in just a few sentences. Many a detective had come unstuck against Emmerson Graff. Jo Jones wasn't about to be one of them. 'You realise you're under caution? It could harm your defence if you fail to mention something that you later rely on in court.' She looked at Richard for a response. He was dumbstruck. *How had this happened?* 'Mr Vigne. Do you understand?' she pushed. Richard nodded. 'Speak for the video, please.'

'Yes. I understand,' he mumbled.

'Do you know this girl, Mr Vigne?' she asked, placing a photograph on the table. The girl was early teens, maybe younger. He looked and shook his head. *Was there something familiar about her eyes?* No. He had never seen her. Was he sure? Yes. 'Do you know her, Mr Vigne?'

'No. I've never seen her before.'

'You're sure?'

'Yes.' Richard felt relieved. They had got this all wrong. He was going to sue the pants off them when they released him. He looked at Emmerson and shook his head. 'I don't know this girl,' he said, clearly. Emmerson smiled, thinly. 'I told you this was all a mistake.' He wasn't as sure as Richard that it was over just yet.

'Her name is Nicola Hadley,' the superintendent said, pushing the photograph closer. Emmerson looked at his notes.

'The name online was Nikki Haley?' Emmerson challenged.

'So, someone spelled something wrong on Facebook,' the superintendent said. 'I'm not online, Mr Graff, and neither is your client. He needs to realise that.'

'Let's keep this cordial, shall we?' Emmerson said, smiling. His eyes were light brown and they narrowed when he spoke. He could feel the superintendent winding up to something and he didn't like what the look of what was coming. She had something. He sensed it. 'There's no need for sarcasm.'

'Nicola Hadley, Mr Vigne?' the superintendent repeated, ignoring Emmerson. She tapped the photograph again. 'Take a good look. Do you know her?'

'My client has clearly stated that he doesn't know her.'

'This is another picture of Nicola Hadley, Mr Vigne.' She placed another photograph on the table. It was a picture of a pretty woman wearing make-up. The superintendent tapped the new photograph. 'Think carefully.' Richard looked from one photograph to the other. It was the same girl, dressed up for a night out. Nicola, the name resounded in his head. She looked much older in the second picture. Her eyes burned into his head. *Nicola*. There was something about her eyes. He felt his intestines clench in knots. Nicola Hadley, not Nikki Haley. A distant memory whispered to him. It was hidden deep in his mind, just out of reach. A cold chill spread through his bones. *Nicola*. Her eyes looked at him from the photograph. They said, 'Don't you remember me?' The superintendent placed another photograph on the table. It was a sucker punch in the guts. The memories flooded back like a tsunami. Nicola Hadley. 'What about now, Mr Vigne?'

The third photograph was of him. He was standing next to Nicola Hadley, cheek to cheek, smiling while she took a selfie. They were both holding Jägerbombs. He remembered downing them and buying more. Nicola Hadley. The name echoed around his mind, deafening his senses. He felt sick. Emmerson looked at the photograph and then at Richard, a concerned expression on his face. The superintendent had pulled it from up her sleeve. His client was on the ropes and he was struggling.

'This is Nicola Hadley, Mr Vigne.' She tapped the photograph again and looked into his eyes. 'You said you had never seen her before.' The superintendent picked up the photograph and waved it in his line of vision. 'Is this you in this photograph?'

'Yes,' Richard said. He looked at Emmerson for help.

'You said you didn't know Nicola Hadley.'

'I didn't connect the name with the face.'

'Really. How does that work, Mr Vigne?'

'I can explain.'

'You can explain?'

'Yes.'

'You can explain why you're hugging a thirteen-year-old girl in a nightclub?' the superintendent asked.

'What?' Richard nearly choked.

'You heard me, Mr Vigne.' She held the image up again. 'Nicola Hadley. A thirteen-year-old.'

'Thirteen?' Richard said, stunned. He looked at Emmerson again. Emmerson looked uncomfortable. 'I didn't know she was thirteen,' he protested. 'She told me she was eighteen.' He looked from one detective to the other and then to Emmerson. Their faces were deadpan. He realised what they were thinking. They were accusing him. The photographs said it all. 'Not that it matters how old she was because I never touched her, but I didn't know how young she was.'

'So, you can remember her now?'

'Yes, vaguely.' Richard swallowed hard. His hands were shaking. His memories of that night were faded and difficult to recall. Alcohol blurred the images and his brain had conveniently buried the memories. 'I didn't know her second name. I never asked her what it was and she never told me.'

'Do you remember where this photograph was taken?'

'It was at a golf club in South Wales, after a charity do.' Richard held the bridge of his nose between his finger and thumb. The pressure was immense. He felt sick; it didn't look good from any angle. No wonder they had arrested him – she was thirteen. The situation was dire at first glance, but he hadn't done anything and he had to make them understand that. That was the crux of the matter: he had never laid a finger on her. 'I can't remember the name of the place.'

'It was at the Celtic Manor,' the superintendent said. 'And this was … three years ago?'

'That's right. It was a two-day charity event.'

'And you met Nicola, when?'

'The second night, after dinner. There was a nightclub on site. We ate and went down to the club after the meal. It was very busy. I think there was a wedding party in there too.'

'Nicola was already in the club when you arrived?'

'Yes.' He shrugged. 'I think so, but I can't be sure. She might have arrived after us, I don't know.'

'Did you approach her?'

'No. Of course not.' Richard shifted uncomfortably in his seat. 'I'm married. I don't approach women in nightclubs.' He glanced at Emmerson. His face was impassive. 'I don't go to nightclubs at all.'

'Of course you don't. Silly me.' She smiled coldly. 'She approached you?' the superintendent asked, sarcasm in her tone. She pushed her hair behind her ears and shook her head.

'Yes. She approached me.'

'Tell me what happened.'

'I was at the bar, buying a drink, and she approached me and asked me to buy her one.' He shrugged. 'She told me she was with her boyfriend, but they'd had an argument because she had danced with another man; he had gone home without her and left her with no money. He was the jealous type, aggressive, apparently. I felt sorry for her so I bought her a drink and we started chatting.'

'That's quite a detailed account, Mr Vigne. Your memory seems to be coming back.'

'It is very hazy, actually. I didn't connect meeting her with the accusations made against me online. It never crossed my mind it was connected to that night.'

'Why not?'

'Pardon me?'

'Why didn't you connect them?' she pushed. 'Someone accuses you of being with an underage girl and you didn't connect it with Nicola?' She paused. Richard didn't know what to say. 'Are there other encounters muddying the water that you had to consider?'

'No. There are not.' Richard was visibly shaken. He could see how this looked. Celia would be furious. It didn't matter that he'd thought she was eighteen. That wasn't the point any more. His stomach was tying itself in knots. 'Look, Nicola told me she was eighteen. I had no reason to think she was lying. The two things didn't pair up in my mind. I had no idea this was why I was arrested. I haven't given her a second thought since that night.'

'Really?' The sergeant spoke for the first time. She had a sly grin on her face. Richard held eye contact with her. She didn't like him one bit. In fact, she disliked him intensely. He could feel it. 'You haven't given Nicola a second thought since that night?'

'No. I haven't. That's the truth.'

'We have evidence that says otherwise,' the sergeant said.

'I think I need a word with my client alone,' Emmerson said. He wasn't happy with where the interview was going. He could feel them leading his client down the garden path where there would be a nasty surprise waiting for them. It was obvious. 'I'd like a break.'

'I'll bet that you do,' the superintendent said, nodding. 'Before you do, look at one more photograph.' Emmerson nodded and sat back. She placed a picture on the table of Richard kissing the girl. Emmerson rolled his eyes skyward and shook his head. They were on a dancefloor and someone else had taken the picture. 'It looks like things were getting steamy in this one,' she commented. Richard had one hand on Nicola's face and the other on her lower back, just above her buttocks.

'I don't remember that,' Richard muttered. He blushed purple. He was in an elevator, plummeting down the shaft with no brakes. He'd had no idea that photograph had been taken. Nicola Hadley had her tongue down his throat. He remembered kissing her for a few seconds before pushing her away. It was only once, and he had no idea someone had photographed him. Trying to convince people that it had happened once, for just a few seconds, would be virtually impossible. The cold facts were, she was a thirteen-year-old girl, and he was a school teacher. There would be no grey areas. How was he going to explain this to Celia and the twins? *Sorry, Celia. I didn't know how old she was, darling.* That wouldn't wash. She would see the photograph and her imagination would run wild and fill in the gaps. He could feel his marriage dissolving around him. All the years of denying any unfaithfulness would be brought into question again. She would never believe him, not in a million years. That photograph would ruin any stability they had left.

Even if she believed him, she would never forgive him. She was insecure enough at the best of times. The photograph was life changing, life destroying, and he had no idea who had taken it. It was the end of things as he knew them. He had the sensation the air had been sucked from the room.

'Would you like to explain this photograph to me, Mr Vigne?'

'I was drunk. I don't remember kissing her.' He shook his head. The detectives had him over a barrel. He couldn't deny it. At the time, it was a nothing moment, but now it was like a nuclear bomb going off in his life. 'She must have grabbed me for the photograph. I didn't even know it had been taken. She must have grabbed me for a second and someone took the photograph.'

'You don't look like you're under duress, Mr Vigne.'

'She must have grabbed me,' he repeated.

'You're a big, fit man, Mr Vigne,' Joanne said. 'Grabbed? By a teenager?'

'I don't remember it.'

'That is convenient.'

'I was very drunk.'

'And that makes it okay, does it?'

'No, of course not. I don't usually drink at all, but I did that night.'

'And what?'

'It was just a dance, she tried to kiss me and I told her no.' Richard protested. 'I pushed her away. That photograph is misleading.'

'So, you do remember?'

'Sort of. It's very hazy.'

'But you said you don't remember.'

'It is very patchy.'

'Patchy?'

'Yes.'

'Tell us what you do remember.'

'We had drinks, shots. Then we danced, but she was flirting and I needed to put her straight,' Richard said, looking at Emmerson. Emmerson nodded for him to continue. 'I told her I was married and that I had kids not much younger than her.' He shrugged. His mouth was dry. He looked at Emmerson again. Emmerson nodded that he should continue. 'That picture was just a moment. It was seconds, honestly.' He shrugged. 'I know it looks bad, but I told her I was married and she backed off.'

'Considering you denied ever seeing her before, I'm struggling to believe a word you say, Mr Vigne.'

'That's enough. We won't be saying any more until I've spoken to my client alone.'

'Wait a minute,' Richard said. Beads of sweat were forming on his forehead. His hands were trembling beneath the table. He was desperate to find the words that could explain the situation but he was struggling to think. 'I want to answer your questions. This isn't what it looks like.' The detectives looked at him, expectantly. Their eyes bored into his. *Fucking liar*, they said. 'I can explain this. Please, let me try.'

'I'm advising you not to say anything at all,' Emmerson said, sternly. 'You would be wise to listen to my advice.'

'I need to clear this up,' Richard said. 'I need to clear it up, right now.'

'We're waiting,' Joanne said, sitting back and folding her arms. 'Are you admitting to knowing Nicola Hadley now?'

'Yes,' Richard mumbled. 'Well, sort of.'

'Looks like more than "sort of" here, wouldn't you say?' she said, pointing at the picture of the kiss. 'This looks like you were getting to know her quite well.'

'It was a drunken moment, nothing more.'

'Nothing more?'

'No. Nothing.'

'Nothing else happened that night?'

'Nothing.'

'Are you sure?'

'Yes.'

'Did you take her back to your room after this photograph was taken?'

Emmerson looked at Richard, thunder in his eyes. He placed his hand on his arm and leaned closer to him, speaking quietly in his ear.

'We are entering the point of no return, Richard,' Emmerson said. 'Think very carefully about every word you say. I am repeating my advice to you, to not say anything at all.' Richard took a deep breath.

'She did come back to the apartment,' Richard said. Emmerson sighed in frustration. 'Let me explain what happened,' Richard stammered. Sweat was trickling down his forehead now. Emmerson looked horrified. He sat back and listened intently, ready to intervene. Richard was digging a big hole for himself; he knew he was, they knew he was. He had to try to convince them his intentions had been honourable. The evidence was damning, and it painted a picture of a sordid encounter that never happened. He had to try and explain. 'It isn't what it looks like. I'll explain.'

'Please do.'

'We were drunk, but at no point did I do anything inappropriate.' He paused. It didn't sound good, no matter how he said it. How could he say it without sounding like a pervert? 'At the end of the night, I said I would make sure she got home safely. We asked reception for a taxi, but they couldn't get one for her.'

'Why not?'

'There was a football game on and Cardiff was busy. They had no cabs available.'

'And she was your responsibility, was she?'

'She was on her own.'

'The hotel receptionist would have looked after her until a cab became available.' The superintendent suggested, shaking her head. 'Why all the concern?'

'I know how this looks.'

'You do?'

'Look.' Richard tried to compose himself. 'She said her boyfriend had left her with no money, so I offered to pay for a cab so she got home safely.'

'So why didn't you give her the money and leave her in reception, or were you hoping for more?'

'It wasn't like that.'

'What was it like?'

'There were lots of people around, men mostly,' Richard said. 'They were drunk and trying to pull anything that moved.' He shrugged and looked from one woman to the other. 'You must know what it's like at the end of the night?' The detectives looked at each other and shook their heads. 'I couldn't leave her in reception on her own. They would have been all over her. I was just looking after her.'

'It's refreshing to hear chivalry isn't dead,' the superintendent said. 'So, what happened next?'

'We tried some more local cab firms but we couldn't get one, so, after about an hour, I said she could sleep on the settee in the apartment and get a taxi in the morning.'

'So, you did take her back to your room?'

'No. Not like you mean.'

'What do I mean?'

'I know what you're implying, but that didn't happen.' Richard wagged his index finger as if she were a pupil misbehaving. She was trying to trap him. He could feel her reeling him in. 'I was trying to help a vulnerable young girl, that's all.'

'She was vulnerable, alright. She was thirteen.'

'I didn't know that at the time. I had no idea how young she was and no intentions of trying anything with her. That was not my thought process.' Richard stressed. The superintendent raised her eyebrows and shook her head. 'It wasn't like I was taking her to a bedroom. It was a two-bedroom apartment, with a living room and a settee.' Richard tried to remain calm as he explained. 'I was sharing with another bloke. We had a bedroom each and there was a shared lounge and kitchen and there was a bed settee in the living room. I said she could sleep there, honestly,' Richard insisted. 'It was perfectly innocent. I did not touch that girl.'

'Nicola Hadley.'

'Yes. Nicola Hadley.'
'That isn't what she says.'
'What do you mean?'
'I mean exactly what I said,' the superintendent said, calmly. 'Nicola has given us a very different version.'
'She can't have because that is the truth,' Richard said.
'She said you had sex with her on the settee.'
'That's a lie!' Richard shouted.
'Why would she lie?'

The comment landed like a sledgehammer had hit him across the back of the head. Everything else could have been verified and forgiven, but not this. The police had a girl saying she'd had sex with a man when she was thirteen years old. No one would believe him. He put his head in his hands. This was the end of everything: marriage, career, friends, family. He had to find a way to convince them he was telling the truth, but how?

'I did not have sex with her,' he insisted. He stood up and tapped the table. 'I am telling you, I did not have sex with that girl.'

'Sit down, Mr Vigne,' the superintendent said, waiting for him to be seated.

'I did not have sex with her, please, believe me.' Richard sighed. He wanted to crawl under the table and die. The resentment he felt towards the police was diminishing. Nicola Hadley had told them that he'd had sex with her when she was thirteen. What else could they do but arrest him and ask the question? He thought about what had been said; the photographs backed up her story. What could he say to prove he was telling the truth? His mind was numb. 'I didn't have sex with Nicola Hadley, superintendent.'

'She says you did.'
'She's lying.'
'Why would she lie?'
'I don't know.'
'She's given a very detailed statement of what you did to her, how long for, and how many times.'

'Fucking hell!' Richard muttered. 'This just gets worse by the second.' His mind was in a spin. It was difficult to comprehend what was happening.

'Would you like me to read her statement to you?'

'No, I would not. I don't believe this is happening,' Richard said, turning to Emmerson. 'I did not touch that girl, but what can I say to prove it?'

'My client categorically denies having sex with Miss Hadley.'

'Does he indeed?' Joanne said, coldly. She sat back. 'Okay. Tell me what did happen, in your own words.'

'Nothing happened,' Richard said. 'We got back to the apartment and I took a spare quilt from the wardrobe. When I went back into the living room, she was already asleep. I covered her up, got a glass of water, and went to bed.' He looked from one detective to the other. They didn't believe a word he was saying, he could see it in their eyes. 'I covered her up and went to bed,' he repeated. 'When I woke up in the morning, I was thirsty and wanted more water. When I walked through the apartment to the kitchen, she had gone.'

'That's it?'

'Yes.'

'You didn't have sex with Nicola Hadley?'

'I told you. No. She's lying.'

'If you didn't have sex with her, can you explain how she got pregnant?'

'What?' Richard asked, his voice a whisper. His blood ran cold.

'Nicola Hadley was pregnant with your baby.' Joanne weighed up his reaction. He could feel her eyes boring into him. He was stunned. Just when he thought it couldn't be any worse, it was. 'She protected you and wouldn't tell her parents who the father was. Her mother and father talked her into having an abortion. She aborted your child.'

'You're not listening to me,' Richard stammered. Saliva clung to his lips. He wiped it away with the back of his hand. 'I gave her somewhere to sleep for the night.'

'You gave her more than that.'

'Superintendent!' Emmerson interrupted. 'A little decorum, please.'

'Your client doesn't deserve decorum,' she snapped. 'He's lied from the minute we picked him up, playing the innocent in all this. The only innocent party in this, is a thirteen-year-old girl, who you groomed with alcohol, invited back to your apartment, and abused.' She glared at Richard. He could feel himself withering beneath her gaze. He wanted to die. 'Your client needs to realise how serious his situation is and admit to what he has done.'

Richard was about to speak but Emmerson silenced him with a nudge of his elbow. He looked him in the eye and put his finger to his lips.

'That isn't the way I'm seeing the situation, superintendent,' Emmerson said. 'May I ask why Miss Hadley has chosen to make a complaint now?'

'What?'

'Why come forward now, making these wild accusations?'

'When Mr Vigne finished the relationship—'

'What fucking relationship?' Richard interrupted. He stood up again.

'Sit down, Mr Vigne,' the superintendent snapped. 'This "little boy lost" act is beginning to grate on my nerves.' Richard couldn't argue any more. His strength was waning. 'I said, sit down.' Richard sat down and put his head on the table. He tried to switch off what was happening. 'As I was saying, when your client ended the relationship, Nicola suffered bouts of depression, and attempted suicide several times. Part of her therapy was facing up to the fact that she was raped at thirteen years of age.'

'Raped?' Emmerson said, calmly.

'She thinks her drink was spiked.'

'What with, alcohol?' Emmerson snorted. 'She was thirteen and drinking heavily.'

'She wasn't old enough to give consent.'

'Rape, is stretching it.'

'Nicola was sectioned for her own safety, which shattered her family. Her father told her story to a predator hunting group online and passed them the information. They contacted us, and we spoke to her family,' the superintendent said. 'We had to investigate the accusations.'

'Have you interviewed her yourself, superintendent?'

'She has been interviewed, yes.'

'That wasn't my question.' Emmerson sat forward and folded his hands. 'Have you interviewed Nicola Hadley?'

'She's not fit to be interviewed at the moment.'

'So, she made the complaint under pressure from her father and the police?'

'She made the complaint when she realised that what happened to her, aged thirteen, was rape. Nicola has had to experience an abortion before her fourteenth birthday.'

'It is a tragic story, only too common in our society I'm afraid, but you have absolutely no proof to back up her story.' Emmerson sat back and shrugged. 'Let's be frank, superintendent,' he said, steepling his fingers. 'Nicola Hadley may have been thirteen, but what was she doing there? She should never have been in that nightclub. She approached a man, much older than herself, and declared herself as eighteen.' He shook his head and pointed to one of the photographs. 'I am sure she will admit she lied about her age. If she had been truthful, my client would never have behaved in this way, in fact, I'm sure he would have pointed her out to the management for her own safety.' He looked at Richard. Richard nodded. It was the truth. 'No one in their right mind would have entertained going anywhere near a thirteen-year-old girl. She lied then, and she is lying now.'

'Ignorance is no defence.'

'Oh, come on, superintendent,' Emmerson countered, pointing at the photographs. 'She looks like an angel here, as if butter wouldn't melt in her mouth. She looks like she has just come out of school, a young girl, not a day over thirteen.' He pointed at the other photographs. 'In contrast, these show a young woman. Her clothes and make-up put years on her. Who would have expected to meet a thirteen-year-old girl in a nightclub?' He shrugged again. 'Add a large amount of alcohol into the mix, and my client is guilty of nothing more than being naive.' He paused. 'Have you verified her story about being at the club with her boyfriend?'

'We're looking into that.' There was a twitch in the corner of the superintendent's eye. Richard saw it. She was off balance. Only for a moment, but he saw it.

'I don't believe there was a boyfriend. We know she lied about her age, and we know she was lying about being there with her boyfriend too,' Emmerson said. 'I think she was there looking for one.'

'Whatever her motives, she was a thirteen-year-old child. She didn't deserve what happened to her.'

'I didn't have sex with her. I was looking after her,' Richard interrupted. 'Honestly, I didn't have sex with her.'

'Someone did. Unless it was the immaculate conception?'

'I didn't have sex with her.'

'She says you did.'

'The fact of the matter is, even if he did have sex with her, you can't prove underage sex with what you have.' Emmerson sighed. 'It's his word against hers. We can't test the DNA if she aborted the child, so you have nothing.'

'Maybe not on that particular night, I agree.'

'Then what are we doing here, superintendent?'

'The first night, it's clear he had a drunken fumble and he thought he'd got away with it.' Richard was about to protest, but Emmerson put a hand on his arm and shook his head. He wanted to hear what the detectives had. 'She told him that she was underage, but he said it didn't matter and he wanted to see her again.'

'What are you talking about?' Richard snapped.

'He continued to have a relationship with a minor *after* he knew her real age.'

'What the fuck are you talking about?' Richard asked again, losing his grip. The blood drained from his face. He was a drowning man being thrown bricks. The situation was going from dire to diabolical. 'What relationship?'

'We've got emails and text messages going back to the day after your first encounter,' the superintendent said. She placed a file containing phone records, and printed emails from Outlook on the table. 'Every time you messaged, rang, arranged to meet up, it's all here. You continued to see her for two years when you knew she was thirteen.'

Richard looked at the phone records. He shook his head. The room began to spin. The numbers didn't make sense; they meant nothing to him. The walls were closing in around him, crushing the life from him. He closed his eyes and looked again. There were hundreds of text messages.

'This isn't my number,' he said, shocked. 'And this isn't my email account.' He looked at Emmerson. 'Look at my profile picture. That's a photograph from ten years ago. This is a fake profile.'

'We wouldn't expect you to use your own phone or email address to set up an account, Mr Vigne. We would expect you to use a burner phone and a Hotmail address to create a profile. I don't think you're a stupid man, Mr Vigne. Not that stupid, anyway.' She opened the file. 'Jvigne at Hotmail dot com, not very imaginative, granted, but it's you. That's the email address that was used to set up this profile.'

'That is not me.'

'Coincidence, perhaps?'

'I have no idea.'

'You can see the email address is a variation of your name?'

'Of course.'

'And the messages are all to Nicola, from someone called Richard Vigne?'

'It isn't me,' Richard muttered. He was losing the will to live. One lie after another were burying him deeper into a hole he would never be able to get out of. 'That is a fake profile.'

'Where did they get the photograph?'

'Online. That's from ten years ago. Someone has copied it from the Internet and set up that profile.'

'This evidence has come from a laptop and a mobile phone belonging to Nicola Hadley,' the superintendent said, tapping the photograph of them kissing. 'The girl that you are kissing on this photograph, and the girl you invited back to your room.' Richard was being crushed by the massive weight of evidence. 'The girl who gives a detailed account of having sex with you, and claims she went on to have a relationship with you.' She paused for the information to sink in. Richard couldn't think straight, let alone explain. 'Two years of communication are right here.' She waited for a response but Richard couldn't think straight. 'Can you explain all this evidence?'

'No. I didn't have sex with her, nor did I see or hear from that girl ever again.' Richard muttered. Tears filled his eyes again. They spilled down his face.

'I assume you have traced the IP addresses?' Emmerson asked. 'That should be easy enough to verify?'

'Mr Vigne has been very smart about hiding his IP address, but we're narrowing it down,' the superintendent said.

'What?' Richard gasped. 'I don't know where to find my IP address, let alone hide it.'

'Like I said, we're narrowing it down.'

'Narrowing it down?' Emmerson repeated.

'Yes.'

'The truth is, you don't know who or where they were sent from, do you?' Emmerson pushed. The superintendent didn't reply; she shifted uncomfortably in her seat. 'This is a fishing expedition. You want my client to crack, and admit everything, because you have nothing but the word of a mentally ill woman scorned, a distraught father, and a fake Facebook account. You need a confession.' The superintendent looked frustrated, her eyes darkened. 'You're not getting a confession from my client today, superintendent.'

'I don't understand this,' Richard said. 'What are you saying?'

'I'll explain outside,' Emmerson said, standing. 'Charge him, or let him go.'

The detectives looked at each other. The superintendent sighed and shook her head. She looked defeated. An angry glance at the sergeant confirmed it. The evidence was full of holes. She placed her hand on the file of messages. Richard held his breath as her eyes stared through him. He was flummoxed. Who had sent all those emails and texts? Someone had, but he knew it wasn't him.

'We'll find out where you sent these from and, when we do, I'll come for you, Mr Vigne.'

'I didn't send them, superintendent,' Richard said, shaking his head.

'You don't have to say anything else, Richard. We'll be going. Kindly order the custody sergeant to discharge my client,' Emmerson said, opening the door. He held it open for Richard but he didn't want to go; he felt there was unfinished business. His need to make the detectives believe him was crushing. 'Richard, let's go.'

'I don't know what is going on here, superintendent,' Richard said, standing, 'but I know I didn't see Nicola Hadley ever again after I went to bed that night.' She looked at him. She didn't believe him, that was clear. 'I can tell you one thing, though.'

'Go on. I'm all ears.'

'I shared the apartment with another man; I'd never met him before and I've never seen him since. We were paired up for the competition, and everyone had to share an apartment with their golf partners.'

The superintendent flicked through her file. She pulled out a sheet of paper that had the Celtic Manor hotel logo on it.

'Ralph Pickford,' she said, reading from the list on the paper.

'That's him,' Richard said. 'How did you know that?'

'I'm a detective, Mr Vigne, we tracked him down. He died in an accident six months ago.' The custody sergeant approached the door. 'Release Mr Vigne, please. No charges for now.'

The detectives walked past him and headed for a stairwell. The sound of their heels echoed off the walls. He could hear the superintendent talking sternly to the sergeant. She wasn't happy at all. Richard was in a daze as he was discharged, Emmerson made small talk but Richard wasn't really listening. The custody sergeant was abrupt but polite as he handed him his belongings, and they were shown out of the rear of the building by a uniformed constable.

'My car is at the front of the building,' Emmerson said. They walked through the back gates and followed the pavement to the main road. Richard was still in a state of shock. He wasn't sure what had just happened. One minute, he was drowning under the weight of the accusations that were being thrown at him, the next, he was being dragged up to the surface for breath. Emmerson had timed his challenge perfectly. He had waited until the detectives had put all their cards on the table, then, when he was sure they were stretched and had no hard evidence to back up their case, he called their bluff. Richard's mind was chaotic. Being outside, breathing fresh air, felt like being born again; it was such a massive relief he was crying again. His emotions were all over the place.

'Richard Vigne?' a voice said from behind them. He turned around and found himself staring into a digital camera. The man had taken a raft of pictures before Richard realised what was going on. 'Kevin Hill, *Liverpool Echo*. Have you been charged, Richard?' he asked.

'No comment,' Emmerson said, grabbing Richard by the arm. He guided him away from the journalist, but Kevin was persistent and he followed them, clicking away on his camera. 'Do not say a single word, Richard.'

Richard was baffled. He allowed Emmerson to lead him, almost tripping over his own feet. The *Liverpool Echo*? *What did they know*? Had the predator hunting group tipped them off, or was it the police? Either way, the last thing he wanted was them writing an article about the accusations against him. His friends and family would be ridiculed; everyone would know what he had been arrested for and they would make up their own minds. Guilty until proven innocent. It seemed no one believed him. *Wait until they see the evidence against you*, his mind taunted. *Nicola Hadley says you had sex with her, explain that, Richard.*

'It's better to give us your side of the story, Richard, or we can only print her side. I'm trying to do you a favour,' Kevin Hill said. He was jogging to catch up. 'Have you been charged, Richard?' he shouted. Onlookers were beginning to stare. 'Did you know she was thirteen?' Richard blushed red. He wanted to crawl into a hole. 'How do you feel about her having an abortion?'

'What?' Richard said, panicking. He stopped in his tracks. 'How do you know that?'

'Richard!' Emmerson shook him. 'Say absolutely nothing to him. I've encountered him before and he's a nasty piece of work. A sewer rat looking for shit to print. Don't give him the satisfaction of twisting your words.' Emmerson spoke loud enough for the journalist to hear him. 'Go away, Mr Hill, or I'll have you arrested for harassment.'

'You call me a sewer rat?' Kevin snorted. 'You spend your life sitting next to drug dealers and murdering gangsters, and now we can add paedophiles to the list. Yet, I'm a sewer rat?'

'I'm not a paedophile,' Richard muttered.

'Go away,' Emmerson repeated. He pulled Richard towards a black BMW. The doors clicked open and the indicators flashed. He opened the passenger door and bundled Richard into it. 'No matter what he asks you, you say nothing.'

'Last chance, Richard,' the journalist called to him. Emmerson closed the car door, muffling his voice. 'Did they charge you?'

Richard looked at him through the window, his mind frozen with fear. The thought of an article about him was the icing on the massive, shitty cake his life had become. If they mentioned the abortion, no one would believe a word he said; Celia and the kids would disown him. The journalist knocked on the window and leaned in, close to the glass.

'Tell us your side, Richard, or it won't look good. People need to read both sides or they'll make their minds up anyway.' Emmerson got in the car and started the engine. 'You can find me online, if you change your mind,' Kevin Hill called, as the BMW pulled away. 'Better to tell me your side of the story, otherwise someone might make it up.' His last words sent a shiver down Richard's spine. It was all made up anyway, could he possibly make things worse? Probably. Definitely.

'How does he know about the abortion?' Richard asked. He was on an escalator to hell. Every second took him further down, deeper into the terrifying darkness where there was no hope left. There was no way of getting off and no emergency stop button. The desperation was seeping into his bones, crippling him.

'It doesn't matter how he knows, what matters is that he does know.' Emmerson glanced at Richard and shook his head. He pulled the BMW into the traffic and headed into the city. 'There is no way to dress this up, Richard. You have had a bad day, but it is about to get a thousand times worse.' Richard slid down in the seat and closed his eyes. He didn't think he could take any more accusations, yet the evidence was there for all to see. 'You have some very harsh choices to make,' Emmerson said. 'Are you listening to me?'

'Yes,' Richard said, opening his eyes.

'You need to decide what to tell your wife and children,' Emmerson explained. 'What was said in your interview is confidential, for now, and I'm not at liberty to tell Celia anything that was said.' He stopped at some traffic lights. 'What you do have to consider, is that it may become public information at a later date, and, if she thinks you've lied, it could make things worse further down the line.'

'I don't think things could be any worse,' Richard said. He stared out of the passenger window, his mind stunned.

'Don't be under any illusion that things can't be worse, because they most certainly will be,' Emmerson said. 'The press will have a ball with this story – the teacher and the child and the baby.

You need to prepare yourself for what's coming, Richard.' Richard was shaking. He couldn't see any way to go. His options were all shit. 'My advice would be to lie low, turn off the phone, and speak to no one except your family.'

'All this for giving someone the settee for the night,' Richard said, biting his nails.

'Unfortunately, Nicola Hadley is saying it was more than that, and there is an abortion to back up her testimony.'

'It's all bullshit.'

'The evidence says otherwise, Richard.'

'Why didn't they charge me if they're so certain I'm guilty?'

'Jo Jones wasn't comfortable interviewing you with what they had, I could see that, but she thought she had enough to make you panic, fold and admit everything. She wanted a confession. You didn't fold and that reassures me you're telling the truth. If you were guilty, under that pressure, you would have confessed.'

'I am telling the truth.'

'I believe you, but we need to discredit their evidence.'

'How?'

'I don't know yet.'

'What shall I do in the meantime?'

'You need to come clean with Celia,' Emmerson said. 'Tell her the truth, straight away, and then there can be no nasty surprises later. If you are charged, it will all come out in court and in the press.'

'I can't tell her everything,' Richard said. 'If I tell her Nicola Hadley had an abortion, she'll leave me before I've had the chance to deny it.'

'From where I'm sitting, the alternative is worse.'

'What's the alternative?'

'Kevin Hill will tell her in the *Liverpool Echo*.'

CHAPTER 8

He was sitting at his desk, staring at his laptop. The predator hunters were in deep conversation on their page. They were talking about Dave Rutland. Apparently, he'd jumped in front of a train at Hough Green Station, shortly after one of their stings had flopped. He laughed. What a fucking shame. If only they knew Darren Parks was being eaten by crabs, while they chatted shit about each other. He wanted to join the conversation, and tell them that he had thrown Dave Rutland on the tracks, and that he had watched him piss himself before the locomotive smashed into his head, bursting it open like a balloon full of rice pudding. Telling them they were all being stalked would be fun too, but not as much fun as watching them from the shadows. That was more fun. He often watched them talking, and viewed their individual profiles for hours – looking, lurking, learning more and more about each individual and their families every time. He trawled through their photographs and became familiar with what they and their families looked like. He especially liked looking at their kids. It was ironic that these intrepid predator hunters were happy to post pictures of their children online, for anyone to look at, copy, download or share. Facebook was paradise for predators. None of the group had their security settings high enough to protect their kids. Idiots. Some of them were family men, playing at being vigilantes, others, loners clinging to the group for company and conversation. He hated them all equally. In a short space of time, he could find out where someone lives, works, and socialises; where they go on holiday, what type of car they drive, what their political views are, and what hobbies they have. It was time-consuming, but simple. Identifying targets who wouldn't be missed was easy. Men with large families and lots of friends were too much trouble. The loners were easier. Easier still were the members who had left the group. They were his favourite. He could kill them with no concern about anyone spotting a pattern. He enjoyed the selection process as much as the execution.

Their chatter about the suicide was comical. There were several budding psychiatrists in the group, a couple of wannabe agony aunts, and some seriously uneducated idiots. Some of them had offered psychological reasons as to why people commit suicide, their posts full of spelling mistakes and the use of wrong words, while others reflected on their analysis as psychobabble, and offered different diagnoses into the mix. Most of the group couldn't spell diagnosis, let alone understand one. Some of the less intelligent members didn't seem to be bothered either way. One of them hit the nail on the head by saying he couldn't give a shit why Dave Rutland had tossed himself under a train, he was weak, and Darwin's theory of evolution was right – the strong survive and the weak die – adding that he was probably a closet gay who couldn't face coming out, and as such, had done the world a favour. He said, with hindsight, he'd suspected he was a bummer all along. His logic was startling. Not surprisingly, that opinion was pretty much the most popular one with many more likes and comments than some of the more thoughtful diagnoses. No one mentioned how much the unfortunate Dave Rutland was liked, or if he had any family, or if he would be missed by them or by the group as a whole. Then one of the admins jumped into the argument, reminding everyone that Rutland was a founder member and deserved some respect. Some of the members told him to fuck off and indicated that he might be a bummer too. They were deleted from the group immediately, but no one cared. Good riddance. There was no loyalty between them. That was because they didn't really give a shit. They didn't give a shit about the people they targeted, and they didn't give a shit about each other. It was all about the adrenalin rush of fishing for paedophiles, hooking them, and finally catching them in their net and handing them over to the police. Adrenalin was an addictive drug, and their veins would be full of it when it was *their* time to die, but it would be a different kind of rush, a rush they wouldn't enjoy.

He clicked on the profile of a man in his thirties: Phil Coombes. He had been watching Coombes for months. Coombes was a creature of habit. Monday to Friday, he worked in a warehouse on nightshift. His weekends were spent fishing, on the canal near St Helens. It was known locally as The Hotties, because the local glass manufacturer pumped hot water from the cooling process into it. Fish thrived in the warmer waters and it was easy to catch them. From Coombes' pictures, his spot had been easy to find; he posted selfies of himself fishing, on both Facebook and Instagram, and it didn't take long to narrow down which stretch of canal he favoured. He also posted pictures of the tins of Stella Artois he drank while he fished. Every weekend, same routine, same place. The only time he deviated was if the predator hunters were on a mission. There had been no mention of an imminent manoeuvre on their page, and Coombes had posted that he was looking forward to fishing at the weekend. As he watched the profile, Coombes posted a photograph of eight tins of Stella in his fridge, with the tagline: fuel for a sex-machine. He doubted that Coombes had sex with anybody but himself.

That made up his mind: Phil Coombes would be the next predator hunter to die. He disliked Coombes immensely. He had been part of the inner core of the group involved in sending him to prison. There were only three of them left. Killing him would be easy and it would be a real pleasure. He would make it slow and painful, and impossible to trace back to him. The list of predator hunters was dwindling. It made him anxious. He wasn't sure what he would do when they were all dead; a man needs a focus in life. He thought about going back to work. That excited him. It had its risks but it paid well, and, ultimately, he loved his work. It was a problem he could debate later, when the predator hunters were dead.

CHAPTER 9

Braddick brought the Evoque to a halt outside a detached house in the Aigburth area of the city. The tree-lined street was quiet. It was the type of street where the neighbours never saw each other; they spent their lives hiding behind electric gates and high walls. Braddick reckoned the arrival of a retired chief inspector would have rattled a few cages – there was a lot of money in the borough, not all of it legitimate. He looked around and took it all in. It was an unlikely place for a detective to retire.

'I'll give you a penny for them,' Sadie said.

'What?'

'Your thoughts,' she said, smiling. 'I'll give you a penny for them.'

'I'm wondering if I'm going to end up somewhere like this when I retire,' he said.

'You won't retire, Braddick,' Sadie said. 'You're a robot.'

'Maybe I am,' he agreed. 'The joints need oiling if I am.' Braddick opened his door and climbed out.

'A squirt of WD40 in the morning, that will do the trick.' She stretched her arms, and smiled as she took off her seatbelt and got out.

'I'm looking forward to meeting Alec Ramsay,' she said, closing the door. 'I've heard so much about him, I feel like I know him already.' She looked at the house. It was a two-storey structure with a slate roof, lots of windows, and a huge conservatory on the side. The gardens were protected by a high wall and solid gates. There were CCTV cameras dotted about. She counted six without really looking for them. 'He likes his security,' she commented.

'Alec Ramsay pissed off a lot of serious criminals, not least the Karpovs and a Latvian organisation called Thr3e,' Braddick said. He walked around the vehicle and headed for an intercom on the gatepost. 'I'm surprised he's not been whacked, to be honest.' He pressed the button.

'Inspector Braddick?' a voice said.

'Yes, sir,' Braddick replied. Sadie saw a camera move and focus on them. The gates opened slowly, allowing them to pass through a gap just big enough for one person. Once they were through, the gates closed behind them. 'He's just being careful,' Braddick said, seeing the expression on Sadie's face. She grimaced and walked up a gravel path to the front door. The lawns were well kept, the borders neatly dug and planted with shrubs. As they approached, the door opened and Alec Ramsay greeted them. Sadie couldn't believe how much he looked like the chef he shared a surname with. She had heard people talking about it, but hadn't realised how uncanny the likeness was. 'Thanks for taking the time to talk to us, sir,' Braddick said, shaking his hand. 'This is Sadie. She's a DS with MIT.' Alec shook her hand.

'It only seems like yesterday that I was knocking on doors as a detective sergeant with MIT,' Alec said, gesturing them in. 'Come in, please.' He closed the door and walked down a wide hallway into the conservatory. 'Take a seat,' he said, pointing to some rattan chairs. 'Can I get you a drink, tea, coffee?'

'We're fine, thank you, sir,' Braddick said. 'We don't want to take up too much of your time.'

'Call me Alec, please. I'm going to make myself a coffee anyway. Are you sure you won't join me?'

'White, with one sugar please, sir,' Sadie said. Alec raised a finger in protest. 'Sorry, Alec.'

'I'll have the same, please, Alec,' Braddick said.

Alec went into the large kitchen, which adjoined the conservatory. They heard cups clinking and the kettle boiling. The view of the gardens was panoramic and had a calming effect. Squirrels climbed the well-established trees; oak and ash stood with sycamore and beech. Rhododendrons thrived beneath the tree canopy, their purple flowers in bloom. They both felt a little bit awkward, like pupils in the headmaster's office. A few minutes later, Alec reappeared carrying three mugs, and placed them down on the coffee table.

'They're yours,' he said, taking one. He took a sip and sat on a rattan settee. The black cushions looked plumped up and new. 'I know you're not here to ask for the office stapler I stole, so, what do you want?' he joked.

'We want to pick your brains on an old case you worked on,' Braddick said.

'Sounds interesting. Go on.'

'Do you remember Hugh Collins and Harvey Fitch? It was a multiple murder case, from seven years ago?' Braddick said, sipping his coffee. Alec's eyes were bright and intelligent looking. He looked at the two detectives, assessing their potential without actually trying to. They were young and sharp, just like he had been.

'It was a Saturday night in October, the thirteenth to be precise,' Alec said. Braddick and Sadie smiled and exchanged glances; it was a Sherlock Holmes moment. 'You want to know how I remember that, don't you?'

Sadie smiled and nodded.

'Don't be too impressed,' Alec said, smiling. 'Normally, I can't remember what day it is, where my glasses are, or whether I've had my breakfast or not, but I remember where I was when Collins was arrested with three bodies in the back of his van. It was called in on my mother-in-law's birthday. It was her eightieth, and my wife had booked a room at a local social club. They had arranged a disco with a break for a few games of bingo. I was bored to tears and losing the will to live. I was surrounded by the in-laws when the call came in.'

'Sounds like a lucky escape,' Sadie said.

'I've never been so happy to hear we had found three dead bodies.' He paused to recall the memories. 'Gail, my late wife,' he said, pointing to a framed portrait of a woman, 'was furious when I said I had to go back to work.'

Braddick felt a tinge of pain for him. They had something in common: they had both lost their partners to fire.

'She was always furious about something,' Alec continued, 'usually something I had done. Anyway, that's why I can remember it so well.' He frowned. 'That, and the bodies of course; it's not every day you see a crime scene like that one.' He paused again. The image of the three bodies, encased in wire mesh in the back of a transit van, played in his mind. 'You haven't found Fitch and Collins after all this time, have you?'

'No,' Braddick said. 'They're in a bar somewhere with Elvis, Lord Lucan and Shergar.'

'I don't think we'll ever find them.'

'Miles and Brian worked the case – the Smiths,' Alec said, laughing. 'Aren't they still with MIT?' He was confused as to why Braddick would come and see him if they were still on the team.

'Yes. It was something they said that prompted me to call you,' Braddick said. Alec raised his eyebrows; his forehead creased with deep lines. 'We've found a body washed up on Crosby Beach.' He handed Alec four photographs. 'As you can see, he was encased in mesh before being weighted and dumped in the river.'

'Any idea where?' Alec asked, studying the photographs.

'We found weeds on the body that suggest he was put into the water upriver. If it wasn't for the storms, we would never have found him.'

'You have no ID?' Alec asked.

'Not yet.'

'And you think the wirework is similar to the Collins Fitch case?'

'We think it's similar, do you?'

'Yes, I do, it's very similar,' Alec said, looking at Braddick. 'But much more detailed.'

Braddick nodded.

'Our thoughts exactly,' Sadie said. 'It's as if he's developed and improved over the years.'

'I'm not sure about that, Sadie,' Alec said, looking up. 'Maybe he had more time with your victim – the Fitch case had three victims to dispose of, more work, less time. Your victim has much more attention to detail; he had plenty of time in a location where no one would disturb his work. Wherever he did this, there's no chance of interruption.'

'Do you think it's the same man?'

'Sorry, Sadie. I can't make a jump like that with just these pictures.' He smiled and studied the photographs. 'This is very intricate, almost arty.' He looked at Sadie. 'I don't think you can assume this is the work of the same person. Not without more evidence.' He slurped his coffee and eyed the detectives. 'You didn't come here just to show me these pictures, did you?'

'Miles and Brian told us you may have had a theory about who was responsible for the wirework?' Braddick said. He saw Alec's expression harden immediately. 'Is that true?'

'Not in so many words,' Alec said, shaking his head. He frowned and thought carefully about how to continue. 'Let me try and explain what I mean.' He took another sip and then put the cup down on the table between them. 'Did Miles and Brian explain what happened when they investigated the murders?'

'They said no one was talking,' Braddick, said, nodding.

'It was more than that,' Alec said, frowning. 'We've all encountered a wall of silence during some investigations, you know what that is like?' They nodded that they did. 'But there is always some chatter going on, somewhere beyond the wall. Some people can't help themselves, they can't shut up.'

'I don't follow, Alec,' Sadie said.

'You know how it works: when word goes out in the underworld that no one is to say anything about a particular criminal or crime, there's always someone, beyond the wall of silence, chattering about it, gossiping in a pub, trying to impress people with their knowledge.' He explained. 'People on the periphery of the crime families, or drug networks chatter, you have met the type that can't shut up.' The detectives nodded that they did. 'Someone will always speculate, no matter how powerful the subject being talked about is, but not this time.' He shook his head. 'There was nothing. No gossip, no chatter, no rumours, nothing. When Fitch and Collins disappeared, it sent a shockwave across the city. The press ran stories on the three bodies wrapped in wire, and put it down to a turf war between the city's gangsters, but the city's gangsters were always at war and everyone connected to them knew that. They also knew that this was something else. Fitch and Collins vanished overnight and were never seen again, and no one knew who had done it. Or, if they did, they daren't say.'

'The victims were Albanians?' Braddick asked. 'Their outfits are pretty brutal.'

'They are brutal, but their ethos is about making sure everyone knows how brutal they can be,' Alec said. 'They dump their victims in plain sight. This was different. Whoever made Collins and Fitch disappear, did it in silence. We spoke to every snout in the city, and every crime family in the county was spoken to, both on and off the record, and we came up with nothing.'

'Why do you think that was?' Sadie asked.

'Fear,' Alec said. 'Pure, unadulterated fear.'

'Of who?'

'That is the million-dollar question,' Alec said, shrugging. 'We didn't know.'

'We're looking back at the investigation, Alec,' Braddick said.

'You're reopening it?' Alec looked excited. He sat forward on the edge of the settee.

'In a manner,' Braddick said, nodding. 'It was reinvestigated last year by the cold case unit, but they hit the same wall you did. They shelved it again as unsolved.'

'What makes you think you can do better than the cold case unit?' Alec asked. 'Have you found something new?'

'Yes,' Braddick said, pointing to the photographs. 'Another victim.' He smiled. 'Plus, we've got something the cold case unit didn't have.'

'Which is?'

'The original investigating officers: you and the Smiths,' Braddick said.

'Good thinking,' Alec said. He laughed. 'I didn't think of it like that, but you're right. It is an advantage.'

'I've got the Smiths re-interviewing everyone they spoke to seven years ago. There may be someone out there willing to talk. The power structure has shifted – local outfits have wrestled the foreign gangs out of the city – people may be more willing to cooperate now. I'm hoping the Smiths will uncover something from the original investigation that will link to ours.'

'Makes sense to me.'

'I'd be grateful if you would cast your eye over anything we find?' Braddick asked. 'Give us your opinion?'

'That makes me sound like a consultant,' Alec said, winking. 'Don't consultants get paid massive amounts of money?'

'You should consult for the other side, they're the ones earning massive amounts of money,' Sadie said. 'You sound interested, though, Alec?'

'Do I?' he said. 'I guess I am. It was one of those cases that got away. The chance to unravel things and put the pieces back together was the part of the job I loved.' The detectives nodded, completely understanding what he meant. 'I used to keep my ear to the ground, for anything about Fitch and Collins, and for years I heard nothing.' He recalled, rubbing his chin. 'A few years before I retired there were rumours of an enforcer, a freelance enforcer, who didn't just dispose of his targets, but enjoyed every second of dispatching them. There were whispers across the city but no one dared speculate who that was or who they worked for. There seemed to be substance to the rumours. I asked the question many times and some of the toughest criminals I've encountered refused to talk about it. That blanket of fear about the case was still out there, smothering the information. It frustrated the hell out of me.'

'Surely you had an inkling about who they worked for?' Braddick asked. 'You know what I mean, which outfits used him?'

'That was one of the conundrums,' Alec said. 'No one ever talked about it. We never got close to finding out who whacked the Albanians in the van, or why. My money was on the Karpovs giving the order, but no one would talk. Fitch and Collins vanished and left us with a complete vacuum.'

'Did you think it could have been someone on the force?' Sadie asked.

'No,' Alec said, shaking his head. The question disturbed him. 'Not necessarily on the force, but it had to be someone who had access to the information we had, someone connected to law enforcement somehow.'

'What made you think that?' Braddick asked.

'Collins and Fitch,' Alec explained. 'Only someone connected to the initial investigation could have known what Collins said in his interview. He blamed Harvey Fitch for the bodies in the back of the van, which made Fitch the link to whoever had killed them. Fitch may have been the only man alive to know who had wrapped those men in wire. Someone leaked the fact that Collins had blabbed.'

'What is the significance of that?' Sadie asked.

'Fitch was loosely connected to an outfit run by a guy called Eddie Farrell, who was backed by the Karpovs. The Russians were heavy-hitters back then. Anyone in their right mind would have made a "no comment" interview, but Collins didn't know who Fitch worked for. I felt a bit sorry for Collins if I'm honest. When he said he didn't know there were three stiffs in the back of the van, I believed him. He was a patsy.' Alec shrugged. 'There was a theory around the Matrix officers, that Collins had pissed off Eddie Farrell, and Fitch was going to use him to drive the van and dump the bodies, then kill him, but as I said, no one was talking. We couldn't get the intel to back it up.' He grinned. 'I guess we'll never know, but, the fact is, no one on the outside knew that Collins had fingered Fitch, so, why take him out?'

Alec looked from one detective to the other. 'Eddie Farrell rated Fitch as a loyal employee, and they're few and far between in that world. He wouldn't have whacked him on a whim.' Alec shrugged and rubbed his chin. 'The speed that Fitch disappeared indicates to me that he was eliminated that night, as soon as Collins had blabbed his name; he was taken out of the game right then. That information could only have come from MIT, or someone connected to the original arrest.'

'Like who?' Sadie asked.

'That list is as long as your arm,' Alec said. 'Could be anyone from the original team of detectives, uniformed officers in the custody suite, the forensic team … I could sit here all night and speculate, but it won't help you.' He paused. 'I can tell you one thing for certain: we had a leak back then and I never could put my finger on who it was. The press were always getting hold of information that only MIT could know. I tried leaking duff information a few times, to try and flush them out, but they were too clever. I never found out who it was.'

'Did you suspect anyone?' Braddick asked.

'I suspected everyone and no one.' Alec shrugged again. There was a thoughtful expression on his face. He was holding something back.

'It sounds like there's a bit of the story missing,' Sadie said.

'You're a very perceptive lady,' Alec said, smiling. He rubbed his hands together. 'Okay. It's been a long time, maybe I should share my thoughts with you.' He considered his next words, reluctant to commit. 'Frankie Boyd,' he said, finally.

'Frankie Boyd? Who is that?' Braddick said, sitting forward.

'Just a man who made my skin crawl,' Alec said. 'There was something very wrong about him.' He frowned as he recalled the images.

'Was he MIT?'

'No. He was a forensic photographer for a Warrington-based company.'

'Intaforensics?'

'That's them.'

'We still use them,' Sadie added.

'Every time the man walked into the same room as me, all my alarm bells started ringing.'

'Why?'

'Instinct maybe. He just wasn't normal, whatever normal is,' Alec said, grinning. 'He would be at a scene for hours longer than he needed to be, hanging around, asking stupid questions. I've never seen a forensic photographer who liked being around dead people as much as that guy did. He would take thousands of photographs, literally thousands.' Alec paused, recalling his memories of Frankie Boyd. 'I remember asking him if he got paid by the image. You should have seen the look in his eyes. He looked through me, like I wasn't there. We've all seen eyes like that, haven't we?'

'Yes. Usually across the desk in an interview room,' Sadie said.

'Exactly. There was something missing from that man, and I began to suspect that he could have been the leak. He didn't fit in. Nobody liked the guy, but he would hover around crime scenes like a bad smell, photographing anything and everything. If there was ever a man that didn't fit in a team, it was Frankie Boyd. I started to keep tabs on him but…'

'But what?' Braddick asked.

'He was fired by the company,' Alec said, shrugging. 'Someone had seen images of crime scenes being sold on Photostock. There were hundreds of them, and although they couldn't nail it down to Boyd, they knew it was him that had uploaded them. On the back of that they found a blog, which featured images from a crime scene investigator. It was anonymous, but some of the scenes were identifiable and they tracked them.'

'Frankie Boyd?' Braddick asked.

'Yes. They fired him for breach of contract,' Alec explained. 'I kept tabs on him, and a few weeks later he upped and took off to South East Asia, Thailand, if I remember rightly. The blog was closed down and I never heard of Frankie Boyd again.'

'And you think he could have been an enforcer?' Sadie asked, confused.

'It might not sound like much, but after he was fired, the leaks stopped.' Alec said. 'I was speaking to a couple of undercover Matrix officers one day and his name came up. One of them asked me if Boyd was working for us on the streets.'

'That's odd,' Braddick said, his eyes narrowing.

'Very odd,' Alec agreed. 'That's what I meant about alarm bells. One of the Matrix officers had seen Boyd on numerous occasions, hanging around places he shouldn't have been. He was always close to trouble.'

'Trouble?'

'You know – pubs where gear is sold openly, street corners where deals are made, red-light areas, car parks where nobody parks their cars. He was spotted around, taking pictures.' Alec could see that Sadie was confused. 'Think about it, Sadie. An expert photographer with a knowledge of forensics. He could have taken pictures of every crook in the city without them knowing – their colleagues, their wives, their kids, their grandparents, their lovers; think about it. I'm not saying that's what he did, but he could have had a hold on every criminal in this city. A photograph says, "I know where your kids go to school". It says, "If I can get close enough to take this picture, I can take everything you hold dear from you in an instant". A picture is powerful evidence too. Take a photograph of someone breaking the law, and you have a grip over them.'

'Hence the wall of silence surrounding the case?' Braddick asked.

'Maybe,' Alec said. 'All my instincts told me it was him.'

'It makes perfect sense,' Sadie agreed.

'When he left the country, things in the city settled down again. Things went back to normal. The jungle drums started beating again, if you know what I mean.' Alec sipped his coffee. 'And we never encountered anyone cocooned in wire mesh again,' he said with a grin.

'Until now,' Sadie added.

'Until now.' Alec smiled. 'It might be worthwhile checking out where Frankie Boyd is. If he is still alive.'

'I can see why you never told the Smiths your theory,' Braddick said.

'It's pure conjecture,' Alec said. 'There is absolutely no substance behind my theory. I always told my detectives not to come near me with "maybe" or "could be" or "might be". I couldn't tell the Smiths about my hunch. Not with what I had.'

'How did you know he had gone to Thailand?' Braddick asked.

'A little birdie told me,' Alec said, tapping his nose with his index finger. He smiled thinly. 'He bought a one-way ticket from Manchester airport.'

'Did you flag his passport, in case he came back?' Sadie asked.

'He hadn't broken any laws, Sadie,' Alec said, shaking his head. 'Plus, he was related to the ACC at the time.'

'Clive Boyd?' Braddick asked.

'Yes, he was his nephew. I've known Clive and his wife, Margaret, for twenty years. I couldn't be seen to take any liberties, besides, I had no evidence of any wrongdoing, not a sausage. It was all just gut feeling.'

'We'll look into his whereabouts,' Braddick said. 'Thanks for talking to us, Alec. It's been very helpful.'

'No problem at all,' Alec said, sitting forward. 'I could have a word with Margaret Boyd, if you like? She was close to Boyd's mother. Off the record, of course.'

'That would be a great help,' Braddick said, standing. 'It might save us some time, thanks.'

'It'll be a pleasure,' Alec said. 'Keep the old grey matter ticking over.' Alec walked them to the door, saw them out through the gates, and watched them drive away. They were nice people, good detectives. He could spot one a mile away. His mind went back to his memories of Frankie Boyd and his expression hardened. He thought about the years gone by. Thailand: a chief constable he knew had gone over there as a consultant a few years back; the Thais were making a concerted effort to eradicate corruption from their force. He smiled as he decided to give his old friend a call.

CHAPTER 10

The lunchtime bell sounded and Jake grabbed his coat from the back of his chair. He was worried about Jaki. The twins had been escorted to the headmaster's office that morning, and the head had chatted to them about what had happened, reassuring them that all the teachers would be briefed, and how they were to report anyone abusing them about their father immediately. He said he wouldn't tolerate any bullying, no matter how petty. At no point did he offer any sympathy for their father's plight, or reassure them it was all a mistake. It seemed that his guilt had already been accepted and his arrest was a great inconvenience.

Double maths had dragged on longer than it usually did. He didn't like mathematics, and the teacher, Mr Beech, was dull; he never smiled and he had a low tolerance level for pupils who struggled to understand things first time around. Jake wasn't one of them, fortunately, but the atmosphere could be tetchy in class, especially if Mr Beech had a hangover. He always stunk of stale alcohol and cigarettes. Boozy Beech, the kids called him. They had a name for most of the teachers, and Jake was just waiting for the first one about his dad to fly around. The rumours about him being arrested in the headmaster's office were rife. He had seen people pointing and staring, laughing and sniggering behind his back. No one had called his dad a paedo yet, but he knew it was only a matter of time.

He stood up; his chair made a nasty scraping noise on the tiles. Something wet hit the back of his head. He knew it was a soggy – a chewed up piece of paper fired through a peashooter. It stung for a second before he wiped it off and turned around.

No one owned up. Everyone was packing up their things, chattering and putting their coats on, except for Tom. Tom Mathews was sitting on the back row where he always sat, feet on the desk, rocking backwards on his chair. Jake made eye contact with him and instantly knew it was him who had fired the soggy at his head. Tom was a big lad, fat but a big lad nonetheless. He wasn't liked and most kids tolerated him so they didn't become a target of his bullying. He was a nasty piece of work. His black hair was cropped close to his head, making his cheeks look humongous, and he had home-made tattoos on his podgy fingers – the four suits of a pack of cards on his left hand and a series of crosses and dots on his right. None of them seemed to have any meaning and they were blurred and ugly. He stared at Jake, a sneer on his lips.

'What the fuck are you looking at?' Tom said. Jake didn't reply; he bit his lip. 'You got a problem, Vigne?' Tom said, a smug grin on his face. Some of the other pupils stopped talking, sensing the tension in the room.

'I haven't got a problem.'

'Apart from your dad being a nonce, that is. No surprise to you though, I bet?'

Jake put on his coat and walked towards the door. Another soggy hit his ear; this time it stuck in his hair. He pulled it free and tossed it onto the floor. The wet paper stank of spit. Some of the other kids laughed. Mr Beech looked up from his marking, disturbed by the racket. Jake kept walking and didn't look back. Tom was chewing another piece of paper, ready to fire it through an empty biro.

'That's enough of that, Mathews,' Mr Beech called out over the clamour. 'You're fifteen, not five, stupid boy.'

'Fuck you, Boozy,' Tom muttered. A chorus of laughter broke out.

'I beg your pardon?' Mr Beech said, removing his glasses. Everyone knew when the glasses came off, Mr Beech was on one.

'I said, sorry, sir,' Tom muttered.

'Get out, stupid boy!' Mr Beech snapped. Tom put up his hand to ask a question. Mr Beech rolled his eyes before acknowledging him. 'What is it, Mathews?'

'Is it true Mr Vigne has been arrested for being a paedo, sir?' Tom shouted with his hand still up in the air. The classroom went silent. Jake was nearly at the door but stopped in his tracks. His face reddened as he glared at Tom. Mr Beech was speechless. He looked at Jake, embarrassed for him. 'Is it true, sir, is Mr Vigne a paedo?' Tom asked again.

'You will be quiet, Mathews,' Mr Beech said, angrily.

'I think we have a right to know if there's a child molester working in the school, sir. I don't know about anyone else, but I don't want to be interfered with by a dirty nonce, sir. It could affect me for the rest of my life, sir.'

'Be quiet!'

'Can't be too careful, sir,' Tom persisted, his hand still raised. 'There are paedos everywhere nowadays. We won't be able to go for a dump in peace, without a paedo teacher looking under the door, sir.'

'Shut up, Mathews.'

'Mr Vigne might have cameras in there, sir, looking at our widgies.'

'Go to the headmaster's office, Mathews,' Mr Beech shouted. 'I'm sick of your insolence. The rest of you, get a move on. What are you all standing around for?' He waved his arms towards the door. 'Get to your next class, all of you.'

'It's dinnertime, dickhead,' Tom said from the back of the class. Laughter erupted again, louder this time.

'Who said that?' Mr Beech stuttered. He always stuttered when he was angry. 'Was that you again, Mathews?'

Jake was grateful for the diversion. He didn't hang around to become the target of Tom's attention again. He opened the door and stepped into the corridor. It was filling up as the classrooms emptied. He was immediately aware of the atmosphere, peculiar glances, and the whispering behind his back. People who normally ignored him were staring, pointing and giggling. Even some of his friends were behaving oddly, their smiles not as warm. They couldn't hold eye contact with him. He knew Jaki would be feeling a hundred times more vulnerable than he was. She was so vain sometimes, always worried about what other people thought of her. This would be her worst nightmare. He walked down the corridor, quickly, heading for the schoolyard where he knew she would be with her friends. There was a crowd of kids near the noticeboards, laughing and jeering. As he approached, his stomach lurched. At the top of the PE board, someone had stuck a photograph of Jimmy Savile over his dad's profile picture. It had begun.

Things were going from bad to worse. He had to find Jaki before she saw what they had done. He looked outside but couldn't see her. April Morris was there, in the spot where they usually gathered, holding court to a semicircle of girls. She was waving her arms about, animated and excited. They were tittering and looking around nervously. He knew they were gossiping about Jaki.

As he reached the crush for the doors, he spotted Jaki walking across the yard. She had her head down, looking at the floor. Her face was red and she'd been crying. It was obvious she had seen the Savile photo. He pushed his way out into the yard and made to intercept her before she reached her group of friends, but she was too quick. The group of girls turned to greet her. Some smiled, awkwardly, others looked at her with distaste, April Morris wore a smarmy grin. She seemed to be loving the news. Jake neared them.

'OMG, are you okay, Jaki?' one of the girls asked. She hugged her and Jaki started crying, sobbing on her shoulder. At least her friends were still her friends, Jake thought, relieved. His relief didn't last long.

'OMG, Jaki. Have you seen the photo of Jimmy Savile on the PE noticeboard?' April said, shaking her head.

'Yes,' Jaki mumbled. Her embarrassment was clear for all to see.

'I do not know how you came to school today. How did you leave your house? I am so embarrassed for you. I would simply die,' April said.

'If I found out my dad was a paedo,' another girl said, her hand covering her mouth, feigning shock, 'I would never come to school again. I would hide in my room for a year at least.' Jaki looked at her, unsure if it was an insult or not. 'You should not be out in public, Jaki. The shame would kill me.'

'My dad is not a paedo,' Jaki said, sobbing. 'It's all a misunderstanding.'

'The police don't arrest people for a "misunderstanding",' a ginger girl called Toni, said. 'My dad is a traffic officer, so I know how it works. They don't arrest people without solid evidence any more, because the CPS kick the cases out before they get to court.' Everyone looked very impressed with her knowledge. 'They must have evidence against him,' she said, confidently, folding her arms across her chest. 'And it will be solid evidence,' she added.

'So, he has done it?' someone asked.

'He must have,' Toni said, nodding.

'Urgh, that's so gross,' April said, pretending to vomit. 'I've stayed at your house and walked around in my PJs.' Everyone took a sharp, dramatic intake of breath. 'I even had a nightie on once – a short one too.'

'Urgh!' they all said in unison. 'That's so gross.'

'I bet he was looking at me,' April said, pouting.

'He was not looking at you, April,' Jaki said, wiping her eyes. 'Don't be disgusting. He is innocent. It is all a mistake.'

'Whatever,' April said, brushing her off. 'Thinking about being in your house makes my skin crawl. My mum said I'm not to go there again, just to be on the safe side.'

'Me too,' Toni said. 'My mum said it this morning. She said I can't stay over again. Not ever.' She lowered her voice. 'She actually asked me if your dad had ever said or done anything weird while I stayed over.'

'My mum asked that too,' another girl added.

'Mine too.'

'OMG, I'm so embarrassed for you,' April said again. Her comments weren't helping Jaki calm down, in fact, they were having the opposite effect. 'If my dad was a paedo, it would be bad enough, but if he was one of my teachers too, I couldn't show my face ever again.'

'Are you okay, sis?' Jake said, approaching the group. He had heard the chitchat and thought it best to take her away from them. Some of them meant well, some didn't. Jaki let go of her friend and hugged her brother. He could feel her sobbing on his chest. 'I think we should go home, don't you?' he asked. She nodded. 'Let's go and get the bus.'

'Isn't that sweet? Look at the little paedo children,' Tom Mathews said, loud enough to attract attention. The other pupils turned to look at what was happening. 'Look at them, hugging in the yard. Incest – a game for all the family, eh, Vigne?' Jake glared at him. Jaki looked up.

'Go away, Tom,' Jake said.

'Hey, Jaki, who fucked you first, your dad or your brother?' Laughter erupted from all sides. Jake was boiling up inside. Jaki's bottom lip began to tremble.

'Leave her alone, Mathews,' April said, suddenly remembering she was supposed to be Jaki's friend.

'Listen to you, April "bury me in a Y-shaped coffin" Morris.' The playground erupted in laughter. 'I saw your name mentioned on Facebook last night,' Tom said, turning to her. 'Are you fucking Mr Vigne the paedo, April "Y-shaped coffin" Morris?'

'You're vile,' April said.

'Why am I vile?' Tom asked. 'It wasn't me who sucked off Liam Wilson behind the sports hall last month. That was you.' April looked stunned that he knew. 'What's wrong? Did you think nobody knew about it? Liam has told half the school.' Tears formed in her eyes. 'Sucking Liam's smelly, little penis, now *that* is what I call vile. You should be ashamed of yourself.' April was close to breaking. He turned back to Jake and Jaki.

'You should be ashamed of yourselves too. Your dad is a dirty paedo.'

'Don't be disgusting, Mathews. Why don't you go and have another bag of crisps, you fat creep,' April said as she stormed off in tears.

'Don't be like that, April,' Tom said, as she ran away. 'Come to think of it, why would he bother fucking a minger like you when there's loads of other girls?'

'Fuck you, Mathews!' April snapped.

'I bet you both do a turn with him, don't you, Jaki?' Tom pushed. 'Hey, Vigne. Do you take it in turns with your sister?' Jake didn't answer. He looked at the laughing faces all around them, some of them so-called friends. Tom laughed; the crowd went wild. Jake thought about running head on at Tom, punches flying, but it would be like punching a beanbag. Taking a hiding from him wouldn't improve the situation. 'Does your mum play, too?'

'Tom Mathews,' the headmaster said, as he approached the crowd. The kids parted like the Red Sea. 'Get to my office, right now, and wait for me.'

'What have I done?' he asked, shrugging. 'I'm just chatting to my friends.'

'You don't have any friends, Mathews,' the head said. 'My office. Now.'

'This is harassment, sir.'

'I won't say it again, Mathews.'

'Oh, alright, sir,' Tom sighed dramatically. The kids were silent, listening to every word. 'If I go to your office, are you going to bum me, sir?' Tom said, turning away. The kids sniggered and tittered. The headmaster changed colour, his anger rising. 'Mr Vigne would probably bum me, sir, because he's a big paedo. I'm very concerned about being interfered with, sir.'

'You're walking a very fine line, Mathews.'

'I think we have a right to know if one of our teachers is a child molester, sir.'

The kids laughed and sneered noisily. Jake wanted to curl up in a ball and protect his sister. He covered her ears with his hands. The headmaster scowled at the crowd.

'Silence,' he shouted. Quiet descended across the playground. 'You should be ashamed of yourselves, encouraging that idiot.' He turned around and made eye contact with as many pupils as he could. 'I will not tolerate bullying of any kind. Do I make myself clear?' No one replied but they nodded. 'I said, do I make myself clear?' he shouted.

'Yes, sir,' they said, almost in unison.

'Jake, Jaki, go to the office and have Mrs Kelly call your mother. I think you should take a half day while I sort out Tom Mathews. That boy will be excluded from this school and he will be lucky if he ever walks back through those gates, and that goes for anybody else who thinks bullying is funny. I will also find out which comedian put the photograph on the noticeboard, and we'll see how funny it is when I show your parents the CCTV footage of you doing it and explain why they'll need to find a new school for you.' He looked around the crowd again, outrage in his eyes. 'That will be hilarious, won't it?' No one dared speak. 'Has anyone else given you a hard time?'

'No, sir,' Jake replied.

'Jaki?'

'No, sir.'

'Good. Go to the office. I'll call your mother at home this evening.'

Jake and Jaki walked through the silent schoolyard, knowing things would never be quite the same again.

CHAPTER 11

Phil Coombes opened another Stella and took a mouthful. Everyone who knew him called him Coombes. Only his mother called him Phil, and he hardly spoke to her. The rest of his family hadn't been in touch for years. There was that thing with his cousin, Susan, when they were teenagers. In truth, he was a teenager at the time and she was twelve. They had been mucking around and he went a bit too far. She'd told his Uncle Adam that he had fingered her, but it was only in there for a few seconds before she'd started balling the fucking house down, and that was that. The family had imploded, his uncle had threatened to call the police, and he and his mother had never heard from them again. Looking back, he wondered if that was where his hatred of paedophiles had developed from. Coombes didn't see himself as a paedo because there had only been two years between him and Susan. They were both kids, playing doctors and nurses, and he had been a little bit too adventurous for her liking. That hardly made him a paedo, did it? He wasn't like the dirty perverts he hunted today. They are grown men, purposely grooming youngsters to have sex with; that is very different. He wondered, if he could have explained the difference to his Uncle Adam over a few pints, whether things might have been different. He had been dead for five years, so it was academic, but he did think about it a lot.

Fuck 'em. He raised one cheek from the camping chair and farted loudly.

'Get out and walk,' he chuckled to himself.

The canal side was empty. He had seen one cyclist, and another couple of fishermen since arriving three hours ago. That was how he liked it. There were a few fishermen closer to the car park, but

Coombes liked to walk along the towpath for about half a mile, to a secluded spot where overhanging trees made shadows on the murky water. That's where the fish liked to hide. There was a tow bridge across the water so he could change sides when the sun moved. There were no canal boats on The Hotties; it was a stretch that had been unused for decades since the coal mines closed. It was a solitary pastime but he enjoyed the isolation. He was awkward in company and struggled to fit in. People found him abrasive and stand-offish, but the truth was he didn't really like people, so it didn't matter. He was happy in his own company. If he was honest, he would have liked to have had more relationships with females, but they didn't like him either. He was a misogynist, and genuinely believed his girlfriends should cook, clean, be willing to give blow jobs whenever, and like it up the bum when the fancy took him – the women in the films he had watched since he was a teenager did. He couldn't fathom the difference between them and the real women he'd attempted relationships with, and the few he'd had were short-lived and dull. Most of them had started with a drunken fumble after a night out and fizzled out from there. Before mobile phones arrived, lots of women he tried to chat up had given him the wrong landline number. It had taken years of being told he had dialled the wrong number before he realised they were taking the piss. More recently he'd tried a few internet dating sites, but every time he approached a woman, usually with a corny line or crude comment about their photographs, they told him to fuck off. In the end he gave up looking and stuck to fishing at the weekends.

He tipped his last can of Stella down his throat and swallowed the warm, fizzy beer. It had been a hot one and he hadn't caught anything. The fish were being lazy today. He looked around his chair just in case he had miscalculated and there was a full can left. There wasn't. He checked the time on his phone and decided to give it another hour. The roads would be quieter then and he had less chance of being pulled for drink driving. He was debating what to have for tea when he heard footsteps approaching and turned around.

'Are they biting?' a man wearing a green wax jacket and a baseball cap asked. He had a fishing pole carrier tucked under one arm and he carried a cool box in his other hand. He smiled, but it was a strange smile.

'Quiet today,' Coombes said, disinterested. The last thing he wanted was to be making small talk with a stranger. All the fishermen he had encountered on the canal were boring fuckers. Boring, or on the other bus. One of them had been very odd and he was sure he had been propositioned by him, but it was in such a subtle way, he hadn't realised until he was sober. This fella looked odd too.

'This might sound like an odd question,' the man said, 'but do you have a bottle opener? I've left the bloody thing in the car.' He opened his cool box and pulled out a bottle of Stella. Iced water dripped from the glass.

'I've got one on my keyring,' Coombes said. He took his keys from his pocket and passed them over.

'You're a lifesaver,' the man said, opening four of the bottles. He placed them back into the cool box. 'I'll loosen the tops on a few so I can twist them off later.' He spotted the empty tins of Stella beside Coombes. 'Do you want me to leave you a couple?'

'I don't mind if you do,' Coombes said. Suddenly, the stranger wasn't so bad. He was a man after his own heart. 'Very kind of you, thanks.'

'Here,' the man said, handing over two bottles. He stood up and started to walk away. 'One good turn deserves another,' he said. 'Enjoy the beer.'

'Will do,' Coombes said, sitting back in his camping chair. He took a long swig of the ice-cold beer and swallowed it, smiling to himself. 'That was a bonus ball.' He closed his eyes and let the sun warm his face. Twenty minutes ticked by. Halfway down the second bottle, he felt very drowsy. He noticed the man in the green wax jacket coming back with a strange grin on his face. Coombes realised he couldn't move his arms, and he suddenly felt very frightened.

CHAPTER 12

Braddick walked into the MIT office and looked around. It was getting late. Most of the desks were empty but there was still a buzz of chatter as information was passed around. There was no sign of the Smiths. They were out chasing down everyone they had interviewed seven years ago. He headed for Google's desk. Sadie was already sitting there, sifting through sheets of information while Google cross-checked the details online.

'How are we doing?' Braddick asked.

'The DNA on our body came in two minutes ago,' Sadie said. 'I was just about to call you.'

'Nothing?' Braddick asked. He knew it was a miss or Sadie would have called immediately.

'He's not in the database.'

'It's never that easy.' Braddick sighed.

'On a brighter note,' Google said, looking up. 'I have narrowed down our missing persons list to two possible people.'

'Two?' Braddick asked, surprised. 'I thought there were hundreds. How have you eliminated the others so quickly?'

'I haven't eliminated them. I've narrowed down our starting number.'

'Okay. How did you do that?'

'Duckweed.'

'Duckweed?'

'Yes. Duckweed.'

'Can you expand for us,' Braddick said.

'Sadie gets it already,' Google said, smirking. Braddick shrugged, his patience wearing thin. 'Duckweed,' Google repeated.

'Get on with it,' Braddick said.

Google stopped smirking. 'Okay, sorry. The weed forensics found tangled in the mesh was identified as duckweed.' He paused. 'And it only grows in fresh water. Are you with me so far?'

'Do I have to shoot you to get the answer?' Braddick asked. He looked at Sadie. 'Do I have to shoot him?'

'Shall I call armed response?' Sadie asked, picking up the phone.

'No need, grumpy,' Google said, taking off his glasses and cleaning them on his tie. 'Duckweed only grows in slow moving rivers, and this strand is only found in freshwater. When I cross-checked that information, there are only two stretches of the Mersey, up river of the estuary, where that could apply.' He pointed to a map on his computer screen. His finger followed a stretch of river that ran from the source near Stockport, to the Mersey estuary where it merged with the sea. Braddick looked at him, eyebrows raised.

'I know what you're thinking,' Google said.

'What am I thinking?'

'You're thinking that's a lot of river, aren't you?'

'I am thinking that,' Braddick said. 'In fact, I'm thinking that's *most* of the river.'

'It is most of the river,' Google said. He raised a finger. 'Technically, it's all of the river before it becomes an estuary.'

'So, you've narrowed it down to all of the river?'

'There's more.'

'Good.'

'Most of the river is slow moving, however, most of the river doesn't have soap residues and metals in it. The duckweed showed traces of both in its cells. This stretch here, after Warrington, has traces of the old industries that used to pollute the river, in the silt.'

'It was famous for wire making and soap manufacturing, right?'

'Right,' Google nodded. 'That narrows it down significantly.'

'To two people?' Braddick was still surprised.

'There are only two people missing in the area after the weir at Wilderspool, here,' he said, pointing to the map. 'Two people in the right age group, fitting the physical description: hair colour, eye colour and significantly overweight. I thought we could start there and work outwards.'

'That's impressive, Google,' Braddick said, patting him on the shoulder. 'Well done. Can we get to their properties tonight?'

'They both lived alone but we've got the local plod onto it. As soon as we can gain access, we'll be there,' Sadie said. 'How did you get on with the Boyd information?'

Braddick pulled up a chair and sat down. He looked around the room.

'I've put out some tentative enquiries. If he has popped up on anyone's radar in the last few years, we should know about it tomorrow. There's no record of him returning to the UK, no tax returns, no bank activity. If he's alive, he's still abroad.'

'Shame,' Sadie said. 'It sounded so plausible.'

'Like Alec said, there's no substance to it. It was nothing but a hunch.'

CHAPTER 13

Richard was sitting at the dining room table. Celia was sitting across from him, Jake to his left, Jaki to his right. Jaki was still sniffling, her eyes red raw from crying. Richard knew it was her reputation she was grieving for, not his. That didn't make her a bad person. She was very sensitive to how the world perceived her. He understood that. The ordeal they had suffered at school wasn't lost on him or Celia. She promised to contact Tom Mathews' parents and threaten them with an injunction. He could feel the tension coming from his family. They blamed him, no matter what the circumstances. It was his fault they were being ridiculed. He wanted to scream his innocence from the rooftops but he knew no one was listening. Everyone questioned it.

'I know this has been a difficult day for you,' Richard said. He looked at them individually. Only Celia held his gaze; there was suspicion in her eyes – they were dark and angry. 'I need you to understand that this has been a difficult day for me, too.' He paused. There didn't seem to be much empathy in the room. 'This is a nightmare situation for all of us, as a family.'

'Are you going to tell us what the police said to you at the station, or not?' Celia asked, angrily. Emmerson Graff had refused to divulge anything until she had spoken to her husband. That didn't bode well in her mind, it indicated there was something of substance to the allegations, they had something she didn't yet know.

'Yes, of course I am,' Richard said, nodding. He didn't know where to begin. There was no way to tell the story without sounding guilty. How could he explain an abortion? 'That is why I've asked for us to sit down as a family, so I can explain to you what has happened.'

'I don't think I want to know,' Jaki said, quietly. 'I feel like I'm going to puke.'

'I haven't done anything wrong, Jak,' he said. 'If I had, they would have charged me.'

'Toni said the police must have had solid evidence to arrest you,' Jaki countered. 'And her dad is a traffic cop, so she knows.'

'They do have evidence,' Richard said, 'lies.'

'What evidence?' Celia snapped.

'Yes, what evidence?' Jaki asked.

'Give him a chance to speak,' Jake said, irritated.

'Well?' Celia said. 'We're waiting.'

Her mobile phone began ringing. She stood up and crossed to the kitchen worktop to answer it. Jake and Jaki rolled their eyes and sighed. The interruption was unwelcome, but Richard felt relieved to be given a few more minutes; he didn't even know where to start.

'Hello, William,' she answered. Richard knew William was her boss. He didn't like him, and William thought Celia was too good for a secondary school teacher. He had been trying to fuck her since she had joined the practice, and he still was. Richard felt his anger rising. He could see the smarmy bastard rubbing his hands together at the news, and could hear his reedy voice in his head: *I told you he wasn't good enough for you, Celia.*

'No. I haven't read it,' Celia said, glaring at Richard. 'I'll take a look now and call you back. Thanks for letting me know, William.'

She put down the phone. Richard felt the tension rising higher. Something was about to happen, he could sense it. Celia turned around and smiled coldly.

'Apparently, your father is all over the front page of this evening's *Liverpool Echo*,' she said. Richard felt his stomach clench and he wanted to scream, as his children ran to get their tablets and laptops to read exactly what the newspaper was saying their father had done.

CHAPTER 14

Coombes watched the man approach him. He was odd, this one, no doubt about it. He was going to ask him what the fuck he was looking at, but his brain wouldn't connect to his tongue. His mouth wouldn't work. There was something about the man's eyes that frightened him, something evil. Coombes felt woozy. He couldn't move. His head lolled onto his chest and he couldn't find the strength to lift it up. The man was in front of him; he put his fingers under Coombes' chin and picked up his head, looking deep into his eyes. Coombes tried to back off but couldn't. The man's eyes were dark. They seemed to look inside his head.

'You'll be feeling very drowsy now,' the man said. Coombes blinked. 'Don't worry though, you'll still feel the pain.' Coombes twitched. 'Do you feel a little vulnerable, helpless even?' Coombes could only dribble in response but the man could see the fear in his eyes and it gave him a warm, fuzzy feeling. 'Good. I'm glad you're frightened – you should be – because what I'm going to do to you will be terribly painful. It will last much longer than you would have thought possible and, of course, you will die somewhere in the process.' Tears formed in Coombes' eyes. 'Weird that,' the man said. 'You can't move, but you can still cry. It's a good thing though, I need to see you're in pain and helpless.' The tone of his voice changed. He sounded like a concerned adult explaining something to a child. 'Helpless is a terrible thing to feel, don't you think?' the man asked. Coombes tried to speak but just gargled. 'Helpless is what you're feeling now. It is how I felt for years. You and your friends made me feel like that, but don't you worry, I'm returning the favour.

One good turn deserves another, don't you think?' Coombes gurgled again. 'Do you remember me?' the man asked. 'You and your friends put me in a position where I felt helpless.' He took off the baseball cap. 'Look at my face. Do you remember me?' he asked again. 'Don't worry if you don't. You probably don't. Do you know why you don't remember me?' Coombes looked at him, eyes wide. 'You don't remember me because you couldn't give a fuck who you damage, playing your little games. Hide and seek for adults. At least, that is what you idiots thought it was. The problem is, the loser of the game goes to prison for a long time, and there's nothing they can do about it. Helpless, you see? Just like you are now. Let me show you how helpless you are.' He smiled and reached down to Coombes' bait box and flipped the lid. Hundreds of blowfly maggots wriggled over each other, searching for something to eat. He picked one out, dangled it in front of Coombes' eyes and carefully put it into his left ear. His pupils dilated as the maggot wriggled further inside. 'I bet that will drive you mad, crawling around inside your head. The itch will drive you crazy but you won't be able to scratch it. Can you feel it wriggling about in there? Do you feel as helpless as you made me feel?' the man asked. 'Four years I served because of you idiots,' he whispered in his ear, before placing another couple of wriggling maggots in there.

The man stepped back and watched Coombes turn red. His face looked tormented. He smiled. Perfect. He was suffering, trapped inside his body, unable to do anything to make it stop.

'They're driving you insane, aren't they?' he said, reaching for some more. 'Let's put some more wrigglers in your other ear, shall we?' He put three in, one at a time, carefully letting them wriggle inside before placing the next one in. 'That must be very uncomfortable. Hold on to that thought, because things are about to get a lot worse.' Coombes let out a sob, a gargle from deep inside. 'I know how you feel,' the man said. 'You want it to stop but it won't. You want mercy, but there is none. Not for you and your friends. Mercy has left the building,' he said loudly, in an Elvis concert fashion. He smiled and looked thoughtful. 'Shall we get on with it?'

The man turned around and took Coombes' line from the murky canal. He dangled the float and hook in front of his eyes. 'This is how the police will say you died: you were pissed on Stella, fell into the canal, got tangled up in your line, and drowned. Just another pisspot dead in the water. Happens every week.' He grabbed Coombes by his cheeks with a gloved hand, careful not to bruise him, and forced open his mouth with his finger and thumb. 'Now, hold still,' he said, concentrating. 'Open wide.' The man pushed the silver barb through the inside of Coombes' cheek, so it popped through his face below his nose. Blood trickled down his chin. 'There we are. I bet that hurts, doesn't it?' he asked, as he wrapped the twine around his neck. Not too tight. He wanted to take his time. Checking the canal bank was still empty, he tipped Coombes from his chair into the water. There was a splash as he submerged and then resurfaced. His feet could just touch the muddy bottom of the canal. The man pulled his head clear of the water with his rod. The twine tightened around his neck. 'Up we come,' the man said, lifting Coombes' head. 'And back down we go again.' He allowed the bubbles to become frantic before pulling him up again. Coombes' eyes were bulging. 'Up we come,' the man said again, his voice soothing and rhythmical. 'Take a deep breath now, back down we go again.'

He let the bubbles froth to the surface for a minute, until they slowed, and lifted him up with the rod once more. 'Up we come again. Deep breath now. How does that feel, Phil?' he asked. 'Not pleasant, feeling like your drowning, with nothing you can do about it, is it?' He checked his watch. 'Down we go again,' he said, smiling. Coombes sank below the surface once more, only his hair showed above the water. Bubbles rushed to the surface and the man waited until they had become more erratic before he lifted his head. 'Up we come, deep breath now, Phil. Three hours until sundown. Let's see how long you can stay alive, shall we? Are you ready?' he lowered the rod again. 'Down we go…'

CHAPTER 15

Richard watched in horror as his family read the news article online. He walked behind Jake, who was reading it on his laptop. The headline read:

Merseyside teacher arrested on underage sex charge

He wondered how far Kevin Hill had gone. It appeared he had gone all the way.

'So, it's true,' Celia said, reading through the article at warp speed. 'Who is this Nicola Hadley?' she said, looking up. 'I thought her name was Nikki Haley?'

'They spelt it wrong on their website,' Richard mumbled.

'Not that it makes any difference what her name is, if the allegations are true.' She was reading the article as fast as she could. 'How could you do this?'

'It isn't true, Celia,' Richard protested. 'Read it properly. It is speculation.'

'Speculation?'

'Yes.'

'That photograph on page two is not fucking speculation. You bastard!' she shouted. Jake flicked the page and they were looking at the photograph of Richard kissing Nicola Hadley. Jake looked up at his dad, disappointment in his eyes. Richard shook his head to reassure him but the doubt didn't budge.

'Calm down, Celia,' Richard said. 'It isn't what it looks like.'

'Is this you, Richard?' she snapped. Richard looked away. 'Answer me.'

'Yes. It is me.'

'And this is Nicola Hadley?'

'Yes.'

'Speculation means there's no proof.' She picked up her iPad and pointed to the picture. 'This is a picture of you with your tongue down a thirteen-year-old girl's throat. What part of that is speculative?'

'Oh my god, Dad, she was pregnant,' Jaki wailed. She had read ahead of the others. 'That is sick! How could you?'

'What?' Celia said, frantically scrolling down. 'Pregnant?'

'How could she be pregnant, Dad,' Jake asked, shaking his head. 'Now this shit is about to get real,' he muttered. He knew his mother was about to go psycho. 'You can't explain that one, Dad.'

'You said it wasn't true,' Jaki said, sobbing. 'You made her pregnant, Dad.'

'It isn't what it looks like,' Richard said, touching her hand.

'Don't touch me,' Jaki shouted. She pulled her hand away and tucked it under her arm. 'You're disgusting!'

'Please, listen to me for a moment.' Richard tried to calm the atmosphere, but the picture and the pregnancy said a million words. It could not be denied. He could explain so much about the circumstances around the photograph but he could never deny it. 'I was very drunk and she grabbed me on the dance floor. It was a second, no more than that. But I didn't have sex with her.'

'She was thirteen, Dad,' Jaki cried. She wiped snot from her nose with a tissue. 'I don't believe it's in the newspaper. Everyone reads the *Echo*. Oh my god, no one will ever speak to me again. This is so sick. She was thirteen.'

'I didn't know how old she was.'

'I hate you. You pervert. You've ruined my life.' She ran out of the kitchen. Richard felt tears of frustration running down his cheeks. He could hear her storming up the stairs to her bedroom. 'I hate you,' she shouted again as she slammed the door. 'I hope you die!'

'You made this young girl pregnant,' Celia said. She was incredibly calm. Too calm. 'It says here that she had an abortion.'

'I didn't touch her, Celia.'

'You can't deny an abortion, Richard.'

'Please believe me. I didn't touch that girl.'

'I have never been more disgusted in my life. You need to leave this house, right now.'

'This is all lies, Celia.'

'She was pregnant for fuck's sake!' she snapped. There was venom in her voice and hatred in her eyes. 'How do you lie about being pregnant, Richard?' She looked at the ceiling. 'You tell me how she lied about being pregnant or fuck off out of this house.'

'I don't know that she was pregnant, neither do you,' Richard said, clutching at straws. 'If she was pregnant, it was nothing to do with me.'

'Get out!'

'Celia, please.'

'Get out of this house,' Celia said, calmly.

'Celia,' Richard said. 'I know how this looks, but it is not what it seems,' he pleaded.

'Why was she even near you, Dad?' Jake looked at him, confused.

'I was drunk and she came up to me at the bar. She told me she was eighteen and that she had been left stranded by her boyfriend.'

'So what?' Celia asked. 'You charged in on your white horse to save her by getting her drunk and fucking her on the settee?'

'Don't be crude. I know you're angry, but that doesn't help.' Richard tried to maintain the fragile peace.

'Don't be crude?' Celia said, angrily. 'You had sex with a child and I'm crude?'

'I didn't have sex with the girl.'

'Child, Richard. She was a child. This photograph tells me you're a liar. Get out.'

'I didn't know how old she was and that photograph is misleading.'

'Misleading?' Celia snorted. 'Taking a drunk thirteen-year-old girl back to your hotel room so she is safe, and then fucking her, is pretty misleading in my book.'

'I didn't know she was thirteen. She was stranded and couldn't get a taxi. I offered her the settee to sleep on. That is all that happened.'

'I couldn't care less if she was 102,' Celia said. She appeared calm on the surface but he could tell she was at boiling point. 'You're a married man, with children older than she is, and you took her back to your room, drunk. You fucked her and made her pregnant. You're disgusting.'

'I know it looks terrible, but it's not what it seems.'

'What do you think it looks like, Richard?' she asked. Her voice was calm but he could feel her anger. She was on the edge. 'Tell me, what can you see here?' Richard couldn't answer. 'I can clearly see you kissing this young girl, and then, according to this article, you invited her back to your room, where you had sex on the settee and she became pregnant and had an abortion. That is what I can see. It is what everyone else will see. The police, the judge, our kids, our friends and family, will all see the same thing.' She stared through him. He couldn't find the words to explain; everything he thought to say sounded weak and unbelievable. 'Tell me what else I should be seeing, Richard.' He couldn't answer. 'Get some things and get out of this house. This is our family home and you don't deserve to be in it right now.'

'I didn't have sex with that girl,' Richard said. His chest was tight and he was finding it hard to breath. The pressure was crushing him.

'Why is she saying you did, Dad?' Jake asked. He was searching his eyes for the truth, almost sympathetic to his plight. 'Why would she say that?'

'I don't know, son. I wish I did.'

'But it says she was pregnant, Dad.'

'I know it does, but that doesn't change the facts. I did not have sex with that girl.'

'Get out of this house!' Celia snapped. She threw a mug across the room and it shattered against the wall, showering Richard and

Jake with shards of pottery. 'Leave now, and don't think about contacting me or the kids until you hear from my solicitor.'

'I'm their father, Celia.'

'You lost that title when you fucked a girl younger than they are,' Celia shouted. Richard looked at Jake and shook his head. 'Don't you dare look for sympathy from your son, you bastard. Get out. Looking at you is making me feel sick. You disgust me!'

'Celia.'

'Get out before I call the police.'

'The police?' Richard said, astounded. 'Why would you call the police?'

'Because you won't leave and I'm concerned for my safety and the safety of my children. You're being investigated as a paedophile. They'll be here like a shot if I tell them that. Get out.'

'Don't be ridiculous,' Richard pleaded. 'I would never harm my kids.'

'I didn't think you would fuck a child, but you did,' Celia said, nastily. 'I don't have a clue who I've been married to for all these years. What else have you done behind my back?'

'Mum,' Jake intervened. 'If Dad says he didn't have sex with her, then I believe him.'

'Shut up, Jake,' Celia snapped. 'Don't interfere in this. This is adults talking.'

'I'm fifteen, Mum.'

'Two years older than the girl your father fucked and made pregnant, Jake,' Celia screamed. 'Get out, Richard, or I swear to god I'll call the police.' She picked up her mobile. 'I'll call 999 and tell them you are threatening us. I mean it.'

Richard held up his hands in surrender. He walked towards the back door and picked up his car keys.

'I'll call you tomorrow when you have had chance to calm down,' he said as he opened the back door. A second mug hit the doorframe next to his head and told him it might take a little longer than that.

CHAPTER 16

Google stood back while a uniformed officer smashed the lock with the big key, the affectionate term for the metal battering ram used to force entry. The door clattered against the wall and he reached inside for a light switch. He found it and flicked it on; a bare lightbulb cast a dull glow over a mountain of newspapers. They were stacked head high on both sides of the hallway, leaving a narrow gap between them to access the house. The stench of decay was suffocating. He took his torch and switched it on, pointing the beam through the gap between the walls of newspapers. Cockroaches scurried here and there looking for darkness. The owner, Reginald Wallace, wasn't a tidy boy.

'Looks like a hoarder to me,' a CSI officer said. The smell reached him and he wrinkled his nose.

'Do you think so?' Google asked, sarcastically.

'Yes,' the CSI said, nodding. 'I've seen it before. Look at all the newspapers. Hoarder, no doubt about it.'

'Thanks for that,' Google said, shaking his head. 'Wait there while we check the place out. You first,' he said, gesturing with his head to the uniformed officer. The officer wasn't happy at the thought of venturing inside. 'Go on,' Google said. 'You're bigger than me and you've got a taser.'

The officer led the way to the first door on the right. Google stepped into the doorway and switched on the light. He was met by a wall of refuse that reached to the ceiling. Binbags, carrier bags, cardboard boxes, and suitcases were piled high to the ceiling. A narrow passageway had been left, which led to a single armchair that was surrounded by plastic Coke bottles, full of amber fluid.

Urine, Google thought. He would sooner piss in a bottle than get up and go to the toilet, or was he so much of a hoarder that he couldn't part with his own waste either? It was obvious that Reginald had a serious mental illness. He had a disorganised mind and attachment issues. A rat scurried from under the armchair, sniffed the air, and then scampered back to where it had come from. The stench of rot was becoming worse.

'I wouldn't want to lose my car keys in here,' Google said. 'I have enough trouble finding them anyway. Let's move on.' The uniformed officer grinned.

They made their way towards a small kitchen at the rear of the house. Every flat surface was covered in takeaway cartons, mouldy plates and pots, and pans of all shapes and sizes that were full of rotting food. The windows had been covered in newspaper, which was taped to the frames so no one could see in. It seemed that Reginald knew he had a problem and wanted to hide it from the world. If they couldn't see in, they would never know how sick he had become. Google looked around for entrances and exits. There was a back door but he couldn't see it: the frame was just visible above the rubbish. The stench was choking now. Rotten food, rotting garbage, and human waste. There was something else too. The cloying stink of a human corpse. He couldn't see it yet, but he knew there was one close by.

'Can you smell that?' Google asked.

'Yes, sir. I don't think our missing person is missing any more.'

'Me neither.'

Google stepped into the kitchen and looked around. There was no other entrance, no cellar door, and no stairs. It was a single-storey flat. He bent low and shone his torch around. There was a tunnel beneath the mountain of debris. At first, he couldn't fathom how it had been made or what it was. He scrambled closer on his hands and knees. The tunnel ran a few metres in before it appeared to take a dog-leg turn to the right. It was supported by a dining table – a long one that could seat six or more. He shone the torch underneath it. The floor was thick with grease and slime.

He could smell human excrement over everything else. His senses were overwhelmed with the stench as he crawled into the tunnel to the turn point. He shone the torch into the darkness and the decaying face of the house owner looked back at him. His skin was green, decomposing, his eyes sunken and blackened. The body appeared to be intact, but it was impossible to tell what had killed him without moving it. Google crawled backwards, overcoming the urge to gag.

'How long have you been there, Reg?' Google said. He reached the end of the tunnel and stood up. His face was smeared with excrement. The uniformed officer wrinkled his nose and stepped back as Google dusted himself down and turned to him. 'Someone at social services wants a massive kick up the arse for this. Poor bloke wasn't missing, he's been dead under there all this time.'

***

Not far away, Sadie was on a similar mission. She put the key into the lock and twisted it. It was a little stiff and needed a bit of persuasion to open. She leaned against the door to move the pile of junk mail that had been deposited through the letterbox while the owner had been absent. The house smelled musty and unlived in. She reached for the light switch; it came on, illuminating a long hallway with two doors leading off it, and the stairs.

'Let me give the place a once over,' she said to the CSI team behind her. 'Once I'm done, I need you to find anything that will link our body to the missing person who owns this place.' The suited officers nodded.

'Who is the owner?' one of them asked. 'Just for our records.'

'Thomas Green, aged thirty-three,' Sadie said. 'He was listed as missing by his employer. Hasn't been seen since. No phone activity and no bank transactions.'

'Sounds to me like Thomas is on the other side,' the CSI said, matter of factly. Sadie glanced at him. The glance was enough to stop him commenting any more. 'Well, that's why we're here, isn't it?'

'It is,' Sadie said, nodding. She had decided a long time ago that she could never date a CSI, they were weird in so many ways; not that the opportunity had ever risen.

Sadie walked down the corridor and glanced into the living room. A sixty-five inch TV screen was mounted on the wall above a gas fire. Attached to it was a PlayStation, with only one controller: the occupant lived alone and no kids visited. She glanced around and saw one photograph of an overweight man with dark hair. He was standing next to Ronaldo, smiling – a Manchester United fan. There was a laptop on the floor next to the settee, and a broadband router was still switched on. He had intended to come home.

She left the room and glanced into a small kitchen. There was one plate and one cup on the draining board. She decided to let the CSIs search the drawers and cupboards. It wasn't important for now. She climbed the stairs and looked into the bathroom. One toothbrush and a razor were on the sink. A bath towel was neatly folded over a rail. The flat was clean, tidy and functional. There were no signs of distress or mental illness. She reached the only bedroom and pushed open the door. The iconic poster of Bruce Lee, dressed in a yellow jumpsuit holding nunchakus, dominated the wall. Beneath it were four different sets of nunchakus, each mounted on brass screws. A set of samurai swords were mounted above the bed, adorned in black suede with gilded handles. Sadie thought they were probably impressive, if you liked swords. She didn't. There was a set of dumb-bells and a sit-up frame on the floor at the foot of the bed. The quilt was tossed back to reveal semen stains on the dark bedding. It was a man cave, which had clearly never had any input from a female. She opened the bedside cabinet and looked inside. A vial of amber fluid was next to a pack of unused syringes, she read the label: Nandrolone. Steroids. Not the hard stuff that the freaks use, but size enhancing nonetheless. The owner fancied himself as an alpha male, and most that did were rarely alphas – they were much lower down the scale. She took a last look around and noticed a sharps bin, which held the owner's used needles. A large poster of MMA fighter Conor

McGregor confirmed her theory: the owner respected aggression and machoism. Thomas Green could have been the type to rile the wrong people. Aggressive people. People far more aggressive than he could have imagined. Thomas Green could have crossed someone who had the influence to pay someone else to wrap him in wire mesh, torture him, and toss him into the sea like garbage, without giving him a second thought. Someone with no empathy.

Sadie had the feeling she was in the right place to match a name to her victim. She walked back to the front door. The CSI team were waiting to be set off the leash.

'You'll save some time if you go straight to the bedroom,' she said. 'There's a sharps bin full of steroid needles, and stains all over the sheets. It's DNA heaven,' she said, reaching for her phone. 'There's a laptop in the living room. I need that rushing through.'

'I'll send it in now before we start,' one of them said.

'Thanks,' she said, as she called Braddick. It was silly o'clock but he wouldn't mind; he never sounded like he had just woken up, whatever time she called. He was a robot, she was convinced of it.

'Sadie?' he answered. 'What have you found?'

'I think we've got our victim,' she said. 'There's DNA all over the place and Thomas Green fancied himself as a bit of a hardcase. He may have pissed off the wrong people. I've had his laptop sent off to the techs so we should know who Green really is in the morning.'

'Good work, Sadie,' Braddick said. 'Get some sleep and I'll see you in the morning.' She hung up and looked at the phone, a little offended by his abruptness. He was often abrupt, and she knew he didn't mean to be, so she wasn't sure why she was offended. 'Goodnight,' she said to no one, and tutted as she went back into the house.

CHAPTER 17

He sipped his coffee as he read the article. A teacher had been arrested on suspicion of having sex with a minor. He had made her pregnant and she'd had an abortion at thirteen. That makes a good story: the teacher and the pupil. Just like the priest and the choirboy, or the television presenter and a vulnerable child. People in power abusing the weak. Makes good reading and has the wow factor.

'How could he do that?' People would ask.

A man in a position of trust betrays that trust with a child. The public would say he deserves to be flogged to death, in front of baying crowds throwing rotten tomatoes. As he read between the lines, his anger rose. The story didn't read right, there was something fishy about the entire article. He read it again. It still didn't read right. There was a blurred photograph on page two, which appeared to be the only thing of substance to the story. To be fair to the teacher, she looked much older than thirteen, but that wouldn't matter. They would crucify him anyway. On the flip side, he hadn't been charged. The newspaper didn't say he hadn't been charged, but if he had, they would have said so. They printed the story without substance because it was a good read. He wondered how damaged the teacher's life had become overnight. Shattered probably. Just as his had been. There was no thought given to the devastation caused when sensationalism is applied to news. None.

He looked for the name of the reporter. There it was, in black and white: Kevin Hill. Bastard. The very same bastard who crucified him years ago. Hill had been like a dog with a bone, it seemed like he was on a mission to destroy every last grain of the man's respect. The arrest, the committal hearing at magistrates' court, the trial, sentencing; he had covered every step of it, and what he hadn't known, he'd made up. Bastard. He was still at it. He ground his teeth together as he read page two, which was basically a summary of the tripe on page one but reworded slightly. He wondered who this teacher guy was. Richard Vigne. A married man with two children who were older than the victim. Great storyline Kevin Hill, you bastard, but did he do it? Who cares? No one gives a fuck what happens to Richard Vigne's life while you sell a few newspapers on the back of his reputation. Bastard. Someone should take you down a peg or two; someone might.

He opened his laptop and logged on. Starbucks' Wi-Fi was the best. He opened Facebook and searched for Richard Vigne; it was an unusual name and his profile came up on the school page. There was a lot of abuse on there. Very nasty. Some people were making threats. That was against the law but no one would do anything about it. The teacher was a paedo, simple as. Threaten him, abuse him, kick his head in – if you want to. He deserves everything he gets. In fact, feel free to set up groups online to trick and trap people. Catch them and hang them from a tree by the bollocks. Do what you want. He felt sorry for Richard Vigne, guilty or not.

Suddenly, the page disappeared. The school had removed his profile. Very clever. He wondered if Richard Vigne had read the comments on his profile. Best if he hadn't, to be honest, innocent or guilty, he wouldn't have enjoyed reading those posts. He searched for Kevin Hill and a raft of links appeared. His Facebook page, his newspaper articles, his Twitter account, everything he needed and more. Kevin Hill was a bastard, a bottom feeder living on people's mistakes, people's misery, people's lives. It was time the bastard was stopped. Someone needed to stop him for good. It was time to shut him up once and for all, and, once he had finished with the predator hunters, he would address that.

CHAPTER 18

Alec heard the landline ringing and crossed the conservatory to answer it. He watched a squirrel performing acrobatics on the washing line as he answered. It was a long-distance call. There was some static on the line and then it connected.

'Hello?' Alec said.

'Alec,' the voice said, 'Peter Bevans here, returning your call.'

'Thank you, Peter, much appreciated. Did you have any luck?'

'That depends on your definition of luck, I suppose,' Peter said. 'Your man Boyd landed himself in hot water a few years back. I didn't have much trouble tracing him.'

'Really?' Alec said. He could feel the tingle: a feeling he got when something new about a case came to the surface.

'Yes. It seems Boyd did a lot of travelling around, hopping from here to Vietnam, Cambodia, Laos, Myanmar, all over the place.'

'Do you know why?'

'He came to Thailand on a tourist visa, which only gives you thirty days in the country, but if you leave and cross the border, you can get another thirty days.'

'I see,' Alec said. Boyd hadn't had time to apply for a visa before he left. That meant he'd left in a hurry. People leave in a hurry when they are running from something. The tingle intensified.

'He worked as a photographer, right?'

'Right. Forensics.'

'That adds up.'

'It does?'

'Yes.' Peter said. 'It would appear Boyd was taking pictures he shouldn't have been, and he was selling them on some very distasteful websites. He was making a lot of money.'

'Without sounding naive, what type of pictures?'

'Pornographic, mostly; prostitutes of all descriptions, women, men, lady-boys, but predominantly youngsters.'

'Youngsters?' Alec asked. There had been no indication that Boyd was that way inclined. This added a different slant to things.

'Yes. That's what attracted the Thai police to him. They're clamping down on paedophiles coming over here as sex tourists. Anyway, their tech teams traced the IP address of who was uploading the images of kids, and Boyd's address came up.'

'An address there?'

'Yes. He was renting a small villa outside Phuket. The local plods went out there to arrest him and said he had absconded, but I'm not so sure that's the truth, looking at the reports.'

'What do you mean?' Alec asked. It was all adding up. He'd known Boyd was a bad egg.

'The reports from Phuket are worthless reading, filled out just to complete the paperwork for their superiors in Bangkok. I think he paid off the Phuket officers who knocked on his door, and then left the country by boat.'

'Where to?'

'I can tell you that without a doubt,' Peter said, proudly.

'You can?'

'Yes. Because he was killed six years ago in a motorcycle accident on an island called Ko Lanta, which is about two hours by speedboat, south of Phuket.'

'What?'

'He's dead, Alec.' Peter could sense Alec's disappointment. 'They have an ex-pats Facebook page and the articles about the accident are on there, if you go back far enough you'll find them.'

'What is the Facebook page called?' Alec asked, reaching for a pen.

'I've written it down,' Peter said, 'Ko Lanta ex-pats news.'

'I'll have a look,' Alec said, sighing. 'Listen, I appreciate your time, Peter.'

'My pleasure. I've asked the authorities on Ko Lanta for the paperwork to be faxed over. I suspect it will be useless, and I'll have to have it translated, but if there's anything interesting, I'll call you. Anything else you think I can help you with, just ask.'

'Thanks, Peter, I will.'

'And come and visit sometime, now you're putting your feet up. You're always welcome.'

'Too hot for me out there,' Alec said. A twinge of sadness pricked him. His wife, Gail, had wanted to go there, but he had always been too busy at work. He wished he had taken her there, maybe things could have been different if he had. Maybe. Maybe not. 'Thanks again.'

'No problem, bye.'

The line disconnected and Alec looked at the handset for a while before replacing it. Boyd was dead. That was a good thing. Boyd had become a predator in South East Asia, and his death had saved others from abuse. Part of him was happy about that, but the other part wanted him to be alive so he could satisfy his curiosity. Was Boyd the enforcer who had wrapped the Albanians in wire mesh, tortured them, and killed them? Was he the man who had silenced an entire city? He would never know.

CHAPTER 19

The MIT office was full to capacity, standing room only. Braddick was standing by a bank of screens showing images of Thomas Green, alive and dead. He clicked the remote and the images shifted from Green's body on the beach to the Albanian men in the back of the van. They were all encased in wire, tortured and killed. It was a rare crime. Too rare to be committed by a random. Braddick and the team knew they were linked, but they didn't know how.

'Okay,' Braddick said, waiting for the chatter to stop. 'Our victim is Thomas Green, aged thirty-three, from Runcorn. He worked for the borough council as a groundsman, mostly grass cutting at the townhall parks here and there.' He changed the images. 'He also worked on the doors at a couple of pubs in the Old Town, for a company we're all familiar with, Premier Security.' A ripple of comments went through the crowd. 'We all know Premier are bent and we all know they control the distribution of drugs in the city centre.' He waited for the derisive comments to subside. 'But, what we need to do now is decide if Premier Security is relevant to this investigation.' He looked around at the faces in the room. They were focused and intense. 'Is the fact that Thomas Green worked part-time for them a coincidence, or is it the reason he ended up in the river?' They nodded in agreement. 'What do we know about him?'

'I've spoken to Matrix, guv,' Sadie said from her desk. 'They've never heard of Green, and they reckon the Runcorn area is a sealed market. It has never changed hands for years. If a small dealer pops up and tries his hand, they get jumped on from a great height. There are some heavy-hitters over there and they don't mess around. Matrix know the hierarchy well. Green has never been mentioned in any of their intel. He's nothing to do with their drugs supply.'

'We're working on the assumption that the cases are linked though?' a detective asked.

'For now,' Braddick said.

'Surely the Albanians were taken out over drugs,' he challenged.

'We have to assume that,' Braddick agreed.

'This is different,' Sadie cut in.

'Why?'

'The Albanians were on the radar. Matrix were on their operation for months, and we know they were in conflict with Eddie Farrell and the Karpovs,' she said. 'It was sharks against minnows. I'm surprised they lasted as long as they did.'

'True,' Braddick said.

'Thomas Green isn't even a blip on the radar for Matrix. No one has ever heard of him. He's no one in that organisation. He may have worked for Premier Security, but a big part of their success has been the legitimate side of their business.'

'Agreed,' Braddick said.

'Green was a part-time bouncer at Wetherspoons in Runcorn. His house was clean and tidy but he certainly wasn't raking in thousands. He was scraping by. I don't think he had anything to do with their operation.'

'Okay, I agree,' Braddick said, nodding. 'Let's not rule out a drug connection, but we'll park it for now.' He looked at the officer from the tech team. 'Did we get anything from his laptop?'

'It's early days, but there are a few interesting things.' The officer checked his notes. 'Green was chatting to a woman on Facebook the week he disappeared. The conversation was flirtatious to say the least, but we only have one side of it.'

'Why?' Braddick asked.

'The profile he was talking to has been deleted. We're trying to get it back from his hard drive but it could take time. We're trying to do it without approaching Facebook themselves, they're a real pain in the arse to deal with and very slow. It could take months that way. The last message Green sent to whoever he was chatting to was "Great, I'll text you now! Xx", so it would appear that numbers were exchanged and the conversation continued offline.'

'Safer if you have something to hide.'

'Exactly.'

'Maybe he went to meet someone. Have we managed to get hold of his network provider?' Braddick asked.

'Now we have his address we're on it; we know he was with Vodafone. We've requested all his messages and call data with a warrant this morning.'

'When will we have the information?'

'Tomorrow, at the latest.'

'Good. We need to know who he was talking to, and if she was genuine or bait. What else have we got?'

'This is very interesting,' the tech said. 'We checked his Facebook footprint and at first we thought it was pretty bland. He doesn't have many friends on there and he rarely interacts with anyone, but then we found he was an active member of a predator hunting site. He was an admin, posted every day, and participated in a lot of the stings they made. He has hundreds of photographs of their operations.'

'Predator hunters?' Braddick said, surprised. 'Flushing out paedophiles online, now that is interesting,' Braddick said. 'How many?'

'How many what?'

'How many stings did they make?'

'Twenty-five in the last five years, leading to fifteen convictions.'

'Wow.' A ripple of chatter spread through the gathering. 'Twenty-five stings. Like or loath vigilante groups, that's impressive,' Braddick said. Some of the gathering agreed but others shook their heads. 'I know what some of you think of these groups, but to run twenty-five operations takes organisation and dedication.' He paused. 'That group was obviously an important part of his life.'

'He posted every day,' the tech said. Braddick looked at Sadie and Google. They were both nodding. 'On the face of it, it all looks to be above board and run with the best intentions,' the officer said. 'But when you look at it from the other angle, there were ten operations they got wrong.'

'This is motive,' Sadie said.

'A thousand per cent,' Google agreed. He began typing on his laptop.

'If someone has been trapped and jailed by this group's actions, they are going to be pissed off, and if they have accused someone wrongly, likewise,' Braddick said. 'Both scenarios are motive to me.' Nodding heads agreed with him. 'I want this group and its active members investigated. Google, I want you to go back through their site as far as it goes and see what you can find.'

'I'm already on it, guv,' Google said, searching the posts on their page.

'Sadie, can you organise splitting up the stings, and investigate each one – especially the ones that ended up with someone doing time?'

'How many admins are there in that group?' Sadie asked.

'Six, I think,' the tech said.

'Get me their details.'

'What are you thinking, Sadie?' Braddick asked.

'We need to speak to each one,' she said. 'There may have been threats made, especially if they got it wrong so many times.'

'Good thinking. Everyone knows what we're looking at here. Let's get on with it. If any one of you have even a sneaking suspicion you're looking at the killer, you call it in and we go in with armed backup. No heroics on this one, understand?'

The nodding heads told him they did. Braddick felt a rush; instinct told him they were onto something.

CHAPTER 20

Richard Vigne woke up and wondered where he was. The surroundings were unfamiliar. His head was pounding and there was a dull ache behind his eyes. He didn't feel rested. Then it came back to him. The pain and emotional trauma of being evicted from his home by the woman he idolised, and shunned by the daughter he worshipped, had broken him. Their words echoed like flying shards of glass, cutting him open. They'd said they were disgusted by him. His own daughter. The woman he had lived with and loved, had children with, couldn't bear to look at him. It was heartbreaking, but how could he blame them? They were looking at the evidence and it was overwhelming. The photo was conclusive evidence of physical contact, it was impossible to explain away. The pregnancy was a fact that couldn't be denied; Nicola Hadley had been pregnant and she had aborted the pregnancy. That was a fact. He couldn't deny it had happened. All the facts were undeniable. The killer piece of evidence was Nicola's statement. She said that he had made her pregnant that night. A thirteen-year-old girl said that he'd had sex with her, on a settee. He said, she said, except for the evidence. There was nothing to support his claims of innocence, not one thing. Celia would divorce him and Jaki would never talk to him again.

He could tell that Jake had wanted to believe he was innocent, but couldn't see past the facts. How could he possibly see past the facts? He was fifteen. The truth was impossible to see when there was so much evidence against his father. It twisted Richard up inside to think that his kids believed he had taken advantage of a thirteen-year-old girl and made her pregnant. They believed it. That was a fact too. A fact that he had to deal with. Jake wanted to believe him. That was the only positive in a lake of negatives. He looked around and tried to recall the night before.

He remembered booking into a Travel Lodge with a bottle of Scotch and a Tesco mobile phone. The police had his mobile and laptop. He remembered drinking the burning whisky and he remembered the terrible anger inside him. The whisky seemed to fuel it. The more he drank, the angrier he became. It had spiralled out of control and he'd wanted to lash out at those responsible for his position. The fucking predator hunters. They had made a mountain out of a molehill and shattered his life in just a few hours. He hadn't done anything to deserve their attention. Everything he had done that night with Nicola Hadley was done with manners and integrity, apart from the kiss, but she had grabbed him. She had instigated it and it was seconds, no more. The photograph said he was guilty but he knew he wasn't. It was all lies and fabrication. Trying to convince other people was virtually impossible because of that image. All those years of doing good deeds counted for nothing. The way he had lived his life should indicate who he was as a man. He had chosen to protect and nurture children as a career, for fuck's sake. He hadn't chosen it for the money, that was for sure, it was his vocation. The thought of crossing the line with his pupils made him feel physically sick. How could anyone think him capable? How could his colleagues, his wife and kids think that of him? Didn't they know who he was?

Hot tears ran from bloodshot eyes and his anger boiled again. He looked at the phone as a message came through. The memories of the night before tumbled back into his mind. He had gone on the predator hunters' page and messaged the admins. In fact, he had messaged as many people as he could before he passed out. He had told them what a bunch of retarded twats they were, and offered to meet up with any or all of them so he could smash their faces in. He said he was going to kill them. His mind went into freefall. Was there a way to recall the messages, delete them before they were read? There must be. The new message was a reply from one of them, telling him that his threats would be passed over to the police investigating his case. His stomach lurched.

That was all he needed. He ran to the bathroom and collapsed, holding the toilet bowl as a bottle of scotch and yellow bile splattered the porcelain. As he remembered how angry he was when he'd written the messages, another contraction spewed acidic vomit into the bowl. He was at rock bottom. Things couldn't possibly get any worse.

CHAPTER 21

He had waited patiently for John Glynn to finish work. He worked at the all night mini-market in the student area of Brownlow Hill, behind the Catholic cathedral. His walk home would take him along the cobbled streets, past the old Victorian terraces on Rodney Street, towards Toxteth. It was the same walk he made five nights a week when he'd finished his shift at 3am. John took the same route every night, never deviating, and he had followed him four times, each journey was identical to the first. The only stop John made, was to light a cigarette when he reached Smithdown Road. There, he would pause, and look down the hill at the Anglican cathedral, which looked majestic at night. The city lights reflecting off the surface of the Mersey were mesmerising. A view John could never grow tired of. He would stare for a few minutes, finish his cigarette, and flick the stump down a grid, before walking the mile to his flat.

It was a dry night and John Glynn had finished on time. He waved goodbye to the morning shift and stepped out into the cool breeze that came from the river. It managed to find its way through any clothing, touching your flesh with its icy fingers. He zipped up his fleece jacket and pulled the collars up to cover his ears and mouth. The man watched him from his white Iveco van. It was a big van, with three panels down the side and a twin wheelbase at the rear. Big, yet almost invisible. It was a white van, they blend into the periphery of your memory. John crossed the road and looked around, nervously. That was unusual. He normally walked as if he didn't have a care in the world. The city was relatively safe at night. Most of the trouble happened in the centre. Tonight, John Glynn looked worried. He wondered if he had a sense that something bad was going to happen. He wondered if he had an instinct that had warned him evil was stalking him. Some people have that, he thought. He had it himself. He always knew when it was time to move on. His instincts had kept him alive. Not always at liberty, but alive nonetheless. Going to prison was the hardest thing he had ever done. He was claustrophobic, so being put in a cage for four years had broken his spirit and he had felt helpless. Once the legal wheels had begun to turn, he *was* helpless – thrown into a cell, then a van, then another cell, each one suffocating. Panic attacks had come frequently but nobody cared. The prison officers didn't give a fuck if he choked on his own tongue, and all the time there was nothing he could do about it. All the time he was helpless, unable to leave until they said he could. That feeling tortured him still. It was a feeling the predator hunters needed to experience themselves. They had to endure the same feelings: the total loss of control of your life, your liberty, your freedom. It had driven him more insane than he already was.

His anxiety levels were rising as he thought about it. There he was, in touching distance. He could almost smell him. John Glynn, just a few metres away from him. He was one of the architects of his incarceration. Him and his stupid idiot friends playing Batman and Robin on the Internet, sticking their big noses in where they needn't be. They were responsible for his torture behind bars. He took a deep breath and tried to control his rage. Killing him here would not help the situation, it had to be done to plan. There always had to be a plan. Pure rage made a mess and left clues; clues are what put people in jail. Stick to the plan and leave no evidence. Savour the moment he realises he is helpless. Watch him suffer and break. John Glynn was in the palm of his hand. One of the founder members of the group. One of only two that were alive. It was his time now.

He waited for John Glynn to reach the end of Rodney Street, before starting the engine and driving down the street that ran parallel to it. There were no cameras there. He waited at the junction for him to finish his cigarette, and then drove up the hill, turning left into an alleyway that ran between the tall houses. He stopped twenty metres in and turned off the lights, climbing out of the van quietly. Glynn would walk by any minute. He waited for the sound of footsteps and took out the taser. One, two, three, four … then nothing. He froze in the darkness and listened. Was Glynn spooked by something? His breath stuck in his chest as he waited. The sound of shoes on concrete started up again. Step, step, step, quicker now. Instinctively, he ducked into a doorway. John Glynn had crossed the road to the other side and was looking over his shoulder at the alleyway. He never crossed the road at that point. There was something wrong. Glynn was behaving skittish, nervously looking around as he climbed the hill towards his home.

He stayed hidden until he couldn't hear footsteps any more. *What had spooked Glynn? Why was he so nervous?* It was inconvenient at best. He ran back to the van and climbed in. Getting close enough to use the taser wasn't going to happen now. There was only one more street where there were no cameras. He started the engine and turned on the headlights, driving slowly to the end of the alleyway before doubling back and getting ahead of Glynn once more. He could see him walking up the hill. There was no traffic and he was walking down the centre of the road, following the white lines, so as not to be near the alleyways. *Why was he being so cautious tonight?* It didn't matter. It had to be done, one way or the other.

Glynn was half walking, half jogging up the hill. His mouth was open and he was panting. The man put the van in neutral, so the engine was ticking over quietly, and let it roll over the crest of the hill. Fifty metres away, Glynn spotted the van coming towards him. The man dropped into third gear and put his foot on the accelerator. Glynn moved over to the right-hand side of the road to allow it to pass, but didn't go near the pavement. He was spooked about the alleyways. Not that it mattered. Ten metres from Glynn, the man swerved the van violently, and smashed into him at about forty miles an hour. The bumper smashed his legs below the knees and Glynn was catapulted into the air. He landed heavily in the middle of the road, behind the van. It took two minutes for him to open the van doors and bundle the injured Glynn into the back of it. It wasn't worth tying him up yet. He would be out for a while, and, from the shape of his legs, he wouldn't be running anywhere. The van drove unnoticed through the streets of Liverpool. He smiled to himself. It hadn't been as simple as he had planned, but life could be like that. The outcome was the same: John Glynn was about to experience helplessness.

CHAPTER 22

Alec sipped his whisky and savoured the flavour – a single malt with one cube of ice, the only way he could drink it. He didn't like the blended brands, no matter how famous or well marketed they were. He didn't like them and that was that. He had been searching the Facebook pages used by ex-pats in Ko Lanta and, so far, hadn't had much luck. The island of Ko Lanta Yai looked beautiful. It was long and narrow and surrounded by secluded beaches that stretched for miles. Although a popular destination for travellers, it didn't appear to be spoiled. Not yet, anyway, Alec thought. Only a matter of time before they ruin everywhere. It's in human DNA to explore, experience, exploit and destroy. There seemed to be some hope for the more remote islands, in the Andaman Sea, at least. Frankie Boyd had chosen to go there because it was remote, yet accessible – Alec would bet his last pound on it. It was probably the reason he'd chosen Phuket in the first instance: it was a busy port with an international airport, easy to escape from if the net was closing in. He had no doubt that Boyd would likely have built up contacts in the local police, long before they'd come looking for him. He seemed to build a protective shield around himself wherever he operated. His escape plans were cemented before he had taken off his shoes and settled there. Alec was convinced Boyd had escaped the clutches of the Bangkok police by bribing their colleagues in Phuket. He hadn't done much travelling himself, but it was accepted that the Thai legal system could be manipulated by cash, as could most of the judicial systems on the planet. He was only two hours away from the mainland but, in effect, he had vanished. No one in South East Asia was too concerned where he was, and they certainly wouldn't have sent out search teams for him. The only reason anyone knew where he had gone was because he had been killed in a motorbike accident. That is one sure way to pinpoint where you are: die abroad. From his research, Alec established that motor accidents were the biggest killer of British tourists abroad; it didn't surprise him, and Thailand being the worst place for them didn't surprise him either. Boyd had become just another statistic.

Alec scrolled though thousands of posts on the ex-pat Facebook page. Most were from small businesses – bars and guesthouses – touting their trade. Others were from travellers to fellow travellers, recommending some places and warning of others. Then there were stories of interest: births, deaths, marriages, and a lot of posts about accidents, *lots* of accidents. It seemed there were six to ten deaths on the island every year, especially through the busy season. The novelty of not wearing a helmet was enough for some people to throw caution out of the window and ride without protection; head injuries were the biggest killer by far. The posts seemed to go on forever, and he was growing tired when a picture appeared that spiked his interest. There was a news report and dozens of posts about it. Three motorbikes had collided with the back of a bus when it had swerved to avoid a child, who had run into the road after his dog. Easily done. It only takes a second and you're gone. It had happened in a remote area of the island. Two British men were killed instantly and a third died in hospital a week later, having never regained consciousness. Their names were listed underneath a follow up article, which included their passport images. The dead men were named as Frankie Boyd, Bill Evans and Carlton Harris. The report said Frankie Boyd was decapitated in the accident. The authorities hadn't wasted any time: his body was burned then scattered at sea as no one had claimed him – scattered at sea was Thai for 'thrown in the bin'. His passport photograph was just how Alec remembered him: his eyes piercing and dark. He read on but could find nothing more about the accident. It was simply another three tourists killed on motorbikes, nothing more. It happened regularly. He emptied his glass and refilled it, disappointed at reaching a dead end. The tingle had gone.

CHAPTER 23

Danny Goodwin listened as the phone connected again. It was the fourth time in the last two hours he had tried to reach John Glynn. The voicemail clicked in again and he swore under his breath. He was monitoring the predator hunter Facebook page and had read the raft of threatening messages again. He replied to just one, informing the sender, Richard Vigne, that he was passing them over to the police. It happened all the time, nonces getting angry about being outed. Serves the little scumbags right, he thought. Don't threaten me because you're a twisted pervert, it's your problem. Vigne had been caught with his pants down and his cock in his hand. His victim had told a sad story. A vulnerable teenager taken advantage of by a predator; groomed, abused, and dumped once the novelty had worn off. At least she had a decent relationship with her father. He had watched her spiral into mental illness and decided to do something about it. Good for him. Vigne was a scumbag. Any father would have done the same. Some would have gone a lot further, fair play to him. It was Mr Hadley who had brought the information to light. He'd had hard evidence, too. Photographs, emails, text messages and medical reports; Vigne was nailed-on fucked, and if he had an issue with what they had done with the evidence, he needed to look in the mirror, fucking nonce. They made Danny sick. He would shoot the fuckers if he could. He would be doing society a favour. There were some in the group who took things into their own hands, but he didn't advocate that. Lock them up, that's fine; setting fire to their homes while their kids are asleep upstairs, not acceptable. He knew it happened, and no one had complained – what would the predators say to the police? 'They set fire to my BMW because I was trying to groom a child online.' Not a chance. It happened, and Danny knew it did, but he didn't condone it. The perpetrators of vigilante violence were on the periphery of the group. They were too stupid to have the patience to trap paedophiles with usable evidence. He tolerated them to a degree, but if they began ranting on their page, he deleted them. He needed to protect the credibility of the group. People took them seriously and he needed to maintain their brand.

Danny listened to John's voicemail again and left a message.

'John, it's Danny Goodwin again. Are you still in bed? You lazy git. Give me a ring when you wake up and let me know you are alright, mate.'

Danny was concerned. He had spoken to John Glynn the previous day and had a serious conversation about what he thought was going on. The group had always been about the six of them, they had started it and they kept it going when others came and went on a whim. For some it was a novelty, short-lived, and fun to say you have done it: 'I was involved in trapping a paedo; the fucker went down because of us'. One to impress people with, a tick in the box and move on to the next thrill, but it was much more than that for Danny and the others. It was their creation and, despite their reservations, it had worked. Fifteen nonces had been banged up for a total of over one hundred years on their evidence. He was immensely proud of that. Danny had always been the linchpin, and he looked out for the others – if he could – although they were oddballs. When he had told John his concerns about what had happened, John didn't get it at first. He had laughed, but eventually listened to Danny's reasoning, and he'd promised to take precautions. Danny had warned him about walking home alone after work, especially when there were so many dark alleyways between the Victorian terraces. If anyone was planning to hit him, it would be there. John had thought Danny was being paranoid at first, but he had explained his theory calmly and it began to make sense. Phillip Coombes' death was the catalyst, although he had been hearing whispers of caution in his mind for eighteen months or so. Coombes' death had cemented his misgivings into something more. Bad things were happening to members of the group, bad things like dying. It could have been a series of unfortunate mishaps, coincidences maybe, but he didn't want to trust to fate. When they had found Coombes in the canal, tangled in his own line, pissed and drowned, he knew it wasn't a coincidence. Coombes liked a beer when he wasn't working, but would he have drunk enough to fall into a canal and not be able to get out? Unlikely. Someone was making their deaths look like accidents. He was convinced, but not enough to share his thoughts with anyone but John. Now John wasn't answering his phone. He had a bad feeling about this. A very bad feeling. John always answered his phone, no matter what he was doing. It was a bad sign. He thought things over again in his mind.

Gary Roberts had gone missing eighteen months earlier, his car was found, abandoned, near Otterspool promenade, with the engine running. The coroner couldn't rule suicide, as they had no body, but everyone assumed he had topped himself by walking into the river. It happened a lot on that stretch because it was secluded, accessible by car, literally a few miles from the city centre, and the water was deep. Not long after that, Thomas Green simply vanished without a trace. Thomas wasn't the adventurous type. He worked for the council, did the doors at weekends for a bit of extra cash, and never went anywhere. There was no way he had jumped on a plane with a pocketful of cash and some sun cream, never to be seen again. Someone had made him disappear. And then Dave Rutland had thrown himself under a train. Dave was a loner and not well-liked by most of the group, but he was alright. Some of the group suspected he was gay, but so what? He didn't do anyone any harm. Dave could be insular, but throwing himself under a train wasn't the way he would go. If Dave Rutland had decided he was going to check out, it would be painless. Dave was squeamish. He had half a tattoo on his left arm because he couldn't stand the pain long enough to have it finished. The artist did the outline, and gave him an appointment to go back and have the shading and colour put in, but he never went. He couldn't take the pain. Danny didn't believe that Dave had chosen that way to die; he would have chosen pills, or booze, or disposable barbeques in his car; it would have been clean, no blood. Anything except being mangled beneath a train. It didn't sit right. He knew Dave Rutland and he knew he hadn't thrown himself under an express train. It was as unlikely as Phil Coombes falling into the canal and drowning. At first glance it wouldn't seem odd – if you didn't know the people, it would be acceptable to believe the coroner's reports, but Danny did know them, and something wasn't right. He could feel it in every bone in his body. They were being stalked and executed, simple as that.

John Glynn still wasn't answering his mobile, which left Danny the remaining founder member. All the others were dead; coincidence? Not a chance, he thought. He grabbed the edition of the *Liverpool Echo* that had covered the Vigne arrest, and opened the first page. Inside were the contact details for all the journalists. He dialled one of the numbers.

'*Liverpool Echo*, Kevin Hill speaking.'

'Hello, Kevin. My name is Danny Goodwin. I started up the predator hunting group that bubbled Richard Vigne.'

'Yes. We've spoken. What can I do for you, Danny?'

'It's more what I can do for you…'

CHAPTER 24

Jo Jones walked into the private treatment room and was surprised by how skinny Nicola Hadley was; her eyes were deep, her cheeks sunken. She was barely recognisable. A plastic tube ran up her left nostril, feeding her nutrients to keep her organs from failing. Her vital signs were being monitored by a machine next to her. Faint marks criss-crossed her forearms, some old, some more recent. She was beyond anorexia. Jo felt a swathe of sadness wash over her. The human mind can be incredibly strong but it can also be incredibly fragile. This young girl was broken, physically and mentally. The doctors said she could be interviewed, they also said she had perked up when they had asked her if she would speak to them about Richard Vigne. Social services were consulted and they agreed to send a member of staff from the child protection unit to supervise the interview. Her father had been uncertain, but was persuaded by Nicola to let it progress.

'Hello, Nicola, I'm Jo. I'm a detective with child protection. I want to talk to you and ask you some questions about your relationship with Richard Vigne. Is that okay with you?'

'Yes. How is he?' Her eyes sparkled momentarily.

'He's in a lot of trouble,' Jo said. 'That's why I am here.'

'My dad hates him. He didn't want me to talk to you about him.'

'I know. Your dad is just looking after you.'

'Don't be too hard on him. I realise now that what he did was wrong, but he was always nice to me.' She smiled, revealing teeth blackened by stomach acid. 'We were in love. He used to tell me all the time.' She twirled her hair with her fingers. Jo couldn't help but see the child in her. After everything she had been through, she hadn't grown any stronger. Her vulnerability was blindingly obvious. Maybe that was what her adult lover had seen.

'You said, "we *were* in love", past tense. Why do you say that?'

'One day he stopped returning my calls and replying to emails.'

'Did they stop suddenly, or did he string you along a little?'

'Suddenly. We were planning to meet, then nothing.' She shrugged. 'I guessed he'd had enough of me and didn't want to see me any more. My dad says it's because I'm older now, and he only wants young girls, but I don't believe that.'

'When he stopped contacting you, is that when you became ill?'

'Yes. I was very sad. When I'm sad, I don't cope very well.' She was intelligent enough to know that she was sick, and what was causing it, but was unable to change anything. 'I stopped eating. I can't help it. When I did eat, I was sick afterwards. The doctors say I have to learn to eat all over again, like a baby.'

'You're in the right place to get better. Take your time and you'll be fine. You have all your life to look forward to,' Jo said. Nicola looked away. She didn't seem convinced. 'Nicola, I need to ask you some difficult questions. Are you okay to answer them?'

'I'll try.'

'I need to be blunt. There is no point in beating around the bush, okay?'

'That's fine. Go ahead.'

'Is this the man you had sex with when you first met?' Jo asked, showing Nicola a picture on her Samsung.

'Yes, that's Richard. He's so handsome, isn't he?'

'And this is the same man you were seeing, up until six months ago?'

'Yes.'

'You're absolutely sure?'

'Positive,' Nicola said. She looked confused.

'Do you remember this man?' Jo asked, showing her another photograph. Nicola looked at the image. The wheels inside her head were turning but nothing was happening.

'Vaguely. I think he was in the club that night.'
'Do you remember his name?'
'No. I was drunk that night.'
'But this is the man you had sex with?'
'Yes.'
'Thank you, Nicola,' Jo said, standing. She gestured to the social worker that she was done. 'You've been a great help.'
'Is that it?' Nicola asked.
'Yes. For now.'
'But what about Richard?'
'I can't say anything about the investigation I'm afraid.'
'Will you at least tell him that I asked about him, please?'
'Yes. Bye for now,' Jo said. She walked out of the room, into the corridor. The social worker and a nurse followed her. 'Can we have a word with her doctor, please?' Jo asked the nurse.

'She's waiting to see you,' the nurse said, smiling. She led them to an office a few metres away, knocked on the door, and opened it without waiting for an answer. 'Go in. Take a seat,' she said.

'Superintendent,' the doctor said. 'I'm Susan Chalmers, Nicola's doctor.' They shook hands. 'How did the interview go?'

'It was informative for me, but not so good for Nicola, I'm afraid.'

'Oh dear. That doesn't sound good.'

'Nicola thinks Richard Vigne stopped seeing her six months ago because he had dumped her?'

'Yes.'

'He hadn't dumped her.'

'I don't understand.'

'The man she thought was Richard Vigne, was in fact Ralph Pickford,' Jo explained. The doctor frowned. 'Pickford was sharing the apartment with Richard Vigne. My guess is, Vigne put her to bed, drunk, and Pickford came back and found Nicola asleep on the settee and took advantage of her. She was drunk and confused, and had been talking to Vigne earlier that night, and probably thought that was his name. Pickford let her continue to think that because she was underage.'

'I see.' The doctor looked disturbed. 'Will he be prosecuted?'

'I'm afraid not.'

'Why not?'

'He died in a car crash six months ago.'

'Oh dear. Nicola doesn't know, does she?' the doctor asked, concerned.

'No, and I can see she's in no state to find out that the love of her life was lying to her all along and is now dead.'

'Thank you,' the doctor said. 'We'll have to choose when to tell her he's dead very carefully.'

'Thank you for letting me speak to her,' Jo said. 'If you'll excuse me, there's an innocent man out there being accused of something he didn't do. I need to break the good news to him and his family.'

Chapter 25

Alec finished off his rib-eye and put his knife and fork together. He wiped his mouth with his napkin and smiled at Margaret Boyd. She returned his smile and raised her glass.

'Cheers, Alec, it's been lovely to see you,' she said. 'Here's to Gail. I do miss her so.'

'To Gail,' Alec said, clinking his glass. He sipped the merlot and refilled Margaret's glass. It was always bittersweet talking about Gail. She had been very popular with all his friends and family and they missed her; he missed her more than words could say. The fact she was found dead in another man's arms sometimes escaped them. He felt very bitter in the early days, but the bitterness had faded into sadness: sadness that he had pushed her into another man's arms. It was his obsession with work that had driven her away.

'I was thinking about her the other day, and how I wish I had taken her to Thailand. She always wanted to go there, you know.'

'Gosh, what on earth made you think about that?'

'Just some research on an old case I worked on.' He smiled. 'But it made me think about her.'

'I'm sure many things make you think about her, Alec.'

'They do.'

'I remember her talking about wanting to go there,' Margaret said. Her mind wandered; she had made the connection Alec had wanted her to. 'My nephew, Frankie, was killed over there. You remember, don't you?'

'I remember hearing something about it, but can't remember the details,' Alec lied. 'Wasn't it a motorcycle accident?'

'That's what the family were told, three months after they had cremated him.'

'What?' Alec said, astounded. 'Three months?'

'We wouldn't have known at all, but his mother contacted the embassy in Bangkok when she hadn't heard from him for a while,' she said, lowering her voice. 'It took them a month to reply to her initial contact.' She leaned closer. 'Between you and me, I think he had got himself into trouble again.'

'What makes you say that?'

'Well, between us and the gatepost, he was sacked from his job in forensics, that's why he went away. We never heard the truth from them, of course, but Clive was told at work.'

'Of course, he would be. That's where I heard about it,' Alec agreed. 'There are no secrets in a police station.'

'Clive always says that,' she said, smiling. 'Anyway, as I was telling you, his mother would never give me a straight answer and she couldn't look me in the eye when she talked about it. I knew he had been up to his old tricks again.'

'Oh, interesting. What made you think that?' Alec asked, letting her talk.

'Her face, whenever I asked if she had heard from him: she would blush and look a little sad. He never kept in touch and I think she was embarrassed. You would be, wouldn't you?'

'Of course you would.'

'When she was told about the accident she was heartbroken, poor woman,' Margaret said, sipping her wine. 'You don't expect to outlive your children, do you?'

'I suppose not,' Alec agreed. He'd been too busy working to consider having children. Another regret.

'I felt so sorry for her. They returned his belongings in an envelope,' she whispered. 'One envelope. Can you imagine all you have left of your son fitting in one envelope?'

'They must have been devastated.'

'Inconsolable, she was. He was the apple of her eye, no matter what he'd done.'

'I'm sure he was.'

'Anyway, the Thais sent her his stuff. There were some travel insurance documents and a driving licence.'

'Was that it?'

'That was it,' she said, shaking her head. 'When she queried where his clothes were, they said they had never found out which hotel he had been staying in, and so had never recovered a suitcase, or anything.' Margaret paused. 'If you ask me, they thought no one would ever come looking for him and his stuff did a disappearing act. There was something dodgy about the whole thing. His name is never mentioned any more – black sheep of the family, and all that kind of thing.'

Alec tapped his nose and winked that he understood. He made a mental note to call Peter Bevans in Thailand again. Margaret was right, there was something dodgy about it all. Suddenly, the tingle was back.

CHAPTER 26

Braddick was looking out of the window as the Liverpool Eye turned slowly; it was bright white against a blue sky. The river flowed silently by, relentless on its way to the sea. His thoughts were of men wrapped in wire mesh, seven years apart. Men who would have been at the bottom of the sea if things hadn't unravelled the way they had. There were many ways to dispose of a body, and, given time, most killers will choose the simplest, safest method with the least risk. Nobody wants to rush getting rid of a body. It is very difficult. Bodies are heavy and bulky and difficult to move. They also stink. Unless they are disposed of cleverly, they will be discovered, eventually. Mistakes are made when things are rushed. He could understand that completely. But, to painstakingly encase the entire body – head, torso and limbs – in chicken wire, while the victim was alive, wasn't disposing of a victim, it was pure evil. It wasn't coldheartedly dumping evidence to ensure they avoided capture, that was understandable; it was torture, physically and mentally breaking down a human until they were a gibbering wreck, and enjoying the process. The victim would be aware that what was happening to them was irreversible, and was merely part of a ritual that would ultimately end with their death, probably much further down the line. They would have time to think about their life, their death, their families, their friends, their good times and their regrets. And he knew the killer would talk to them all the way through. He knew that, because it would give him a buzz – telling the victims what was going to happen next, savouring their terror, was what turned the killer on. The anticipation of their pain would be mind-bending. He told them what was coming and he fed off their terror. Braddick knew that 100 per cent.

The killer may well have slipped into their role as enforcer, or cleaner, or silencer, whatever they wanted to call it, but fundamentally he was a narcissistic psychopath, who enjoyed killing immensely. He killed for the sake of killing. He wanted to inflict pain, panic and fear so he could witness human suffering up close. Killing can be profitable, and money may be a by-product of his passion, but it certainly wasn't his motivation. Whoever he was, it would take some stopping him, and he would have to be stopped as there was no way he would stop himself. He liked killing too much. A knock on the door disturbed Braddick's thoughts.

'Come in,' he called.

The door opened and Sadie walked in with Google behind her. She was flushed with excitement. Braddick smiled, he loved her mannerisms. She reminded him so much of someone he once knew.

'We're onto something,' Sadie said, putting a pile of news reports on his desk. She opened her laptop and put it on his desk. Google did the same with his.

'You were right,' Google said. 'You were right,' he repeated, as if he was surprised.

'About what, exactly?'

'Motive,' Sadie said.

'Let's hear it,' Braddick said, looking at their screens.

'There has been a string of incidents and accidents, and when you look at them in isolation, they aren't significant, but together, it's a different story.'

'Okay,' Braddick said.

'Eighteen months ago, uniform found a car abandoned, with the engine still running, down by Otterspool prom,' Sadie began. 'The owner, Gary Roberts, was never seen again. He was a founder member of the predator hunters. There was no phone or bank activity and no body was ever found. It was put down to suicide, although the coroner left an open verdict on file.'

'That doesn't seem too odd, in isolation,' Braddick agreed.

'We know Thomas Green was murdered and dumped in the river, but it was a fluke that we found him,' Google said, taking over. 'What is new to us is, a few months ago, a man called David Rutland threw himself under a train at Hough Green Station, following a failed sting by the predator hunting group. Another suicide. There was no note and no sign of distress at his home. He had no debts, and a reasonable amount of savings.'

'Okay, I'm following,' Braddick said, nodding.

'Last week, a dog walker found this man, Philip Coombes, another founder member, drowned in a canal near St Helens in a freak fishing accident.'

'What happened?'

'He was drunk, slipped into the canal, and became tangled up with his line. He drowned. Allegedly.'

'Okay. There's a pattern emerging.'

'There is. They were all the original members of the group. It's too much of a coincidence,' Sadie said. Her complexion was returning to normal: alabaster white.

'That leaves John Glynn, who lives in Toxteth, and Danny Goodwin, who lives in Allerton, as the only surviving founder members of the predator hunters,' Google said.

'Good work,' Braddick said. 'Have you contacted them?'

'Both mobiles are going to answerphone at the moment, but we've sent uniform to their homes and we'll keep trying.'

A knock on the door interrupted them. It opened and one of the detectives from night shift poked his head around; he was about to start his shift.

'Sorry to bother you, guv.'

'No problem, Carl. What is it?'

'Have you read the local rag today?'

'No. Why?'

'The paedophile hunter group that we're looking at are all over the evening edition of the *Echo*,' he said, holding up a copy.

'Jesus,' Braddick hissed. 'What does it say?'

'One of the group, Danny Goodwin, reckons there's a serial killer out there picking them off, one by one.'

The detectives looked at each other. Google put his head in his hands.

'All that work gone to waste,' he said. 'All we had to do was wait for the *Echo* to come out.'

'It certainly reinforces what you've found – that story could only have come from one of them,' Braddick said, angrily pointing to the pictures of John Glynn and Danny Goodwin. 'They must have worked it out together. If the killer didn't know we were onto him, he does now. Find out which idiot published the story and get in touch, will you? I want to know who he spoke to, Goodwin or Glynn.' He pulled up the online version and they read it, skimming the speculative bits.

'It gives a few names, guv.'

'What names?'

'The names of the people who have made threats to kill them.'

'This is a vigilante nightmare,' Braddick said.

'One guy specifically has made threats to kill them all, as recently as yesterday,' Google said.

'Where are you reading that?'

'Third page.'

'There are three pages?' Braddick said, sighing.

'A teacher they outed this week for having underage sex with a thirteen-year-old. He's been contacting members of the group and threatening to kill them.'

'Richard Vigne,' Braddick said.

'That's him.'

'Who's investigating the underage sex charge?'

'The child protection unit,' Sadie said. 'That will be Jo Jones.'

'Find Danny Goodwin and John Glynn and speak to them, and arrest Richard Vigne, let's put some pressure on him.'

'What for?'

'Making threats to kill will do for a start. If he's our man, we'll soon know.'

'I'll speak to Jo Jones and see what she thinks about our Mr Vigne.'

CHAPTER 27

He read the newspaper and shook his head; that sewer rat, Kevin Hill, had done it again – printed a story full of speculation and coincidence. Danny Goodwin had spotted the pattern before the police had, but they would be onto it now. That changed the dynamic of the game. It would speed things up and make them complicated, like a multi-ball feature on an old pinball machine. He loved those things. The game was hard enough with one ball, but when the multi-ball feature kicked in it was such a rush. The machine would go batshit crazy, lights flashing, sirens blaring, with three balls in play at once. He remembered the first time it happened when he was playing, he'd nearly pissed his pants, he was so excited. The rush was incredible. The adrenalin had taken him so high that, when it was finished and all the balls were lost, he'd felt drained – mentally and physically. This would be the same. Kevin 'twatty-bastard' Hill had just flicked the switch. It was multi-ball time and he didn't even know what he had started, but he would. Both he and Danny Goodwin had conspired to expose the plot, not realising what that would ignite. They would, when it was too late to stop the wheels from turning. There was no need to live in the shadows, planning, plotting and sneaking about in the undergrowth any more. It was time to up the ante. There was no need to make events look like something else – not now. Things would have to be done sooner rather than later, and probably with a little less finesse than he would have liked. No matter: the end result was all that mattered. He picked up his tools, gloves and balaclava and walked to the garage at the rear of the farm. A side door led him into the parking bay. He climbed into the van and put his equipment on the passenger seat.

'How are the legs feeling?' he said to John Glynn. 'Sore, I bet.' John was sitting upright in the back of the van. He was tied up and gagged. His face was swollen and bruised but his legs were much worse. The left was twisted the wrong way round and the right was swollen so much it looked like it might explode. He could see John Glynn was suffering badly. 'Your friend, Danny Goodwin, has been talking to the press.' He said, looking in the mirror. John tried to ask for help but he couldn't. The pain was unbearable. His eyes were red from crying. The man started the engine and the garage door opened automatically; when it had fully opened he drove out. 'Did Danny warn you about what he had worked out?' he asked, conversationally. 'He did, didn't he? That was why you were so skittish last night, isn't it? He told you to avoid the alleyways on the way home, didn't he?' John began shaking as the van moved out of the garage. The man slammed on the brakes, sharply, sending John sliding into the bulkhead. His muffled screams were tragic. The sound would break the heart of the strongest men. Not the man's. He closed his eyes and listened. It was beautiful.

'That hurts, doesn't it, John?' he said. John was shaking and sobbing, choking on the gag. His eyes begged for mercy. 'It is only just beginning, John,' he said. 'You have no idea how much worse it is going to get. You have no idea, honestly.' He smiled coldly. John was hysterical. 'I need to sort those legs out for you.' He reached into the tool bag, picked out a six-inch nail, and held it up for John to see. 'We could try nailing them together, couldn't we?' John's eyes bulged as if they might pop from his head, he shook his head manically. 'No? You don't think so?' John gurgled at him. 'I'll think about it,' the man said.

He turned round and put the nail back in the bag. The sound of muffled sobbing grew louder as he steered the van down a narrow farm track. Rocks and rubble made it a rough ride. The vibration sent John's pain to a whole new level. He was slipping into shock. His heart was pumping at a million miles an hour. The pain was incredible. 'Your friend Danny Goodwin is a smart boy. How long has he known, I wonder?' He spoke into the mirror again. 'I knew something was wrong when I followed you. Your friend was right. I'm not sure what he told you, but he told the *Echo* there was a killer stalking your shitty Facebook group, slaying members and making it look like an accident or suicide. He is right: I did kill your friends and I am going to kill you, and then I'm going to kill Danny, and then I'm going to kill Kevin Hill,' he said, angrily. 'And then, I'm going to fuck off somewhere hot for a while.' He paused. 'Listen to me, waffling on. You don't know why you're here do you? Rude of me not to tell you, sorry. Very remiss of me. Let me explain, you're here because you're a cunt.' He looked at John in the mirror and smiled. 'You think you and your cunt friends can take the law into your own hands and ruin people's lives, and that is what you do, when you trap people by playing your little games online, pretending to be Looby fucking Lou, aged twelve.' He banged the dashboard. 'That is what happens when you fuck about with people's lives: you ruin them. You make them helpless. Do you know what helpless feels like yet, John?' He looked at John, his eyes closed, wincing in pain. 'Are you listening to me, you little fuck?' he shouted. John didn't open his eyes. 'Listen to me, John.' He stopped the van and climbed into the back. 'Are you feeling helpless yet, John?' he shouted. John opened his eyes, tears running down his cheeks. He nodded yes, he was feeling helpless. Very helpless. 'Are they hurting, John?' he asked, pointing at John's legs. John whimpered and nodded again. 'Good.' He kicked him in the left knee and was surprised how spongy it felt. There was hardly any bone intact. 'I'm sure it is very painful, but not as painful as it's going to be. Are you ready, John?' John looked at him, his eyes begging for mercy. There was no mercy. The man began stamping on his broken legs and white-hot lightning bolts of agony seared through his brain. Eventually, after what was an eternity, his heart gave up the ghost and John Glynn left the pain behind.

CHAPTER 28

Richard Vigne felt sick as he walked along the river near the Albert Docks. Although the fresh air made him feel better, the whisky taste was still in his mouth and on his skin, despite brushing his teeth and taking a long shower. His stomach grumbled, reminding him that he hadn't eaten anything solid for days. He decided to try a late breakfast with some coffee – if he could keep it down it would aid his recovery. He didn't cope with hangovers well, he never had. That was probably why he didn't drink very often: the fear of the next day. Some of his friends at university had been able to drink themselves into a coma then go to lectures the next morning after eating a tin of cold beans; Richard could never think straight until teatime the following day. Alcohol wasn't his thing: not then, not now. He turned away from the promenade and walked towards the brick archway, which led to the interior of the docks where all the bars and restaurants were.

It was a warm day, and when he emerged from the archway the sun was beaming down on the water. Yachts and old sailing ships were anchored around the wharfs and people were milling around enjoying the sunshine. It was hard to believe the last few days had happened, and that the world was going about its business, despite the nightmare he was going through. He had been happy and healthy all his life and then, wham, it was all gone in a flash. A bolt from the blue had shattered his world to pieces. Walking amongst others, in such a tranquil environment, felt surreal, almost like nothing had happened at all. It lifted the gloom for a moment and he welcomed the relief.

He walked along the docks, enjoying the sun on his skin. Ten minutes on he spotted a café, and looked at the menu in the window.

The description of the full breakfast made his mouth water. It had everything on it but the kitchen sink, and it came with toast. His stomach lurched slightly at the thought of eating fried food but it was a kill or cure moment. He could see there was one table free; he pushed open the door and the smell of bacon and strong coffee hit him. He sat down and picked up a menu. A young waitress walked over to take his order.

'What can I get you?' she asked. She had a city centre accent: harsh and guttural.

'I'll have the full English and a mug of coffee, please,' Richard said. She smiled, and reminded him of his daughter. The sick feeling descended again. Jaki's words echoed around his mind. The waitress looked over her shoulder as she walked away.

He took out his mobile and checked the messages: nothing. That was good. He was worried about the backlash from the threatening messages he had sent; there would be some comeback, somewhere. They had said they would hand them to the police and he had no reason to think they were lying. He regretted it. It was a stupid thing to do and he knew it was wrong, but whisky and anger don't mix. He thought about turning himself in to the police and apologising, at least he wouldn't have to worry about it any more – even if they did charge him. But what would they charge him with? Threats to kill were serious, but would they take them seriously? He wasn't a violent man; he had only said it because of the trauma and because he was drunk. It had made him act differently. Surely, they would see that. Then he thought how people had reacted when he was accused of being a paedophile. No one had given him the benefit of the doubt. He was guilty until proven innocent, so why would that be any different this time? It wouldn't be.

'Are you that teacher, Richard Vigne?' A woman's voice disturbed him. She was standing next to his table, wearing an apron, arms folded across her chest. She glared at him with disgust.

'Pardon?' he said, shaken by the question. The other diners were looking over.

'Shelly, the girl who served you, said you're that pervy teacher who has been in the *Echo*,' the woman said. Her accent was harsh too. 'Her friends all go to the school you teach at.' She put her hands on her hips. 'Are you sure it's him, Shelly?'

'Yes. That's him, Aunty Sue,' Shelly said, scowling. 'His picture has been all over Facebook. Dirty paedo.'

'You should be ashamed of yourself, pervert. Get out of my café,' Aunty Sue said.

'What's up, Sue?' a man asked from the corner. He was a big man, dressed in hi-vis clothing and a vest. His colleagues looked on from the same table.

'This fella here, is that paedophile teacher from the news,' she said. Richard thought it was time to make a sharp exit. He flushed with embarrassment and headed for the door. His guts were cramping again. It was the worst feeling in the world. 'Yes, go on, dirty paedo!' she called as he opened the door. 'Having sex with a child, you should be strung up by the bollocks.'

'What did he do?' the builder asked.

'He was having sex with a young girl, nonce.'

'How young?' another asked, scowling.

'Thirteen she was. He got her pregnant.'

The builders stood up as one and headed out of the door. The customers in the café watched through the window.

Richard had only taken a few steps, glad to be away from the accusing eyes. He had never been so embarrassed. It was a dreadful feeling to be ashamed of who he was, despite being innocent. The sense of hopelessness smothered him. He could feel his eyes filling up.

'Hey, paedo!' a voice growled.

Richard turned around into a fist. The punch landed square on his nose, breaking it. He was knocked backwards, blinded by the force of the blow. Another punch landed to the side of his head and he collapsed on the concrete.

'Someone call the police!' said a passer-by.

'What are you doing, you animals?' another voice shouted. 'Leave him alone, you bullies.'

'Piss off and mind your own business,' one of his attackers growled. 'He's a paedophile!'

'Kick him harder,' another voice piped up.

Kicks landed to his ribs, hips and thighs. He curled up as tightly as he could to protect himself. A well-aimed boot landed on his testicles and he doubled over, gasping for breath. White light flashed in his brain. The faces around him blurred into one. Women shouted and screamed for the violence to stop, but no one was listening. The kicks didn't stop and the onslaught gathered momentum. He slipped and his head became exposed. His skull was kicked like a football and he felt his jaw crack. The pain was debilitating. He couldn't move. He cried out for them to stop but the kicks carried on, accompanied by a torrent of abuse. Richard knew he was going to die right there unless he moved. He struggled up but was knocked back down, repeatedly. He crawled blindly on all fours as fast as he was able, deflecting blows when he could. Suddenly, the concrete beneath him disappeared and the beating stopped. It was a blessed relief. He felt himself falling and he opened his eyes. He realised, as he slipped into unconsciousness, he was heading into the deep, dark waters of the dock.

CHAPTER 29

Alec dialled the number in Thailand and listened to a series of clicks before the ringtone began. It was answered after the fourth ring.

'Peter Bevans.'

'Peter, it's Alec.'

'Hello, Alec, I was going to ring you,' he said.

'That's a likely story,' Alec joked.

'Seriously. After we spoke the other day I looked through the paperwork that was sent over from Ko Lanta, and I've been through it with my interpreter. It makes interesting reading.'

'What do you mean, "interesting"?'

'It's a typical *farang* versus Thai, crash report.'

'*Farang*, meaning what?' Alec asked.

'Sorry, local speak for foreigners.'

'I get it. Go on.'

'The entire thing is a whitewash.'

'No surprises there,' Alec said. 'Go on, tell me more.'

'Over here, if there is a road accident involving a *farang*, everything is whitewashed so the Thais are never at fault. Whoever is at fault foots the bill here, so they tend to stitch up the *farang* wherever possible. Anything involving dead bodies is very expensive here; removal, cremations, burials, all cost a fortune, especially for foreigners. I think this report has been doctored to claim the costs from the insurance companies.' Peter explained. 'The Ko Lanta police claim a child ran into the road after his dog, which had run into the path of an oncoming bus. Neither the child nor the dog were insured, so the next best culprit is the bus driver, but he isn't at fault because he was driving safely enough to stop without killing the child or the dog. The persons at fault were the motorcyclists, who were travelling too fast to stop and weren't wearing helmets. Apparently, it was carnage. They never found Boyd's head. So, because it was deemed they were at fault, the authorities can claim from the *farang* rental company that hired the bikes to them and didn't make them wear helmets. They claimed the bus was a write-off, and claimed the costs for disposing of three dead bodies and sending their belongings back to where they came from.'

'I thought they didn't have to wear helmets over there,' Alec said.

'You don't, unless you're in an accident, then you do. The point is, the accident was on the east coast of the island, as far south as the road goes, and it took the first responders forty-five minutes to get there. By the time they arrived, most of their identification – credit cards and such – had vanished, and so had the hotel keys from their pockets.'

'That's why there were no belongings,' Alec said. The tingle was back with force.

'There's very little listed on the reports – basically, what they had in their pockets, minus anything valuable.'

'And their identification was missing?'

'Yes.'

'Except for Boyd's driving licence.'

'Yes. How do you know that?'

'A friend of the family told me.' There was a suspicious tone to his voice.

'And you think that's suspicious, Alec?'

'Don't you?'

'Yes.'

'Why was Boyd's licence the only ID found?'

'You don't think this Frankie Boyd character died on Ko Lanta, do you?'

'No, I don't,' Alec said, 'not for one second.'

'What is this about, Alec?'

'I think Boyd may have taken the opportunity to vanish, and turn himself into someone else.'

'By leaving his driving licence on a dead body?'

'Easily done in a situation like that, in a foreign country.'

'Okay, it's feasible,' Peter said. 'Let's say your man stumbles across the accident. It was very remote.'

'He could have been visiting the area.'

'He may even have witnessed it,' Peter said. 'He goes to help the injured, realises they are dead, and sees the opportunity to change his identity.'

'He may even have been a passenger on one of those bikes,' Alec said. 'He could have been with them.'

'Maybe. There were no other witnesses.'

'If he was a passenger, we have to assume he would have known the men. He may have befriended them at some point,' Alec mused. 'He would have known where they were staying and where their money, passports and IDs were.'

'That's feasible. Either way, witness or participant, he could have seen it as an opportunity to stop anyone from looking for him.'

'Exactly. A decapitated body and a missing head. Is the head missing because he made it disappear?' Alec asked.

'He would have had plenty of time.'

'He could have placed his driving licence into the pocket of the dead man, taken his ID, and turned himself into someone else, all in one instant. Frankie Boyd is dead and he becomes the other guy.' Alec was convinced.

'So, who was the other guy?' Peter asked.

'That is the question I need to answer. If Frankie Boyd didn't die on that island, I need to work out who he became,' Alec said.

'The other two fatalities, Bill Evans and Carlton Harris,' Peter said, 'that's where I'll start.'

'They may have been travelling together,' Alec agreed.

'I'll check – they could have been travelling together, or they could have been travelling with someone else, assuming they knew each other before that day, of course.'

'Do you have the name of the company they hired the bikes from?' Alec asked.

'It will be on the accident reports.'

'You said they were a *farang* company.'

'Yes.'

'They may be able to tell you how they paid – together or separately,' Alec said. 'They may even have payment details.'

'I doubt that,' Peter said. 'Things are done differently here, Alec. Cash is king. It was a long time ago, and the seasonal workforce are transient. Most bike hire companies are run by bar or guesthouse owners as another source of income. Businesses don't keep records here, but I won't rule it out. It might be worth making a few phone calls.'

'I could do it, if you like?' Alec said. 'I'm asking a lot from you and, if you give me the company details, I can follow that lead while you look at the police records. It would save time.'

'Okay. I'll dig it out and call you back. I still think the missing persons route offers the best chance. If the guy had family, they may have made enquiries about him when contact stopped. It happens all the time here,' Peter said.

'Would there be a record of such an enquiry?' Alec asked. 'Can you check the Thai missing persons reports online?'

'There are some websites for missing tourists but the police are not really interested. People come here and never go home.'

'I could check the websites myself,' Alec said.

'Good luck with that one. Some people go to those islands to disappear. They don't want to be found. It would be like searching for a needle in a bucket full of needles. Let me search the reports for the Andaman coastal areas for that period, but don't hold your breath, Alec.'

'I won't. I appreciate your help.'

'No problem.'

'If you get any possible names, let me have them,' Alec said. 'I can pull a few strings and see if they ever flew to the UK. You never know your luck.'

'I'll see what I can find.'

'Boyd has a problem with staying out of trouble. He may already be back inside somewhere. If he has been in trouble, I can find him, but I'll need a name.'

'I'll do what I can for you, Alec.'

'Thanks, Peter.'

'Can I ask you a question?'

'Of course.'

'Why are you tracing this Boyd character?'

'He's a very bad man,' Alec said. 'A very bad man indeed.'

CHAPTER 30

Danny Goodwin tried to call John Glynn again: voicemail. He now knew something had happened to him, it had been too long without contact. The police had been to his home and there was no reply. That was a bad sign. Work said he had finished on time the night before and left for home as usual. Idiot. Danny had warned him not to walk home alone. John had laughed it off at first, but, eventually, he'd managed to make him see sense. The suicides and accidents were too much of a coincidence. There was a crazy nonce out there hunting the hunters. He had warned him but he hadn't listened. Silly bugger. He'd said he couldn't afford to get taxis home, as he was only earning minimum wage. It seemed like a solid investment from where Danny was sitting. Pay for a taxi, or end up dead – no brainer.

The police had called earlier about the article and given him a bollocking for going to the press; they asked him a load of stupid questions and told him they were bringing him in for questioning. They also told him he might be a target. No shit, Sherlock. He didn't need to be a detective to work that one out. They warned him to sit tight until a uniformed unit arrived at the back door. That might have frightened a lesser man, but not Danny Goodwin. He had a samurai sword, two machetes, a taser, and a baseball bat on standby. Any dirty paedo coming for him had better be ready for a good hiding. He thought about what Kevin Hill had written in the *Echo*. The article had rattled some cages, which was what he had wanted to do. If he had walked into a police station and told them his theory, they would have laughed him out of the door or sent him to the asylum. His theory was fact based. It was solid.

Kevin Hill had sensationalised the facts, but that was his job. It had done the trick and given the group some well-deserved publicity; any publicity was good publicity in his mind. Their YouTube videos, of paedos being arrested following their sting operations, had over two million hits, and had generated him a lot of money. He had made over forty grand from the advertising royalties in the last twelve months. None of the other members knew they were making any money, he'd kept that to himself. He had started it off, and he selected their targets and planned each mission in fine detail. It was his creation and he was proud of it. He deserved every penny. The *Echo* article had sent their Facebook page into meltdown. Messages of support were coming in their hundreds and YouTube was being hammered. It would generate thousands in royalties. He chuckled to himself, bitterly. Their exploits had attracted the attention of dozens of angry paedos. They all made threats, but this one was in a different league. He was the real deal. A real-life serial killer nutcase. He had taken out five of the original six members, but he hadn't got to Danny Goodwin. Danny was too sharp, too aware of what was going on. He analysed everything then analysed it again. The others dying had solved one problem: the YouTube money would never be questioned now. John had once asked how many hits you had to achieve before advertising revenue began to generate – that was before they had started generating a penny. Danny had laughed it off at the time, but his plan was always to keep building the revenue stream. Kevin Hill said he wouldn't be surprised if the nationals didn't pick it up; it was big news if it could be proved as being true: five of the six original members of online predator hunting group dead, in suspicious circumstances. The story would generate thousands of pounds of income. Every cloud has a silver lining, he thought.

A knock on the kitchen window made him jump. He looked up to see a man staring in at him through the glass. The man held up an ID card and gestured for Danny to open the door. Danny froze for a second and glanced at the baseball bat next to the back door. The man rapped hard on the window and gestured frantically to the door again. He tapped his watch, to say, 'hurry up', and his face darkened, impatiently. The plod weren't big fans of vigilante groups. This one had an attitude on him. Danny walked to the window and inspected the ID. He had seen enough fake IDs to spot them a mile away. It was genuine. He nodded his head and walked to the back door, opening it with one hand, turning off the light with the other. He blinked and felt a sharp flash of pain across his throat. Arterial spray splattered the kitchen walls. He put his hands to his neck to try to stop the bleeding, but the slash was too precise and too deep. Blood sprayed the ceiling, windows and door, as he staggered around aimlessly. Air hissed from his windpipe and he made a gurgling sound as the blood rushed into his lungs, choking him.

'Hello, Danny,' the man said. 'Nice to meet you again.' Danny looked at him, confusion and panic in his eyes. 'It's okay to be frightened, Danny. You're dying and there's nothing you can do to stop it.' Danny collapsed to his knees, still holding his throat with both hands. His eyes were wide with panic. 'Do you feel helpless yet?' the man asked. Danny fell backwards. The man stood over him and watched him bleeding, a warm smile on his face. 'It's not a nice feeling, is it, Danny?' he cooed. 'Helplessness. I need to be quick, because I want this to hurt a lot.'

CHAPTER 31

Braddick looked through the window and watched the doctors trying to keep Richard Vigne alive. They prepped him for theatre and took him away for emergency surgery. He had been kicked in the head so hard that his brain had swollen. They said they needed to drill a hole in his skull to relieve the pressure, or he would have no chance of survival. Four men had been arrested at the Albert Docks, on section-18 charges, much to their dismay. They couldn't see what they had done wrong. One of them found it amusing, until he was told they could be looking at a murder charge and he vomited on the custody suite floor. The chances of Richard Vigne surviving were slim. Jo Jones was there when he'd arrived but had gone to make a call. Richard's wife was on her way to the hospital with their children – twins apparently.

'Any news?' Jo Jones asked when she returned.

'No, not yet,' Braddick replied. 'They have taken him down to theatre.' Jo looked concerned. 'Thanks for meeting me here. I want your take on Richard Vigne.'

'No problem. I want to speak to the wife and children anyway. I phoned her earlier, to let her know the good news about him being innocent, and the next call she receives is from the hospital, saying her husband is in intensive care. She has a lot of questions.'

'I bet she has.'

'The guilt is kicking in – she didn't believe him and she booted him out.'

'Now he's in intensive care.' Braddick sighed. 'She'll never forgive herself if he doesn't make it.'

'Let's hope he does.'

'You know he's been making threats to kill, against the predator hunting group who gave you the information?'

'I heard. It was mentioned in the newspaper that he had made threats,' Jo said.

'I've heard them,' Braddick said.

'And?'

'He was pissed out of his mind, could hardly speak. Some members of the group have been spooked and are blowing it out of all proportion.'

'Are you seriously thinking they're being killed off, one by one?'

'Yes, it looks that way,' Braddick said. 'Too many coincidences to be anything else.'

'And we don't do coincidences.'

'We *don't* do coincidences.'

'He's not your man,' Jo said, nodding towards the empty space where Richard had been. 'Never in a million years. When do you think it started?'

'Roughly, eighteen months ago.'

'Way before Richard Vigne was mentioned to the Facebook group.'

'I know, but we have to check.'

'He's been through enough without being fingered as a serial killer too. In hindsight, we never should have pulled him. If the girl had been interviewed first, we never would have.'

'Why?' Braddick said. 'I thought it was a nailed-on case?'

'It looked that way with a first glance at the evidence.'

'Sounds like there's a "but" coming?'

'There are a lot of "buts".' Jo spotted Celia and the twins arriving. They were ushered into the relatives' room by a nurse. 'The wife and kids are here. I'll let the doctors speak to them before I go in there and apologise for fucking up their lives.'

'You can't blame yourself.'

'I don't,' Jo said. 'I blame the press.'

'Let's go and get a coffee,' Braddick said. He gestured to the vending machines nearby. They walked over and he put enough money into the slot for two white coffees with sugar. 'You still take sugar?'

'I never took sugar, but you always forgot. Don't worry about it,' she said, shaking her head. She sipped the hot liquid and grimaced. 'It's not great but it will do.'

'Tell me what happened.'

'At first, we had all the evidence we needed to bring him in,' Jo explained. 'The victim, Nicola, told her father she had been in a relationship with an adult since she had become pregnant at thirteen. We had emails, we had text messages, and we had photographs.'

'Anyone worth their salt would have brought him in with that.'

'On the face of it, I suppose.'

'So, what is the truth?'

'He went to a golf tournament in Wales, got pissed, and ended up letting a young girl sleep on the settee because she couldn't get home. He was sharing the apartment with another guy, Ralph Pickford,' Jo explained, her voice hushed. 'I think Pickford comes back to the apartment, finds the girl on the settee, and has sex with her. She thinks his name is Richard, because she's drunk, and he lets her believe that.'

'Because she's underage?' Braddick said.

'Not just underage, pregnant.'

'Nightmare.'

'Anyway, she doesn't tell her parents who the father is, has an abortion, and keeps seeing him. Pickford carries on seeing her, up until six months ago when he's killed in a car crash. The girl thinks he's dumped her, becomes ill, suffers a breakdown, and spills the beans to her dad about who the father of her baby was. He goes ballistic and passes the information to the predator hunters, they pass it on to us, with photographic evidence and years of emails, texts and so on.'

'It would look cut and dried.'

'It was, but we couldn't speak to Nicola. She was too ill to be interviewed.'

'You were damned if you did and damned if you didn't,' Braddick said.

'I interviewed Vigne myself because I didn't like it. He didn't seem the type to me. I believed him when he said he was innocent. I went to see Pickford's brother, he was the only relative. They had given some of his stuff to a charity shop and sold some on eBay.'

'Nice,' Braddick said.

'We traced his laptop and downloaded the hard drive. All the emails he had sent were there. When I finally got to speak to Nicola, she identified Pickford as her lover. Richard Vigne was innocent the whole time.'

'Poor man,' Braddick said. 'His face has been splashed across the newspapers. They won't run a story about him being innocent, will they?'

'Not a chance,' Jo said. 'That's not a story. He'll have to live with the whispers and comments for a long time to come.' She paused, and looked at Richard Vigne's empty bed. 'If he pulls through.'

CHAPTER 32

Alec dialled the number of the Easy Bar on Ko Lanta. It rang for a full three minutes before it was answered by a local lady who spoke no English. He tried very hard to ask for the owner and eventually she went looking for help. He waited patiently and after a few minutes longer heard footsteps approaching.

'Easy Bar,' a man with an Australian accent said impatiently.

'Hello. I am trying to speak to the owner, a Mr Gerrard.'

'You're speaking to him.' The abrupt reply came.

'My name is Alec Ramsay, I'm a detective from the UK,' Alec lied. There was no need to be retired at this point in the conversation.

'What can I do for you, detective?' he asked, amused. 'Half of my customers are on the run from something, usually their wives, the other half are too drunk to know their names.'

'I can imagine,' Alec laughed. 'I am trying to trace a British man who was on the island six or seven years ago. Where you the owner then?'

'I've been here for twenty years,' Gerrard said. 'I've drunk a lot of Chang since then though.'

'Maybe you can help,' Alec said. 'The man I'm looking for is called Frankie Boyd.'

'Never heard that name, sorry.'

'Do you remember renting some motorcycles to three men who were killed in an accident with a bus, in the south of the island, about that time?' The line was quiet. 'Hello?' Alec said. 'Are you still there?'

'I'm still here.' Gerrard's voice was flat, suspicious. 'What do you want, exactly, Mr Detective?'

'Two of the men, Bill Evans and Clinton Harris, hired scooters from your bar.'

'What about it?'

'According to the police, the third man killed that day was Frankie Boyd, the man I am trying to trace. Can you remember any of the men they socialised with? Maybe someone they were travelling with?'

'Like I said, I've drunk a lot of Chang since then. People come and go here. I've seen a million faces over the years and they all start to look the same, eventually.' He sounded bitter. 'I don't remember the men who hired those scooters; I remember renting out scooters that never came back, and I remember having to bribe the police to fuck off and leave me alone because they wanted the insurance company to pay out. Lots of tourists die on scooters here, detective. It's just part of the job. You're going a long way back.'

'Yes, I realise it is a long time ago, I appreciate it would be impossible to remember everyone.' Alec sighed. 'I thought it might be worth a try.'

'Sorry.' Gerrard paused. 'There's one thing I do remember.'

'Really?' Alec said.

'I remember they were sent here to hire my scooters because the bar where they drank had hired all theirs out.'

'Can you remember what the bar was called?' Alec felt a twinge of excitement.

'I can,' Gerrard said. 'It was called Pangea Bar.'

'Can you spell that for me, please?'

'It won't help you, detective. It burnt down three years ago.'

'Ah,' Alec said, disappointed, 'seems like a dead end. Thank you very much for your time.'

'No worries. Sorry I couldn't be more help.'

Alec heard the line go dead. He felt disappointed and frustrated, but that was the lot of a police detective. Good detectives didn't give up. Each dead end was just the elimination of one line of enquiry. It wasn't the end of the case. He put down the phone and walked to his laptop. It was open on the Ko Lanta ex-pats site. He searched for the Pangea Bar and looked at the photographs of the fire and the burnt-out shell that was left behind. The owner hadn't insured his stock and fixtures and fittings, and couldn't afford to rebuild it. Alec scrolled back through the months before the fire. Pictures of tourists holding cocktails and beers seemed to go on forever. When he reached the posts from six years ago, he decided a glass of scotch would make his search more bearable.

CHAPTER 33

Braddick nodded a hello to the uniformed officers manning the cordons. He climbed into a blue protective jumpsuit and pulled on overshoes. Sadie was waiting at the front door. She looked grey. The scene inside had shocked her. He ducked beneath the crime scene tape and walked towards her. They didn't speak as they stepped into the hallway and nodded to Graham Libby. He was finishing up his notes.

'There are no great mysteries here,' Libby said. 'There is arterial spray on both the outside and inside of the back door. My guess is, he opened the door and was immediately slashed across the throat while his hands were busy. There are no defensive wounds – he didn't try to defend himself because he didn't have time. The killer used a Stanley knife of some description, severing the jugular, trachea, and carotid arteries with one blow. He slashed right to left, so is probably right-handed. There are no obvious prints that I can see and the footprints are flat so he wore overshoes, or similar. The victim staggered backwards into the kitchen where he collapsed, and that is where the killer cut out his tongue, sliced off his genitals and stuffed them into his mouth. Your killer is a very sick puppy.' He shrugged. 'There's a lot of blood but there's none beyond the kitchen. The killer entered and exited through the back door.'

'Who found him?' Braddick asked.

'The uniformed unit sent to pick him up and bring him in,' Libby answered. 'They said the blood was still pumping when they arrived. The killer had been there minutes before they arrived.'

'Did they look for him?' Braddick asked.

'One of them stayed with the body, the other drove around the area, apparently.' The doctor gestured to the kitchen. 'They're out the back, waiting for you. One of them doesn't look very well, to be honest. I'll have my report with you this afternoon.'

'Thanks, doctor.' Braddick walked into the kitchen and looked around. 'He didn't last long,' he said, looking at the arterial spray. It arced up the walls and onto the ceiling; blood splatter was visible on all four walls, the ceiling and the windows. 'He must have opened the door himself. That means either he was unaware the attacker was there, or he felt safe opening the door.'

'He was expecting uniform to knock on the back door,' Sadie said.

'It's no coincidence that the killer used the back of the house.'

'Agreed,' Sadie said. 'How did the killer know he was expecting someone to knock on the back door?'

'Police scanner, maybe,' Braddick said.

'There's no other way of knowing.'

'He's becoming reckless,' Braddick said. 'All the other murders were planned and executed with patience and precision. This was panic. The first cut was enough to kill Goodwin, yet he risked being caught at the scene to indulge himself, knowing the police were on their way. Why would he take that risk?'

'Hate,' Sadie said. 'He wanted to hurt Goodwin, no matter what. That is rage: he hated him.'

'I agree. What set him off?'

'The newspaper article,' Sadie said. 'It has rattled him. He's been able to operate in the shadows, move around freely. Suddenly, his crimes are in the press and he must know we're onto him. He had to act before we brought Danny Goodwin in.'

'What's his next move?' Braddick asked.

'I don't know.'

'If it was me, I'd be getting on a plane.'

CHAPTER 34

Alec scrolled through pages and pages of posts from the Pangea Bar. He took off his reading glasses and rubbed his eyes. They were tired – they seemed to be tired more often these days. Old age was creeping up fast. He sipped his scotch, put his glasses back on, and returned to his relentless search. The Pangea was an open-air beachside venue, with a thatched roof supported by coconut tree trunks. The images posted were of white sands, idyllic sunrises and sunsets, beach parties and barbeques; happy people drinking cocktails from coconut husks. He gazed at a thousand smiling faces but didn't see any he recognised. Then a post appeared that had names tagged, he didn't understand what tagging meant. He clicked on one of the tags and it took him to posts with images of the same person. A lightbulb came on in his mind.

'Why didn't I think of that before?' he scolded himself. He went back to the Pangea Bar page and typed the name Carlton Harris into the search bar. Half a dozen posts appeared with photographs attached. The images showed groups of men posing with local girls. Alec shook his head, fat middle-aged men with pretty Thai women, it didn't sit right with him. The images were all group shots. He identified Harris in the crowd of faces, and spotted Bill Evans in two of them. The two photographs had been tagged to some of the people in the pictures. One name was on both photographs with Evans and Harris: Noel Cook. He typed Noel Cook into the search bar; nothing new. The same two photographs returned. Alec sighed and sat back. He exited the Pangea page and returned to the main Ko Lanta site. It had to be worth a shot. He typed Noel Cook into the search bar again.

The page reloaded with a raft of posts and he scrolled through them. There were photographs of Cook scuba diving, cycling, riding a moped, and drinking with local girls. Then it hit him.

Frankie Boyd was standing behind Noel Cook, talking to Bill Evans. He was standing side-on and probably didn't know he had been photographed. Boyd did know the men that had died, the photograph proved it. It was too much of a coincidence, otherwise. Alec continued to scroll down but couldn't find anything else of any use. He thought carefully about his next step; he could call Peter in Thailand and ask him to run the name through missing persons, but that would take time. Peter had said there were missing persons pages on Facebook. Alec typed: missing persons, Thailand, and hit search. The page opened and it did what it said on the tin. He searched for Noel Cook. Three posts came up asking for information about him, they had been posted six months apart by his daughter. No one had interacted with the messages. That was it. Boyd knew the men socially, and Noel Cook had gone missing when Frankie Boyd died. He didn't need any more evidence.

Alec picked up the telephone and dialled Braddick. It rang twice.

'Alec,' Braddick answered. 'What can I do for you?'

'I might have a lead for you,' Alec said. 'I think Frankie Boyd is still alive.'

'What?' Braddick asked, shocked. 'How can he be?'

'It's a long story, so I'll cut it short,' Alec said. 'He was involved in an accident in Thailand but I don't think he died.'

'Okay. I'm listening.'

'I think one of his friends died and Boyd switched driving licences to make it look like he had been killed. It gave him the opportunity to disappear and become a ghost.'

'Sounds feasible,' Braddick said. 'Do you have a name?'

'Noel Cook,' Alec said. 'I don't want to insult your intelligence, but Frankie Boyd has a habit of getting into trouble. Changing his name won't change that.'

'I'll run a PNC check on him and see what comes up,' Braddick said. 'Are you okay to wait a minute or do you want me to ring you back?'

'Yes, I'm fine to wait,' Alec said. The tingle was there again. He could hear Braddick typing then there was nothing. He must be reading something, Alec thought.

'Alec,' Braddick said. 'You won't believe this.'

'What is it?'

'Noel Cook was arrested during a sting conducted by an online predator hunter group on Facebook,' Braddick said. His mind was whizzing at a million miles an hour. 'They groomed him and then set a trap. He served four years of an eight-year sentence. Guess what for?'

'Have you got all night?' Alec said. 'Nothing would surprise me about that man.'

'Possession and distribution of indecent images of children.' Braddick was excited, Alec could hear it in his voice. 'The group set him up, pretending to be a paedophile ring looking for child porn, and passed all the information on to us. He was arrested in a dawn raid and sent on remand immediately. This is motive, Alec.'

'Have you got an image of Cook?'

'Yes,' Braddick said. 'It's him alright.' The sound of typing again. 'He's still in the system. I've got an address.'

'Where?'

'Chester. I know the area. It's bedsit-land for students.'

'What are you going to do?'

'I'll put someone on the address while I sort out a warrant,' Braddick said excitedly. 'I'll call you back when I can.'

'Good,' Alec said. 'Be careful, Braddick.'

'Always,' Braddick said. 'Thanks, Alec.'

CHAPTER 35

Frankie Boyd was sitting in his white Iveco, waiting for Jane Hill to finish her shopping. She shopped at Aldi most days on her way home from the gym; Kevin Hill earned enough to allow her to be a full-time housewife. She dropped her three children at school at eight thirty, Monday to Friday, went for coffee at Starbucks with two other mothers from the school, Sarah and Leanne, then she would go to the gym before shopping for tea on the way home. It was amazing how easy it was to map out someone's routine, just by following their social media accounts. Names, dates, times and habits were available for all to see. Most of the time it was safe to post about who you had coffee with in the morning, but not when Frankie Boyd was hunting you. Then it was dangerous. Not that she would know he was hunting her until it was too late. He planned to take Jane Hill and her children first. That would make it easier to control Kevin Hill. It was time for Kevin to feel helpless; it was time for all the Hills to feel helpless. Jane and her children were guilty by association. They would learn how it felt to watch a family fall apart around them. It would be a lesson they wouldn't enjoy, but one they needed. They had to experience helplessness before they died.

He thought back to when he became Noel Cook. He had grabbed the opportunity with both hands and tried to rebuild his life. It was a magical time, like another life. He had been given a chance to be free from the scrutiny of the law. Getting caught was his downfall. It was his obsession with photographs that dropped him in the shit every time, but he hadn't learned his lesson. Photographs were his living, but they were the evidence that exposed him, yet he couldn't leave them behind. The residual income was all he had to live on. He had made a lot of money from his photographs when he was Frankie Boyd; his time working in the city was his favourite. He had invested weeks and months following the major players, building portfolios of them and their families, friends and associates. Blackmail was a lucrative business. That had led on to rivals buying the evidence that he had on their enemies, and so he slipped into a world of crime lords and criminals. His knowledge of forensics was the tip of the wedge that allowed him into the even darker underworld of murder for money. Selling information about the disposal process, to men desperate to make people disappear, was easy. He helped some of them, made money, and his reputation grew. It wasn't long before they skipped a step and paid him to take care of everything. Killing was simple for him. He enjoyed the suffering of others. Disposing of bodies was academic, he knew how to do it. When the heat of the law came a little too close for comfort, he could apply pressure from the top down and his tracks were covered by a blanket of silence. Everyone knew he had evidence on everyone, and no one wanted to risk it. His reputation as an accomplished assassin was cemented in folklore. He was untouchable then, but it couldn't last. Nothing does. It was his legitimate job in forensics that exposed his alter ego. He should have given it up and moved into the shadows, but he left it too late. Being around the dead made him happy.

His time with forensics was enjoyable. He loved the smell of death. Some of the crime scenes he had photographed were fascinating. It was amazing what one human could do to another, and he employed some of the killing techniques he had witnessed himself. That was fun. Experimenting was educational. He was amazed by the human body's resilience: if it is fed and watered, it will repair and regrow; its healing capability is nothing short of miraculous. The human spirit, however, is much weaker, and he discovered that breaking the spirit was easier than breaking the body. Things at that time were perfect. It was disappointing when his websites were discovered and traced back to him. Fucking photographs again. He couldn't leave them alone.

When he was fired, he knew the spotlight would be put on him. That twat, Alec Ramsay, was already sniffing around. He knew he was having him followed. It was time to go away, so he borrowed some money from his darling mother and went to Thailand. Being an only child had its advantages. He had money but it was always better to spend hers. His mother doted on him and gave him whatever he asked for. Silly bitch. South East Asia had opened a whole new world of filth for him. The poverty meant that people would do pretty much anything for a handful of dollars and there was a lucrative market for depraved images, and he had thousands and thousands of them. His library was growing all the time. Of course, all good things come to an end; he wasn't sharp enough to move to the dark web before they were onto him and the money trail got him. Leaving Phuket had been a trauma. He paid a local sergeant to turn a blind eye while he headed to the port and boarded a boat to Phi Phi Lai. The island was an hour from Phuket. He stayed there for a month and then became bored of the busy, narrow lanes crammed full of tourists. Another boat took him to Ko Lanta, which was quieter. He became a tourist, drinking heavily and sleeping late, waiting for something different to happen. It was Groundhog Day in the sun.

There were times when he'd thought being arrested would be preferable to the monotonous fun. He craved depravity, and missed the stench of decomposition and the games of cat and mouse with the police. It was a small island and everyone knew everyone else. The social circles were incestuous. After one particularly heavy drinking session, he decided to strangle the girl he had paid to take home. He needed to kill someone and she was there. His usual checks and balances were skewed by alcohol. She fought like a tiger but eventually passed out. He had thought she was dead and went to sleep. When he woke up the next morning, he had a panic attack. He couldn't believe what he had done. There was no dead body in the bed next to him, but there could have been. There should have been. It was luck that she'd survived.

The girl had made a holy fuss about it and threatened to go to the police, but the bar owner, an Australian guy, paid her to shut up. Frankie made a joke of it, saying it was a sex game, but he could tell by the change in attitudes towards him that no one believed him. The local girls wouldn't go anywhere near him and the ex-pats were cool in his presence. He was close to leaving when some casual acquaintances invited him to the south of the island for a few days. It was the perfect chance to escape the accusing eyes for a while. Things would calm down eventually and it would be forgotten. That was the trip that changed his life and gave him an opportunity. They had stopped at too many bars along the way, drinking in the sunshine. To say they were over the limit would be a massive understatement. His friends were racing each other when the accident happened. The crash was catastrophic, but he had been fifty yards behind the others. He had hired his scooter from another bar and it was old and slow. By the time he'd caught up with them, they were either dead or dying. The bus driver ran off down the hill to get help, and the kid ran off with his dog. There he was, standing over the headless body of Noel Cook, in the middle of nowhere; it was an opportunity he couldn't miss. He rolled the head like a bowling bowl, down a steep gulley into a stream, planted his driving licence on Cook, and stripped the bodies of valuables and hotel keys. His life as Frankie Boyd had ended. A few hours later, he had a large sum of cash and a dozen credit cards, and was on a boat heading back to Phi Phi. He had stayed there for a while, keeping his head down and planning his journey home.

He had made his way to Cambodia by sea. Flying home from there was safer: he could avoid Bangkok immigration checking his passport photograph. Going home seemed to be the natural thing to do. He wanted to go home as a different person and start again. He had enough money to live for twelve months or so, without struggling, plus his photographs would bring him residual income.

It was the perfect opportunity to live a normal life without looking over his shoulder all the time. He stayed away from his old haunts and grew facial hair. Nobody would remember the odd crime scene photographer he used to be.

Everything was good for a while, but he soon realised being Noel Cook was boring as fuck and became restless. He was considering going back to crime, and then he met Cathy. Cathy was a section manager at the local supermarket and sometimes worked shifts. She was pretty, intelligent and hardworking, and he'd fallen in love with her in a heartbeat. They were the perfect couple when they were alone. It was a whirlwind romance and they fell for each other hook, line and sinker. The problem was her baggage: she had kids, and an ex who didn't want to be her ex. Her ex-husband had hated him with a passion. Their two kids were still young, six and eight, and he was still deeply in love with Cathy and tried everything to put her off being with Noel Cook. Her kids weren't keen either and they sided with their dad. The kids were a massive stumbling block, but she stood up to her ex and, after seven months dating, he moved into her home. His life became as normal as normal could be. He won the kids over and they began to warm to him being there. The urges faded and he supressed the darkness within him. Everything was perfect, until the predator hunters targeted his website. The dirty bastards. They groomed him, and bought bits and pieces, before upping their orders and asking for darker material each time. He didn't see the deception and he walked right into their trap. They passed all their information to the police, and their cybercrimes unit followed the money trail to his IP address. He could still see Cathy's face when they smashed in her front door and stormed up the stairs to arrest him. The guns had frightened the life out of her and the kids. She was devastated. When she was told that Noel Cook was to be charged with the manufacture and distribution of indecent images of children, she was sick in her hands. He could hear her sobbing as they dragged him into a van. Dirty bastards.

Frankie had tried to contact her from remand but got nowhere. A week later she slapped a court injunction on him, put her house up for sale, and moved back in with her ex-husband. Losing Cathy broke him. He blamed himself, he blamed karma, he blamed the police and the press, but, most of all, he blamed the predator hunters. They would pay dearly and he wouldn't rest until they were six feet underground; he would kill them all, even if it took him a lifetime.

Movement brought him back to the present.

Jane Hill came out of the supermarket holding a single carrier bag. He checked his watch; she was right on time. His plan was simple: Jane would arrive home at four o'clock, with her children, and she would drive the people carrier into the garage; the doors would close automatically. He would be waiting in the kitchen for them. They would be like rats in a trap. Kevin Hill would arrive home at six thirty, by which time his family would be bound and gagged and well on their way to being broken. He would taser Hill when he stepped through the door, and take them to his cellar. He could take his time there without being disturbed. Everything was going to plan. It was time to teach Kevin Hill what it is like to lose the woman you love and the kids you treasure. He would protect them with his life; watching them in distress would break his heart. Hill would suffer as he had, but worse. Much worse. What he had in mind for Hill would be his finest moment. He was looking forward to it so much, he could feel himself growing hard. His heart beat faster, he needed to calm himself. One wrong move and it would all come crashing down. Calm down, Frankie. It's time to go to work.

CHAPTER 36

Chichester Street was noisy. There were students on both sides of the road, singing and generally being drunk. They were staggering home from the George and Dragon. It was kicking out time, the perfect cover for a forced entry. Uniformed officers sealed off the top and bottom of the street and signalled when it was safe to proceed. Braddick watched the forced entry unit approach number 5. It was a run-down Victorian terrace, four storeys high, with sandstone steps leading up to the front door. It was the only house in the street with no lights on. The paintwork was blistered and peeling, and one of the windows had been broken and was patched up with a bin bag. The other houses had been kept in good condition to attract students to rent them, number 5 was dilapidated in comparison. They had tried to contact the owner of the building, but to no avail. Looking at it, the building was hardly his pride and joy.

The order was given and the front door disintegrated beneath the weight of the big key. The entry team poured inside and Braddick listened to the shouts of 'clear' from inside as they searched each floor. Torchlight flashed behind dirty curtains. There was a moment of silence then an armed response officer gestured him in.

'No one home?' Braddick asked.

'Someone is home, but we won't get a lot out of him. You had better come and see for yourself,' the officer said, his face drained of colour.

Braddick walked up the steps and into the hallway. Low wattage bulbs cast long shadows on the stairs; a threadbare runner covered terracotta tiles that were cracked and broken. He could smell death. The living room door was open and he looked inside. An analogue television stood in one corner and an old hi-fi stack was in the other – every student's dream, in the eighties. The suite was faded and worn and black mould covered the armchairs. Thick drapes stopped any light from seeping into the room. The smell of damp and must was oppressive. Fungus was growing on the exterior wall, beneath a poster of a whale diving. He walked back into the hallway and looked up the stairs. A corpse has hanging from the second-floor bannister rail: the neck was broken, the teeth bared. Braddick reckoned the man had been dead for weeks.

'Is that your man?'

'No,' Braddick said, shaking his head. The corpse looked to be Asian. 'Although, I have a feeling our man might have had something to do with him being here.'

'None of the rooms have been occupied in a long time,' one of the entry team said. 'Cook's room is at the top of the stairs.'

'Check him for ID,' Braddick said, climbing the stairs two at a time. Sadie followed him. A uniformed officer put on rubber gloves and checked the pockets of the corpse.

Braddick stepped into the room that had been rented by Noel Cook. A single mattress was bare and stained with damp. The floorboards were dark and dusty. A small rug next to the bed was the only sign of furnishings. The drapes were thick and heavy and ripped at the bottom. He looked behind the door.

'Sadie,' he said, 'look at this.'

'Fucking hell,' she said.

The wall behind the door was covered from floor to ceiling with photographs: Danny Goodwin, John Glynn, Thomas Green, and David Rutland. The others were strangers to him. There were dozens of faces. It sent a shiver down his spine. *Had he already killed them, or were they targets?* The hunters being hunted, unaware of how close a killer was to them.

'We need to get these to the office and cross-check them against the dead members of the group.' Braddick studied some of the faces. Boyd had taken the photographs up-close. He was skilled, that was obvious. To take shots like that, without the subject being aware, was a talent. He looked around again. The room had been vacated in a hurry, probably around the same time the body in the stairwell stopped breathing.

'The victim is Ahmed Ashkani,' a uniformed officer said from the doorway.

'That figures,' Braddick said. 'He's the landlord. No wonder we couldn't reach him.'

'Another faked suicide?' Sadie asked.

'It certainly looks that way,' Braddick agreed. 'Get Graham Libby down here, he'll know if it is or not. Not that it matters. We still have no idea where Frankie Boyd is. We need to find out who all these faces are and warn them that Boyd is on a mission.'

***

Alec pulled up on the main road and looked at the farm track opposite. It was dusty, and pitted with rocks and boulders; a strip of grass ran up the middle. There were no street lights, but he could see a light burning in the farmhouse at the top of the lane. He gauged it was a half mile or so away. The tingle was driving him mad. He had to take a look at the place. Something was bothering him and he couldn't put his finger on it; instinct had told him to come here. Braddick had found the arrest report for Noel Cook and it was a baby step to trace an address, but it didn't feel right. Frankie Boyd was not likely to be sitting at home with his feet up, watching Netflix, or whatever psychopaths watch these days. He would be executing plan B. The *Liverpool Echo* had exposed his crimes and he had reacted badly. Killing Danny Goodwin the way he did, confirmed what Alec had always suspected about him. He had madness behind his eyes, the kind of madness that left him devoid of empathy or sympathy. Boyd would be well aware it was only a matter of time before the net closed in, and that this time would be the last. He would go away for life. They would throw away the key. That made Boyd's options limited: he was cornered, and cornered animals are dangerous and unpredictable. Boyd was evil, total evil. What would a totally evil man do, if he knew he didn't have long before he would be killed or locked up for the rest of his days? That was a question with many answers, none of them good. He could choose to escape, but that was almost impossible. Both his identities were now flagged to every law enforcement agency in the land, and would be worldwide by the morning. He was going nowhere. Would he try to cause as much damage as possible before they dragged him away, or would he hide until they came to arrest him and go quietly? He didn't think Boyd would go quietly, it wasn't his style.

Alec shivered. It wasn't cold yet but he felt a chill touching his bones. Were his instincts warning him to go home and be a retired detective, safe and warm in his bed? Evil was radiating from that farmhouse. He checked his watch and his phone; the phone had a signal and it was fully charged. He zipped up his coat and trudged up the lane. The single light was still burning in the farmhouse window, drawing him to it like a moth to a flame.

CHAPTER 37

Nicola Hadley's heart was going to break. The doctor had told her that the man she had known as Richard Vigne, was actually Ralph Pickford. It was difficult for her to comprehend. Her dad hadn't been there, thank heavens. As a long-distance lorry driver, he could be away for days at a time. He would have flipped out and become angry and aggressive, and that would have increased her angst. His first reaction was always aggression. He said it was because he was protecting his daughter, and there was nothing wrong with that, but it made her anxious. Right now, her anxiety was off the scale. The news of Pickford's death had hit her hard. She was crushed. Her brain felt numb and the drugs weren't helping at all. She was on the verge of having a panic attack, a coiled spring inside her was ready to release.

Her father had questioned their decision to tell Nicola the truth, but the doctor thought it was better for them to tell her, rather than risk her finding out from the newspapers or on television. She had wanted to tell her in a controlled environment, where Nicola's reaction could be monitored and professionals were on hand. As she explained the situation, she re-enforced the fact that Pickford had not dumped Nicola; she deemed that as being very important. Emotionally, that information should make her feel better about herself: it wasn't her fault. It meant he hadn't rejected her, or stopped loving her – he had died. She seemed to think Nicola should see this as a positive, that she hadn't been dumped, and he had still loved her when he drove under the back of a stationary lorry and cut himself in half. Like that mattered. Nothing mattered. It had all been a big lie anyway. She hadn't even known his real name.

Lying in bed, dwelling things over, things were falling into place. The clock on the wall ticked slowly. Every minute seemed to be an hour. She looked again and the hands hadn't moved. The sleeping pills weren't working. She had asked the doctor for an injection of stronger drugs – they always worked – but the doctor told her she was too weak for them; her heart wasn't strong enough. She said the pills would work, but they were slower to act. They had spoken about her future treatment plan, and the doctor arranged for a support worker to stay with her while her psychiatrist offered her grief counselling. She had taken everything in her stride. What other choice did she have? Ralph Pickford was dead, and that was that. The name didn't mean anything to her, even if it was his real name, Richard had been her lover. She couldn't swap the name in her head. It would not sink in. Richard had never existed and Ralph was dead, they were the facts. She was ill and suffering mental trauma about a lost love who never existed. It twisted her fragile mind into knots. With hindsight, she wished she hadn't let her father talk her into having the abortion. She thought about her baby, and what might have been, every day. Thinking about it made her terribly sad. She had killed their child – Richard's child, not Ralph's. They had talked endlessly, mostly on the Internet, about having more children, and had hoped to get married when she was old enough. She thought she could replace the pain of aborting their baby, with the birth of another child. That was the hope she had clung to; she'd thought the pain would go away. It hadn't gone away and, now he was dead, it never would. Hope had gone too. Without hope, what did she have? The thought of becoming Mrs Vigne, Mrs Richard Vigne, was her only ambition. There was nothing else. She had wanted to be Mrs Vigne, with a gaggle of little Vignes running around her feet. That had been her dream, but her dreams had been lies. Richard had never existed. Every word out of that man's mouth had been a lie. She thought about the times they had shared with each other. It had all seemed so right. Not now. Now it all seemed so wrong. Her hopes and dreams were gone. Her baby was dead, and so was Richard. She knew what she had to do. Before the night was done she would join them, and be with them forever.

CHAPTER 38

Alec stopped when he reached the edge of the farmyard. The darkness was impenetrable. He looked around. Dark shadows shifted and merged; his eyes couldn't make out any solid shapes. He had the feeling that someone was watching him from the darkness; his nerves were on edge. The sky was black and overcast, there were no stars to be seen. An owl hooted from the woods behind the farmhouse. There were no signs of any vehicles, animals, or people, yet the solitary light still burned in a bedroom window. He didn't know why he had come here. It had been a hunch. Another hunch. Over the years he had learned to trust his instincts. It was a feeling he couldn't ignore, he had to investigate. He knew the farm had belonged to Boyd's mother. She was a widow and he was her only son. The news he had died would have left her distraught. Alec figured if Boyd had contacted her, and told her it had been a mistake and he needed sheltering for a while, his mother wouldn't have turned him away. No mother would. She wouldn't know anything about what he had done or what he was capable of. Frankie Boyd was her only son and she missed him desperately when he went travelling, and then she was told he was dead. Alec had a hunch that, when the shit had hit the fan, Boyd had scurried home to mummy, and she would have been so overwhelmed by his return to the living, she wouldn't deny him anything. She would be old and vulnerable by now. Boyd could hide out of sight on a farm for years and no one would know any different. Boyd was a chameleon, changing to adapt to his surroundings, blending in while he waited to strike. He would take advantage of his mother as easily as the next person. Alec pitched him as a psychopath with no empathy for other humans, including his kin. It made sense that he would return home for shelter.

Alec checked his phone again. The signal was weaker, but it was there. He walked quietly across the farmyard and approached a downstairs window. The yard was muddy and it stank. Years of rearing cows and geese had deposited a thick layer of animal shit that never hardened, no matter how little rain there had been; it squelched beneath his feet. He looked inside and saw a metal range cooker set into an arched brick recess. An antique shotgun hung above the mantelpiece; logs were piled in a basket next to it. There was a glow from the embers beneath the range. Someone was home. He tiptoed to the next window and peered inside: a living room, complete with a fireplace, Welsh dresser, and floral-patterned furniture. Painted plates adorned the walls and Staffordshire pottery lined the mantelpiece. A wooden magazine rack was next to the armchair. He imagined the old lady sitting there, reading in front of the fire. It was like stepping back in time. All seemed normal, yet it didn't feel right. There was tension in the atmosphere, like the minutes before a thunderstorm. He looked over his shoulder, something was skirting the farmyard. A rat, maybe. Or a fox. The woods would be full of nocturnal critters. He listened as the four-legged creature ran through the undergrowth. His mind was telling him to leave. *Leave this place, Alec, and explain your hunch to the youngsters in the morning.*

He couldn't leave. Not until he was sure. Alec investigated every window on the ground floor. Everywhere was in darkness and appeared to be as expected. It was an old farmhouse, owned by an old lady, furnished with antiquated furniture. There was no sign of Boyd or his mother. There were no sounds, no television or radio, no lights flickering on the ceilings. All was still. He checked his watch, it was getting late. His nerves were on edge as he made his way to the back door. A hoot from the trees disturbed sleeping birds and they flapped, noisily, skywards. His heart was racing, pounding in his chest. He wanted to walk back to the car and leave, but something was telling him to go inside.

All his instincts agreed there was something amiss, yet he couldn't enter the property. His common sense was telling him that he was no longer a detective, and he had no grounds to enter the building. He could call Braddick and tell him about his hunch, but if Braddick knew where he was he would flip. His presence at the farm could jeopardise the case against Boyd. A good barrister could have any evidence found at the farm made inadmissible if it was known that Alec had been there, sniffing around illegally. It was time to go and leave the police work to Braddick and the MIT. He was about to leave when a muffled cry from inside changed his mind. He took out his mobile and found Braddick's number. It was time to call the cavalry. He had pressed dial and heard it ring twice, when a heavy blow to the back of his neck stunned him. He dropped the phone and it was smashed to pieces in the mud by a weighty boot. Another hammer blow landed on the back of his skull and he collapsed, face down in the sludge.

CHAPTER 39

Frankie Boyd whistled an inane tune as he dragged Alec down the basement steps. Alec was aware he was being moved but was still unconscious. Frankie sat him on the floor and fastened his hands and feet with zip ties to a thick metal pipe. There was blood coming from an indented wound at the back of his skull. Jane Hill saw the blood on his hands and started crying again. She had been hysterical earlier and her muffled sobbing had distressed her children. Frankie had to threaten to set fire to one of her children to shut her up. Kevin Hill had been surprisingly quiet, considering his family were tied up and gagged in a cellar. They were sitting in a line, their backs against the wall. The only light in the cellar came from the kitchen above; it was impossible to see into the corners of the room. The Hill family were oblivious to the gentle sobbing coming from across the cellar, their own peril was far more important to them. The arrival of Alec hadn't changed the dynamic, they were still terrified beyond description. Mrs Hill's distress was becoming uncontrollable again. Frankie switched on the light.

'Shut up, Jane, or I'll kill the fat kid,' Frankie said, matter of fact. He looked at her and smiled. 'Don't look at me like that, he is fat.' He shrugged. 'Do you feed him more than the others, or does he steal from the fridge?' Jane Hill closed her eyes and tried to pretend she was anywhere else. She stopped crying to protect her child. 'There, that's better.'

The Hills blinked against the glare. As their eyes adjusted, the figure across the room came into focus.

'This is my mum,' Frankie said, smiling. An old lady looked back at them. She had been crying for a long time, her eyes swollen and red. 'Say hello, Mum,' Frankie said. His mother was sitting in an old armchair, tied to it with sisal rope. She blinked and scowled at him. Seeing the family sitting on the floor, opposite her, had confused her. She focused on the children. 'Don't be rude, Mum. Say hello.'

'Shut up, Frankie,' she snapped. 'You let those children go this minute. What do you think you are doing, for heaven's sake?'

'Are you going to say hello?'

'No, you idiot. You've gone too far this time.'

'My apologies for her rudeness,' Frankie said to the Hill family.

Alec groaned and began to focus. He looked around and analysed the situation. It wasn't good. Frankie Boyd looked as if he had lost his mind completely. The air of menace that surrounded him was like an aura of evil. Alec tested his bonds but he was fastened tightly. There was no way to escape them. A sculpture across the room caught his eye, making his heart beat faster. It was an angel made from wire mesh, standing six feet tall, at least. The wings were intricately crafted from thin wire, weaved and threaded with skill. There were others behind it. A full-size horse was next to the wall. Each sculpture could have been shown in any reputable art gallery.

'Look who is awake.' Boyd kicked Alec's feet. 'I'm glad you're awake,' Frankie said. He followed his gaze to the statues. 'Are you impressed?'

'Very,' Alec said, nodding. 'You obviously have a talent with wirework.'

'It was a hobby but it didn't pay as much as photography.'

'You are obviously skilled at it,' Alec said.

'I think you knew that anyway, detective.'

'No. I didn't know anything.' Alec looked at the statues. 'Not until now.'

'But you don't seem surprised to see me, Detective Ramsay?' He frowned. Alec didn't answer. 'You're *not* surprised to see me, are you?' Alec shook his head. 'That was your biggest problem. You always were a smart-arse.'

'And you were always trouble,' his mother said, interrupting him. 'From the day you were born, you were trouble. No wonder your father left us. He couldn't stand you.' She shook her head and talked to the Hill family. 'His father said he was wrong in the head before he could speak, and he was right.'

'Shut up, Mother,' Frankie said. 'If you can't say anything nice, don't say anything at all.'

'Nice?' she said. 'You don't know the meaning of nice. You wouldn't know nice if it came up and bit you on the arse.'

'Shut up, Mother.' Frankie flushed red. 'You're getting on my nerves.'

'Someone needs to get on your nerves,' his mother said. 'What on earth do you think you're doing?'

'I'm teaching Mr Hill a lesson in humility,' Frankie said. Kevin Hill looked up and listened; Alec watched in silence. The atmosphere was tense and explosive. Boyd was on the edge, he could sense it. 'He wrote some terrible things about me, didn't you, Kevin?' Kevin shook his head. 'I lost everything. It's time to set the record straight.'

'Who is he?' his mother asked, confused.

'He's the newspaper reporter who slated me all the way through my trial,' Boyd said, childlike. 'He lied about me.'

'He told the truth,' his mother disagreed.

'He lied!'

'Enough of this nonsense, Frankie,' she said. Her face darkened in anger. 'Let those children go, immediately,' she shouted.

'Be quiet, or I'll slit your throat right now.' Frankie looked at her and she glared back. Alec didn't think he was bluffing. His eyes were void of emotion. The woman in the chair may have been his blood mother, but it meant nothing to Boyd. Alec could see that. She was purely the means to an end. Her loyalty to him had been repaid by him strapping her to an armchair in the cellar. He didn't care who she was.

'You don't frighten me, Frankie Boyd,' she said. 'You're a bad egg, always were, but you don't frighten me.'

'I won't tell you again, shut up.' There was menace in his voice now. Alec knew the old lady was pushing her luck.

'I will not. This is my house.' She shook her head. 'All those years I thought you were dead, I never for one minute thought I would wish you were. Well, I do. I wish you were dead.'

Frankie walked over to the armchair and stood next to her. She looked up at him with angry eyes. He tilted her head back and drew the Stanley knife across his mother's throat. Jane Hill began to struggle violently against her ties, flapping around on the floor like a fish out of water. Her children were screaming, their muffled voices distressing to hear. Blood gushed from the wound and Boyd held her head still until the light had left her eyes. When she had stopped twitching, he let her chin fall to her chest. The sound of her blood dripping on the cellar floor filled the air. Frankie looked disturbed. He frowned, and looked around the cellar as if it was the first time he had seen it. The knife in his hand dripped with his mother's blood. Alec shuffled up against the pipe and tried to move his wrists. He tried to stretch the zip ties, but they were strong. Boyd looked his way and he stayed still. He didn't want to attract his attention at the moment. One wrong move could set him off.

'There was no need for that, was there?' Frankie said, shrugging. 'I told her to shut up.' He wiped the blood from his hands onto his trousers. 'She never did know when to be quiet.' He shook his head. 'You heard her, she blamed me for my dad leaving. That's bullshit. He left because she didn't let him get a word in edgeways.'

Jane Hill was trying to hold it together but her panic was coming in waves. She was choking back sobs, her breath short and sharp. Kevin Hill kept eye contact with her, trying to reassure her. Exactly what he could reassure her about was beyond Alec. Their position was dire. As bad as it gets. The chances of any of them getting out of the cellar alive were zero. Boyd had moved from being a stalker, picking off his prey at will, to snatching a family and killing his own mother. His demeanour was that of a man who was disintegrating from the inside out. The consequences of his actions were no longer of any concern to him, and that was the problem. Alec had encountered men who no longer cared what happened to them, and the ending was never good. Jane was jabbering again.

'I can see you're not happy, Jane,' Boyd said. He sounded concerned. 'But if you don't stop all that fucking noise, I swear, your kids won't last five minutes. You're making me edgy and I'm not at my best when I'm edgy. Do you want me to slit their throats right now?' Jane Hill shook her head, her eyes were bulging. She stopped struggling and tried to calm down. 'Good, that's better.' He walked over to Kevin Hill and removed his gag. 'Now then, Kevin. Here we are, face to face after all this time,' he said, smiling coldly. Kevin Hill licked his lips, his mouth was dry with fear. He tried not to make eye contact with Boyd. Alec thought that was a good thing. Boyd was slipping further into madness, his grip on reality was loosening. 'This is all your fault, Kevin. I hope you realise that, Jane,' Boyd said, looking at her. 'This is not my fault. You have been very nasty to me, over the years. I had a family once, you know?' He chuckled, dryly. 'Of course you know I had a family, don't you?' Boyd asked. 'I was Noel Cook then. You called me a sick monster. When they arrested me, you said I was a paedophile. Can you imagine what that did to Cathy and her children?' Kevin Hill shook his head. 'No, you can't. Not that you give a shit about what happens to the people you write about. I lost my woman and her children. They were my family. I loved them.' Boyd stood up and strutted back and forth across the cellar. He was becoming agitated. Alec could feel the mood darkening. 'They weren't mine, granted, but I loved them all the same.' He pointed a finger at Hill. 'You insinuated that I may have interfered with her children. I never touched those kids. The thought never even crossed my mind. You called me sick, you're sick.' Boyd began to shake and had to take a breath to calm himself. 'You made that up. That came from your mind, not mine. You took my family from me.'

'I didn't,' Kevin tried to object.

'Shut your mouth,' Boyd snapped. 'You insinuated I had sexually abused my step kids, and that was one of the reasons Cathy wouldn't speak to me.' He paused. Kevin didn't speak – he daren't. 'She fucked off back to her husband, and I never heard from them again because of what you said. You took them from me. She wouldn't even speak to me.' He sighed and shook his head. 'Do you have any idea how that made me feel?' Boyd asked. Kevin shook his head. Alec watched Jane and the children. They were terrified, transfixed on the conversation between Boyd and their father, fear in their eyes. 'It made me very sad. It made me feel helpless, Kevin, because there was nothing I could do about it. Nothing at all. Have you ever felt helpless, Kevin?' Kevin didn't answer. 'I doubt it. Not like that. Not like losing your family and not being able to stop it. That is what helpless feels like, Kevin.' He took a deep breath. 'You need to know how it feels,' Boyd said, nodding. 'I've thought about how to teach you what helpless feels like.' Kevin shook his head. He didn't want to hear Boyd's idea. Alec tensed and waited to see what depraved bullshit was going to come out of his mouth next. 'I don't want to kill you, Kevin,' Boyd said. He sounded calm. His eyes were dull and dark. 'I want you to understand what helpless is; I want you to suffer like I had to, but I don't want you to die.'

'Good, because I don't want to die,' Kevin said. He was trying to communicate, but Alec didn't think it was the best move. One wrong word could tip the scales. 'Look, I was doing my job and I'm sorry for what happened to your family.'

'Shut up,' Boyd shouted. 'I don't want to hear "sorry".' His lips were opening and closing but no words were coming out. His brain was in neutral. 'You have no idea what sorry means, not yet, but you will.' Boyd took a deep breath. 'I'm going to be fair – I want you to have a choice, Kevin.' Kevin looked at Boyd as he walked over to the corner of the cellar; he picked up a sledgehammer and carried it back. Jane Hill began squealing. 'Shut up, Jane!' She tried to calm herself.

Guilty

'Take it easy, Jane,' Kevin said. She looked at him, teary eyed. He tried to smile but it didn't work. 'Please let my family go,' he said to Boyd. Boyd frowned. 'It is me that did you harm. They have done nothing to you,' Kevin said. His voice was shaky. 'Keep me, but let them go. My kids have never harmed you.'

'You're right,' Boyd said, 'but you did.'

'Please, Frankie.'

'Shut up,' Boyd snapped. He shook his head. 'I can't think straight with you whinging like a bitch.' Kevin looked at the floor, realising he was pushing Boyd too far. 'I'm going to kill your family, but I want you to have to make a choice.'

'Don't hurt my family,' Kevin said. Jane was blubbering again. 'Please, don't hurt them.'

Boyd looked at Alec and walked over to him. 'You're very quiet, Detective Ramsay,' he said. 'Will you please explain to Kevin that he's annoying me?'

'I would listen to what Frankie has to say, if I were you,' Alec said, calmly. He looked Kevin in the eyes, to reinforce the message.

'I'm sorry,' Kevin said. 'I'm listening.'

'Good. I'm going to give you a choice.'

'What choice?' Kevin asked. His bottom lip quivered. He was close to losing it. 'Please, don't hurt my family.'

'Shut your face,' Boyd said, lifting the sledgehammer above his head. 'You are not listening to me.'

'Stop, stop, please!' Kevin pleaded. 'I'm listening. I am.' He waited for Boyd to calm down. 'Tell me what the choices are.'

'Okay.' Boyd lowered the hammer; Kevin sobbed but choked it back; Alec listened. 'Here's the choice you have to make: option one is they all go together, here. It will be reasonably quick.' He explained calmly, as if he was talking about the weather. 'One or two blows with the sledgehammer, and they'll be gone. You choose which order the kids go in, and Jane goes last, of course.' Jane Hill was hysterical. The kids were wailing. The noise was deafening. 'You watch them die, but you live.'

'Don't do this, please,' Kevin said. Tears ran down his face.

'Listen to him, Kevin,' Alec said. He wanted Boyd to keep talking. He was calmer when he was talking. 'Let him finish.'

'Thank you, Alec.' Boyd nodded. He seemed to lose his thread. 'Or, option two, you can all go together, but that will be long and slow and cold and wet, and you'll have to choose who dies first because you won't be able to keep them all afloat.' Boyd smiled thinly. 'You'll all drown eventually, but you'll have to choose who you let go of first.' He smiled again, and shrugged as if the choice was obvious. 'Make your choice, Kevin. Shall I bash their brains out right now?' He lifted the sledgehammer above his head.

'Let him choose, Frankie,' Alec said. He sensed Boyd was about to flip.

'No!' Kevin shouted. 'We all stay together.' He was shaking now. Tears flowed freely. 'We will stay together as a family.' Kevin was angry now. He couldn't contain it any longer. 'I was right when I said you were a sick monster,' he said, his voice breaking. 'They were the truest words I have ever written.' Frankie shook his head and frowned.

'And there I was, being reasonable and giving you a choice. If you can't say anything nice, don't say anything at all.' He swung the sledgehammer down in an arc. The hammer struck Kevin Hill on the top of his skull. Blood and brain matter splattered Alec and Jane. Pink goo ran down her cheek. Kevin Hill toppled over and landed on her lap, and his brains spilled onto her legs. Alec closed his eyes as her muffled screams reached epic proportions. He heard the sledgehammer coming down, over and over, with a sickening sound. Jane Hill stopped screaming, and, one by one, her children did too. It was the soundtrack from hell.

***

Braddick was disappointed. They had another body and nothing else. There were still more questions than answers. Google and his team were sorting through the photographs they had recovered, trying to identify who was still alive and who was already dead. It was a jigsaw puzzle, which had more pieces now than it did when they began. It became more complex with every hour that passed; their image of the killer blurred with each murder. He was unravelling, now he was in the wind and could be anywhere. It was a waiting game until they uncovered something that gave them a clue; that was all he needed, just a sniff of Boyd. He looked at his phone to see he had missed a call from Alec; it was late and it unnerved him. He checked his watch. It was very late. He thought about leaving it until the morning to call him back, but something rankled him. There was no message. *Why hadn't he left a message?*

Braddick called Alec's number. The automated message told him it was not possible to connect the call. Alec was a retired detective. Detectives never turned off their phones, ever. He instinctively knew something was wrong. It took the communications section an hour to ping Alec's phone and pinpoint its location. When Boyd was confirmed as the name of the property owner, Braddick knew where he was, and why he had gone there. He could only hope he was unharmed.

CHAPTER 40

Frankie Boyd heard the sirens coming, they seemed to bring him back to earth. He studied the carnage around him – Kevin Hill and his family were no more; blood soaked the cellar walls and floor; his face was red with the sticky fluid and his eyes looked uncannily white in contrast. He seemed surprised at what he had done. Alec watched him, his heart racing. The police had traced his call, he knew they would. Boyd appeared bemused by the situation. He looked at Alec and shook his head.

'Look at what he made me do,' he muttered. He listened to the sirens. 'Sounds like your friends are on their way. I guess it's time to say goodbye.' Alec pulled his knees up to his chest. Boyd went to the far end of the cellar, where Alec couldn't see him. He heard a key in a lock followed by a door creaking open. There was a click. Boyd returned with a double-barrelled shotgun. He broke it and fumbled two shells into the barrels. 'No more prison for me, Ramsay. I can't do the time. If you can't do the time, don't do the crime, eh, Ramsay?' He laughed dryly. 'Isn't that what they say?' He snapped the shotgun closed. The sirens were louder now. 'It has been interesting. I would say it has been nice to know you, but it wasn't. You're a cunt, Ramsay,' Boyd said. He aimed the shotgun at Alec and pulled the trigger. Alec heard it roar and felt the force of the blast slam him into the wall, blood running from a dozen wounds, his body peppered with shot. The sound of the front and back doors being breached, echoed through the farm.

'Armed police!' He heard. The light was fading. He felt himself sliding away. Boyd put the shotgun in his mouth and pulled the trigger. Alec saw the top of his head splatter all over the ceiling. His body crumpled to the floor as the first policemen stormed down the stairs. Darkness descended.

CHAPTER 41

One month later

Richard Vigne kissed Celia goodbye. She held him tightly, with meaning. They had become much closer since the nightmare of Nicola Hadley. It had made them appreciate how much they loved each other. He finished his orange juice and grabbed his laptop bag.

'Hey Dad, what are we doing in PE today?' Jake asked. 'I want to know what kit to bring.'

'What would you like to do most?' Richard asked, taking a bite of Jaki's toast.

'Dad,' she moaned.

'Football, of course,' Jake answered.

'Football it is,' Richard said, ruffling his hair. 'Don't tell your friends I let you choose.'

'I won't,' Jake said, fist-bumping his dad. 'See you later.'

'How come he gets to pick what game you're playing?' Jaki asked, pouting. 'I never get to choose.'

'Yes, but you're orange,' Jake said, leaving the breakfast table.

'Knobhead,' Jaki shouted after him.

Richard smiled as he opened the front door; the twins made him chuckle. He thought about Nicola Hadley, the poor girl had taken her own life. Despite never knowing her, her death had disturbed him greatly. He was a father first, and the thought of losing a child was unbearable. The entire episode was a struggle to overcome; the ramifications were still taking their toll. His life had disintegrated overnight and it would take a lot of time to rebuild it. The police had uncovered the truth too late.

Richard was vindicated and the local press printed a retraction, which was a paragraph on page ten, and the school apologised unreservedly and offered him the deputy head post again; this time, he accepted it. Events had taught the Vignes to look forward, not back. The murder of Kevin Hill and his family had made them realise that family was everything, but it was as fragile as everything else in life, there were no guarantees; it had made them value what they had. They had pulled through as a family and they were lucky.

Richard shouted goodbye to the twins and walked to his car. The summer was waning but it was still light in the morning, and it was warm, and the trees were still green. He unlocked the car, the lights flashed. A siren blared in the distance. He slung his laptop on the passenger seat and went to open the gates at the end of the drive. Their neighbour across the road waved. He had blanked Richard for weeks, until word had spread that he was innocent. Things were returning to normal. He heard an engine roaring and turned around. They had been fighting the council for a traffic calming scheme for years. He looked up the road and froze. The Scania truck hit him at fifty miles an hour, demolishing the gateposts and crushing him before careering into his car. Richard Vigne didn't have time to blink.

When the articulated lorry stopped, the driver's door opened and Billy Hadley climbed down from the cab. He walked to the back of the truck and looked underneath it; Richard Vigne was mangled beneath the back wheels. His wife and kids ran from the front door. He heard them screaming and shouting, phoning the police and an ambulance. It had no effect on him. Richard Vigne was as guilty as Ralph Pickford for Nicola's death. There was no doubt about it. Vigne was the one who got her drunk, and he was the one who took her back to the apartment. Neither of them would see their children again, unless there was an afterlife, and he seriously doubted that. He walked towards the road and waited for the police to arrive.

EPILOGUE

Alec brought three mugs of coffee from the kitchen and put them on the table. The trees were bending in the wind, their leaves beginning to brown. Sadie was staring at his scars. They had made a mess of his face, but weren't as bad as the ones on his neck and chest that he'd covered up. Alec noticed her looking. She looked saddened by the sight of them.

'They're not as painful as they look,' Alec said. He smiled at Sadie and she blushed.

'I'm sorry,' she said, 'I didn't mean to stare.'

'I do it myself sometimes,' Alec said. He chuckled. 'In the mirror, of course. I'll get used to them.'

'I'm glad you're okay,' she said.

'That's because of you guys getting there in time,' Alec said.

'Not soon enough,' Braddick said. The sight of the Hill family, bludgeoned to death, had been enough to cause three officers to seek counselling. 'Are you sleeping better?'

'That depends on how many whiskies I've had,' Alec joked. He picked up the local paper. 'I read about the teacher being killed – Richard Vigne. Makes you think.'

'You followed the story?' Braddick asked.

'Only once I'd realised the connection to the Facebook group,' Alec said. 'I've become a bit of an expert on social media.'

'The young girl that Vigne was accused of abusing, took her own life in hospital. William Hadley, the girl's father, couldn't accept the facts,' Braddick said. 'It seems he blamed Vigne for her death. He ran him over on his driveway then sat on the pavement and waited for the police to arrive.'

'How sad,' Alec said. 'Just shows how differently we're all wired.'

'Doesn't take much to push people over the edge,' Braddick said.

'True,' Alec agreed. He sipped his coffee and touched the scars on his face. 'Some people don't need pushing. Some of them are born on the edge of insanity.' He smiled. 'Spotting them is the key.'

'Amen to that,' Braddick agreed.

Printed in Great Britain
by Amazon